BURIED ALIVE

She looked up to see a black shadow filling the sky. It hovered there, above the canyon rim. At first, Nick couldn't understand what she was looking at, then the shadow slowly resolved itself into a helicopter, its rotors kicking up dust and debris. Small rocks began raining down.

"Don't they see us?" Nick shouted.

Her father's answer was lost in the rotor roar as the chopper descended even lower. The increased downdraft beat at her. A dust devil swirled to life on boot hill, sandblasting Nick from head to foot.

"Get down!" she shouted at her father.

An instant later, Nick was hurled flat by flying debris. Instinctively, she wrapped her arms around her head and curled into a ball.

Pain blossomed everywhere, her arms, her legs, her head. Dirt filled her eyes, blinding her. Dust choked her. She couldn't breathe. She was being buried alive.

FLIGHT
OF THE
SERPENT

VAL DAVIS

BANTAM BOOKS
New York • Toronto • London
Sydney • Auckland

FLIGHT OF THE SERPENT

A Bantam Book / December 1998

ISBN 0-553-57803-0

Published simultaneously in the United States and Canada

Bantam Books are published by Bantam Books, a division of
Bantam Doubleday Dell Publishing Group, Inc. Its trademark,
consisting of the words "Bantam Books" and the portrayal of a
rooster, is Registered in U.S. Patent and Trademark Office and in
other countries. Marca Registrada. Bantam Books, 1540 Broadway,
New York, New York 10036.

PRINTED IN THE UNITED STATES OF AMERICA

OPM   10 9 8 7 6 5 4 3 2 1

To the memory of Collin Wilcox,
who offered encouragement on
a rainy night so long ago

and to Grady Martin,
whose laughter made it all worthwhile

ACKNOWLEDGMENTS

The author is indebted to Frank Ashley, Ralph Minor, and Joseph Marasco; World War Two pilots whose expertise and memories made this book possible. Joan Nay did her bit, too, sharing her knowledge so graciously, as did Marilyn Knowles. If technical gremlins persist, they are strictly the author's and not theirs.

FLIGHT
OF THE
SERPENT

PROLOGUE

She waited. She knew what she had been born to do and she hadn't done it in a long time. Men had laughed, wept, and died in her arms. She missed them. But one man in particular still came. He had rescued her in her darkest hour. He had not forgotten. But he never touched her. Not the way she wanted.

He would spend long hours talking, but she was impatient with talk. She longed for more. She felt it in the deepest recess of her being. They would be together again, the way she wanted. She remembered his soft touch and firm command. She remembered the joy and the fear they shared together, and his total dependence on her. No, that wasn't true. It was she who was dependent. She who needed him, to be free.

She was born female and deadly, but now she waited.

1

Nicolette Scott had made a ritual of climbing boot hill late every afternoon. From the top, she had a panoramic view of Ophir, Arizona, her ghost town. Sitting on the huge mound of ore tailings helped Nick shake the claustrophobia she experienced working in the historic town perched on the side of the ore-bearing escarpment.

Choosing a spot near her favorite tombstone— *HERE LIES BESS HARRIS AND HER DOG, WHO KEPT HER COMPANY TO THE END*—she planned the next day's activities. With the coming of sunset the air was beginning to cool and Ophir, built in a narrow gorge cut into the foothills of the Mescalero Mountains, was already deep in shadows. In the canyon there was the smell of moisture in the air, tantalizing with false promise. The nearest water was miles away. The temperature hovered somewhere in the nineties.

To the west the escarpment slumped into the great Sonoran desert, still baking in the last rays of the setting sun. The flat western horizon, framed by the canyon walls, was unbroken except for a dark monolithic shadow that seemed to float above the dancing heat waves. The air was so clear that the great monolith appeared to be within a few minutes' walking distance, but Nick knew that the dark shadow was the geologic phenomenon rising two thousand feet above the desert floor known as Mesa d'Oro, and was fully thirty-five miles away.

Opening her notebook, Nick grabbed the pencil from behind her ear and absently finger-combed her short red hair. She had a dozen students to keep busy, though most of them weren't actually going for academic degrees. For some people an archaeological dig was part vacation, part wish fulfillment. Forty years ago they would have been content with dude ranches. These days, they dressed like Indiana Jones and expected to discover lost treasure each time they turned a shovel full of earth. But they hadn't counted on Ophir, scorching by day, teeth-chattering at night.

The class description in the university's brochure hadn't helped matters any. "*And they came to Ophir, and fetched from thence gold,*" some romanticizing publicist had quoted from the Bible. "*Spend six wonderful weeks searching the glorious Southwest just as Coronado once did, each day filled with lectures and the promise of discovery.*" As a result the students blamed Nick for the heat, the bugs, the ever present sand and grit, the canned food, and the lack of television.

Even to Nick, Ophir, Arizona, was anything but romantic. Following the discovery of gold in the late 1880s, the town sprang to life at the mouth of Sulphur Canyon as a collection of ramshackle buildings tucked under the ore-bearing cliffs. For a brief time riches had poured from the mines that honeycombed the surrounding land. Tailings were dumped everywhere, the highest pile becoming boot hill.

At the height of the boom, Ophir's population rivaled the likes of Tombstone and Bisbee. Now all that remained were a few sun-blackened clapboard relics that had escaped the great fire of 1922.

Technically Ophir wasn't a true ghost town. It still had residents, diehard prospectors mostly, squatting in the best of the surviving shacks.

Last year those diehards had been joined by Zeke Moyle, who'd bought Ophir lock, stock, and barrel. Moyle was a refugee from California where, he said, smog and cigarettes had turned his lungs into Marlboro Country.

Upon taking possession of the town, Moyle named

himself mayor and declared Ophir a tourist mecca in the making. His first official act was to rename the largest surviving shack the Emporium General Store. As meager and bedraggled as the place was, it served as a gathering spot for Nick's students in the evenings after work. There was no place else.

At first Moyle had been more than friendly, possibly because he thought Nick was there to help him realize his dream. But he was quickly disillusioned. Her interest was in what lay beneath Ophir, the artifacts that had been lost in the great fire. Her quest had been triggered by the discovery of pioneer diaries found in the archives at the University of New Mexico, where Nick's father, Elliot Scott, headed the Department of Archaeology. The manuscripts were part of a bequest dating from 1936. They were, according to their own prologue, one of the few things salvaged from the fire.

When Nick's father came across them, they were buried in the basement of the university library, still in their original hatboxes. The diaries had been the life's work of two sisters, Pearl and Lillian Benson, who'd come to live in Ophir in 1885 and stayed until the fire burned them out. Since Elliot's field of expertise was the ancient Anasazi Indian culture, he turned the find over to Nick, whose speciality was historical archaeology, the study of the near past. Many classical archaeologists sneered at this speciality, considering anything that happened within the last two thousand years not worth bothering about.

With her father's backing, Nick had been named head of the Ophir dig for the University of New Mexico while on the summer break from her own employer, the University of California at Berkeley. If the dig went well, she hoped to publish a portrait of pioneer life that might help her gain tenure at Berkeley at long last, despite the fact that she topped her department chairman's enemies list. Ben Gilbert had never forgiven her for having a world-famous archaeologist as a father.

Reading the Benson sisters' account of everyday life had made Nick realize that the image most people had of the old west came from movies, and had nothing to do with the day-to-day reality that confronted the two women. Nick wanted to change that misconception. Using references from the diaries, she hoped to locate their homesite and excavate the immediate area. Already, she'd uncovered numerous artifacts from the townsite: tools, metal buttons, glass bottles purpled by the sun, and a twenty-dollar gold piece that collectors would kill for.

Today's excavation had been special. She'd uncovered an artifact that had made the whole trip worthwhile. Her father was going to be surprised, though he probably wouldn't admit it. To him, the gold at the end of the rainbow was a thousand-year-old Anasazi Indian relic. But for Nick, the study of the recent past rivaled any ancient civilization. To her, unearthing a covered wagon, or even an old airplane, was every bit as magical as walking into Tut's tomb.

When she'd explained her intentions to Mayor Zeke, he screamed duplicity. He'd only gone along with the university's request to dig up his town because they'd enticed him by mentioning the gold of Ophir. Moyle had confused Ophir with one of the Seven Cities of Cibola, whose fabled wealth had lured the Spanish Conquistador Coronado to explore the Southwest in the sixteenth century.

Sitting there now, atop boot hill, Nick blamed such tales of gold on early real estate agents, possibly the forebears of the one who'd sold her the musty place in Berkeley he'd called "a buried treasure of a condo."

How anyone could think a desert like this could support a civilization built of gold defied imagination. Even the cactus had a hard time surviving. As for wildlife, most of it had six legs or slithered.

As she went back to her sketch of the town, weighing tomorrow's likely excavation sites, Zeke Moyle appeared and shouted up at her from the foot of boot hill. "Stay put, Missy. I'm coming up."

With clenched teeth, Nick tugged the Cubs baseball hat from the back pocket of her jeans, and pulled its brim down over her eyes to hide her annoyance. Calling her Missy was typical of the man. His western drawl was pure Gene Autry; his bib overalls pure Rodeo Drive.

He arrived out of breath, collapsed onto an overturned tombstone, coughed viciously, and lit a cigarette. He looked to be in his mid-fifties, with skin tanned like Beverly Hills leather.

After a moment, he blew a stream of smoke. "If you people are going to dig holes all over my town, you might as well do me some good and discover something I can sell to tourists." The comment left him wheezing.

"We're going to be working around the old church tomorrow," she said. In her diary, Lillian Benson had said she felt close to God, being a close neighbor of His church. The only problem was deciphering Lillian's definition of closeness, not to mention the fact that Nick was running out of time. In two days, the six-week dig would come to an end. Her students would go home, having paid handsomely for two units of credit, and she'd be left to do all the grunt work herself.

Moyle dug the toe of his boot into the sandy soil. "What's wrong with right here?"

"I've told you before. Digging up ancient civilizations is one thing, turning a spade on twentieth-century cemeteries can get an archaeologist into big trouble."

He stabbed a finger at a cluster of decaying wooden markers. "Who's to say how old those are?"

"We're standing on mine tailings from the 1890s," Nick said. "We'd have to go down twenty feet to hit the original strata that the Spanish conquistadors would have encountered."

"Okay, forget Coronado. All I'm asking is that you find me somebody famous enough to bring in tourists."

"Sure," Nick said, envisioning a tombstone marking

the death of her career. *Here lies Nicolette Scott, archaeologist turned grave robber.* "Who do you have in mind?"

"Tombstone's got the OK Corral to bring in the customers. That's what I need, somebody like Wyatt Earp."

"He's buried in California."

"Billy the Kid, then."

"Try the cemetery in old Fort Sumner."

"Okay. Make it Wild Bill Hickok."

Nick shook her head. "Deadwood, South Dakota."

"Somebody important must have died here," Moyle said, exasperated. "You tell me. You're the expert. Or so you say. What is it you call yourself exactly, a historical archaeologist? Well, we're sitting on history, aren't we?" He looked skeptical.

"I've told you before. Historical archaeologists deal with the recent past. In this country, that means the period after Columbus arrived."

"Gunfighters fit into that category. Or maybe . . ." He scratched his chin. "Some famous Indian warriors. That might help. The whole town could dress up in war paint and put on a show for the tourists."

"I told you before, Zeke. My project is life in a turn-of-the-century mining town. Maybe you ought to re-create that."

He scratched his head.

"It wasn't exactly romantic, of course," she added, to pay him back for the Missy comment. "There was no electricity, no air-conditioning, no plumbing. Wells were dug by hand, and pumped by hand if the windmills weren't turning."

Moyle shook his head. "Just find me a body and I'll come up with a famous name to go with it. Outlaws are what sells."

Nick couldn't help laughing. When it came to archaeology, Moyle was closer to the mark than was comfortable. Potential commercialization often played a major part in funding expeditions.

"Maybe you ought to do your own digging," she suggested. "With luck you might find some of Coronado's gold."

"The gold here ran out a long time ago."

"You never know. Coronado led an army right through here more than four hundred and fifty years ago, fighting hostile Indians all the way. Would he have done that if there hadn't been something to find?"

He squinted. "Are you putting me on?"

Nick coughed to keep from laughing. "In my business you never know what you're going to dig up."

"What would happen if you did find some old Spanish stuff?"

"Do you know where Ophir got its name?"

Moyle shook his head.

"The Bible says King Solomon's mines were in Ophir."

"And you think that's what those Spaniards were looking for?"

Fighting to keep a straight face, she nodded.

"There's some old Indian ruins farther up Sulphur Canyon," he said. "Maybe Coronado left something behind out there." He gestured toward the canyon mouth. "Of course, I own that land out there too, so anything you find we'd have to divvy up."

Suddenly suspicious, she said, "How far are these ruins from here?"

"Maybe a mile."

"I've been over that ground and didn't see anything like that."

He lit one cigarette from another. "These days, there's not much left standing out in the canyon, but there used to be. It was ten years ago, maybe more, when they found the Indian ruins. For a while now, me and the boys have been using them for target practice." He shrugged. "Hell, I didn't think anybody'd care about them."

Chances were he was making the whole thing up. On the other hand, she was willing to go for a walk before dinner, especially if there was the possibility of an archaeological rainbow at the end of it. "Maybe I'll take a look right now. Tell me again. Where are these ruins exactly?"

"In a cave in the side of the cliff, just beyond where the canyon gets real narrow. It's pretty high up, but you can't miss it. There are some faded markings on the sandstone walls right below the cave opening. Squiggly lines, circles, stuff like that."

"Why don't you show me?"

Moyle coughed. "I'm not up to walking that far in this heat. Even this time of day, it'll be a bitch out in that canyon. It's thin as a needle out there, and runs east to west so the sun bakes it nearly all day."

Nick stood up and patted her jeans to satisfy herself that her pocket flashlight was where it should be. "Tell my students I'll be late for dinner."

"You wouldn't catch me wandering around by myself. The radio said it hit a hundred and five today. Those canyon walls hold heat like an oven. If you wait for morning then maybe I'll guide you in myself." Zeke looked uncharacteristically concerned.

She shook her head. "I'll be fine." The man didn't understand what a real find meant to an archaeologist. To lay your hands on a centuries-old artifact was like touching history itself. That was worth taking most risks, including chasing fairy tales.

"Suit yourself, Missy." Moyle raised his hands as if to say she was just another foolish woman. "Just remember, that canyon can be a killer this time of year."

For an instant, she had an urge to wipe the smirk off his face and tell him about the courses she'd taken in desert survival. Graduation had been a solo trek across thirty miles of badlands.

"I'll tell your students to send out a rescue party if you're not back by sundown," Moyle said as he ground his cigarette butt into boot hill.

"You do that," she replied dryly.

Nick watched him on his way before returning to her tent to pick up a larger flashlight and a canteen of water. Water was rule one in desert survival. Carry your own. Never depend on finding it.

Then, moving quickly, she bypassed boot hill and headed into the canyon. She was fairly certain that the Indian ruins were nothing but a tall tale. It was too far south for the Anasazi, the "ancient ones" that her father loved with the same obsessive passion that she had for planes. But she had run across ruins in less likely places and this was the land of the Hohokam, "those who have gone before."

At the canyon's mouth, the sandstone walls were wide apart. A quarter of a mile farther on, they closed in to form claustrophobic, hundred-foot vertical barriers. At that point, Nick had the sense that the walls were leaning inward, reducing the bright blue sky overhead to a narrow slit.

She slowly scanned the sandstone walls as she moved deeper into the canyon. At the same time, she reminded herself that a man like Moyle wasn't above salting a ruin with fake artifacts when profits were at stake.

After a mile, by her estimate, she hadn't seen anything more interesting than a few small lizards and one diamondback. Moyle and his cronies at the Emporium were probably laughing at her wild-goose chase right now.

She checked her watch. She'd been walking for half an hour, following one switchback after another. She pulled off her Cubs cap and mopped her forehead. The radio had been right. The day had been a scorcher. And like Moyle had said, the surrounding sandstone was radiating enough heat to microwave her. Besides, the shadows were deepening. In another half hour, the canyon would be blanketed in darkness.

Sighing, she took a sip of water from her canteen and started back toward Ophir. She hadn't gone more than a few yards when she caught movement out of the corner of her eye. A shadow, like that of a great bird of prey, swept quickly across the canyon's sunlit rim and was gone. She shook her head, fearing that the heat had gotten to her and that she was seeing things. But the impression wouldn't go away. The bird—the shadow, whatever it had been—appeared to have had something clutched in its talons.

She rubbed her eyes. The shadow reminded her of the bedtime stories about the powakus, the Hopi sorcerers, that her father had used to scare her with. Oh Elliot, she said to herself, you thought you were telling me exciting stories about the descendants of the Anasazi and instead you were half-scaring me to death.

Come on, Nick, she admonished herself. Drink some more water and cool off. You're hallucinating.

Then she heard it, a rumbling sound that reverberated down the canyon. It grew in intensity until the ground beneath her feet resonated with it. For an instant, she thought it might be the precursor to an earthquake. Then the sound changed. The roar settled into a rhythmic thumping.

She looked up, expecting to see a helicopter. But only a sliver of bright blue sky was visible between the sheer canyon walls. There could be hundreds of helicopters hovering nearby, but she wouldn't be able to see them unless they flew directly overhead.

With a shrug, she gave up watching the slit of sky and picked up her pace back toward Ophir. If she didn't hurry, her students might actually send out a search party.

Above her, something crashed violently against the canyon wall, so close she reflexively ducked her head. The agonizing scrape of metal on rock bounced back and forth between the canyon walls. The long jarring note ended in a impact solid enough to feel through the soles of her desert boots.

For a moment, she thought she heard rotor sounds

again, distant and fading. Or was that only an echo? Then there was silence.

One thing was certain. No rock slide had made that sound. A chopper had gone down. But where? Sound was impossible to pinpoint in a twisting canyon like this. For all she knew, the echo had traveled miles. Yet that seemed unlikely.

Nick took a deep breath. There was no smell of smoke, but any kind of aircraft disaster was sure to include spilled gasoline. And what if the pilot was trapped inside?

Nick knew better than to run. That kind of exercise spent too much energy and too much water. But she set a good pace as she turned back to move deeper into the canyon. She'd keep it up for another half a mile, she told herself. After that, she'd go back to Ophir for help.

2

Judging from the wreckage, the aircraft had struck the lip of the gorge, then tumbled from one rocky outcrop to another, until it burst apart on the canyon floor. Several huge red-rock boulders had come down with it.

Survival looked impossible. Even so, Nick jogged the last fifty yards, stopping just short to study the wreckage. She'd heard a helicopter, only this was a small airplane she was looking at, a single-engine Cessna. And for an instant the image of that shadow came back to her, a bird of prey with something clutched in its talons. But that didn't make any sense. The heat is getting to you, she told herself. You're a scientist, for heaven's sake. Don't let your imagination run away with you.

But one thing was certain. Imagination had nothing to do with the Cessna's ruptured gas tanks. Fuel was everywhere, spilling down the wings and along the crumpled fuselage, its smell so overwhelming she could taste it. One spark and there'd be nothing left but a fireball.

Cautiously, she circled to her left to get a look inside the cockpit. The door on the passenger's side hung on its hinges, giving her an unobstructed view of the pilot, who was held in place by his seat belt. For an instant, she thought he was alive. Then she saw his dead eyes, a clouded blue. She stepped forward and gingerly felt the carotid artery. There was no pulse and the skin was strangely cold and clammy in the desert heat. His complexion looked raw and angrily sunburned, as if he'd been the victim of exposure rather than a fatal crash.

Behind him, red plastic fuel containers filled the back of the plane, and judging by the sound of liquid gushing into the cockpit, at least one of them had broken open.

Something clicked, metal on metal. Startled, Nick lurched backwards.

In the same instant, the fuel exploded. The force of its eruption sent her head over heels. After that, she kept going, scrabbling along the rocky canyon floor to escape the searing heat. By the time she was far enough away to sit up, Nick realized that all the hair had been singed from her arms, and only her Cubs cap had saved her head from the same fate. Her face felt sunburned, her cheeks tender the moment she touched them. Only then did she realize that her hands were scraped raw and bleeding, as were her knees.

By now there was nothing to be seen of the plane but its tail, though the flames were quickly spreading that way. She made a mental note of the serial number before it was consumed by hungry flames, then scrambled to her feet and headed for Ophir.

From Zeke Moyle's Emporium, Nick called the county sheriff's office. Moyle, a prospector named Dobbs, and Nick's entire student body listened in, hanging on every word as she recounted her discovery.

The moment she hung up she said, "They want us all to stay put and wait for help to arrive. They don't want us disturbing the site before the NTSB investigators get here."

"And just who the hell are they?" Moyle demanded.

"The National Transportation and Safety Board."

"Shee-yit. Feds. That's all we need around here." He raised an eyebrow in Dobbs's direction. "The first thing you know, they'll be checking our tax returns."

"I think we should ignore them and go look for that helicopter the lady heard," Dobbs said.

"It will be pitch black soon," Nick pointed out. Besides, she added to herself, maybe all she'd heard was the Cessna's engine going bad. Certainly, the deputy she'd just spoken with hadn't sounded convinced that there'd been a helicopter involved. *You say you heard a chopper, lady, but found a Cessna airplane. This isn't some kind of prank, is it?*

"Sound plays tricks in these canyons," Moyle said, looking to Dobbs for corroboration. "Who could tell one engine from another anyway?"

Dobbs closed one eye as if taking a bead on some unseen target. "I seen one of them whirlybirds out in the desert the other day."

"Sure," Zeke put in, "and giant ants too."

"I'm over that," Dobbs said, looking hurt.

"There *was* a helicopter," Nick insisted. "What about the rest of you? Did any of you hear it?"

Around the room, the students' heads shook in the negative.

Perfect, Nick thought. If people who knew her reacted with skepticism, the NTSB investigators would think she was a total crank. Ophir's image didn't help either. It was like one of those desolate towns you see in horror movies, the kind where UFOs invade and turn everyone into zombies. Even the Emporium looked spooky, a one-room shack, no more than twelve feet square, with its back wall carved into the cliff face. Nick suspected that the entire structure would have collapsed if it hadn't been for the floor-to-ceiling shelving which held Zeke's meager supply of canned goods.

"The helicopters I seen were out near the mesa," Dobbs clarified.

Moyle scratched the tip of his chin. "That's a long way off. That far, I can't see anything but mirages."

"There's a few buildings left out there from the old army base," Dobbs insisted. "Some are on top of Mesa d'Oro, though I seem to remember more being down below it."

"For Christ's sake," Moyle said. "They haven't been used for fifty years. It's nothing but a no-man's-land out there."

"After the war, Indians used to camp in those old barracks sometimes."

"Squatters," Moyle said.

"Is there a road to the mesa?" Nick asked.

"That's gone along with the army."

Nick shrugged. "We'll let the professionals worry about the helicopter when they get here."

"Suit yourself," Moyle said. "Far be it for me to tell you what to do, but I wouldn't mention a helicopter no one else has seen or heard."

"You must have seen them before?"

"Not me, Missy."

She stared at the man. He'd been living in Ophir for more than a year. She'd been here only six weeks and she'd seen choppers on two separate occasions. So chances were, he'd spotted them too. But if so, why would he lie about it? Nothing plausible occurred to her. Unless he thought the existence of helicopters might hurt business.

"From now on," Nick said. "I'll keep a camera with me. Maybe I can capture one of those birds on film."

Moyle shook his head in obvious disgust. "I hope you don't come up with any flying saucers. Ophir doesn't need that kind of publicity. And I hope that plane's where you said it is, too."

"It's there all right. I got its serial number before it went up in flames," she assured him.

Dobbs sighed. "I feel sorry for that pilot. It sounds like he didn't have a chance."

"He was dead when I got there," Nick said.

"I sure as hell hope so," Moyle answered. "Burning's a bad way to die."

3

John Gault came awake at the first ring of the phone. The lighted numerals of the digital clock next to his bed blazed a red 3:47.

Jesus, it had to be bad news. A call at midnight, even one A.M., could be a former lady friend, or a war buddy wanting to reminisce. Maybe even someone needing to make bail. But 3:47. That was the dead time of night.

He switched on the light, swallowed against the growing tightness in his throat, and picked up the phone. "Gault."

"John, it's Curt Parker."

Cold crept over Gault, causing him to grit his teeth against the spreading chill. Parker worked for the Federal Aviation Administration out of the Salt Lake office.

They'd known one another for years, ever since Gault taught the man to fly.

"Who went down?" Gault asked calmly. At the moment, three of his planes were out on charter, one to his grandson.

"John, the NTSB has men on the ground, but no formal identification has been made."

Parker's tone confirmed Gault's fears. "It's Matt's plane, isn't it?"

"A witness gave us the call letters, November, two-two-four-seven, Zulu."

"Oh, god," he said shakily.

Parker was a long time responding. "I'm sorry, John. The plane burned."

Jesus. Fire was the worst. Better to die on impact. Gault ran a shaky hand through his already disheveled hair.

"An archaeologist found the wreckage at the bottom of a ravine in southern Arizona," Parker went on. "In the middle of nowhere, if you look at the map. A place called Ophir."

"What the hell was Matt doing there?" Gault wondered out loud.

"That's what the NTSB boys want to know."

Gault took a deep breath. It didn't stop his hands from shaking, but his voice remained calm. "Matt was working on a story for the paper, though he didn't say anything to me about flying to Arizona. Where's the nearest airport to this Ophir?"

"A flyspeck called Mescalero."

"The twin-engine's due back late this morning. I'll be flying there as soon as we service it."

"I've known you a long time, John. As a friend, I'm advising you to stay put and wait till the investigators do their job."

"Matt was a damned good pilot. I have to know what went wrong," Gault insisted.

"A day or two won't make any difference. After that,

I'll get somebody to fly you there. Hell, I'll do it myself if I have to. That's a promise."

"Goddamit, Curt, would you wait if your grandson had crashed?"

Parker sighed. "I know you well enough not to waste my time arguing, John, but I'd leave right away if I were you. There's a bitch of a storm coming our way."

"I'll have to wait for the twin-engine. I haven't got anything else available at the moment, not with the 150 down for its annual overhaul. Now tell me exactly what the archaeologist found."

"Strictly speaking, I'm violating notification protocol by talking to you. That's not my job."

"I appreciate that, Curt. So just tell me what you can. Tell me about the archaeologist," Gault said impatiently.

"The report I got was pretty sketchy. His name's Nick Scott. I know that much. He's with some university, so he can't be a crank."

"Do you have a phone number for the man?"

"I have a contact number in Ophir. As I understand it, that's walking distance from the crash site."

Gault wrote down the number, hung up, and tried it immediately. There was no answer. He'd try it again when he got to the airport.

On shaky legs, he walked to the open bedroom window to check the weather. Beds of geraniums and pansies glowed softly under a bomber's moon.

He shook his head. It was early summer, time for things to grow, not die. There was no sign of a storm, but life had taught him that bad luck was always out there, waiting.

Gault Aviation showed only night-lights at five in the morning. One of them spotlighted the sign over the door. SERVING UTAH AND THE INTERMOUNTAIN WEST SINCE 1946.

Gault had hammered up that sign himself all those

years ago. He'd been fresh out of the service then, a demobilized Army Air Corps captain who'd gone into hock to buy a war surplus building and the two bomber-size hangars that went with it.

Now, staring at the twice-remodeled office, he could only shake his head. The success of his business meant nothing. What good was it without Matt?

He took a deep breath and caught the smell of jet fuel from the nearby National Guard parking strip, where a four-engine Lockheed Hercules transport was going through a preflight check. His planes used a lower octane gasoline, which had its own distinctive smell.

He started for the Hercules, thinking it might be his future granddaughter-in-law's plane, but abruptly stopped in mid-stride. Now was not the time to tell her about Matt. Nothing had been confirmed, as far as he was concerned.

Gault clenched his teeth. Stop kidding yourself, old man. You're alone now. The last of the Gaults.

His shoulders slumped. Whatever his future held now, it wasn't likely to be Paula Latham. She'd be someone else's granddaughter-in-law eventually.

He turned away from the Hercules, searching the horizon for the dawn. But darkness continued to hide the Wasatch Mountains, Salt Lake's ten-thousand-foot eastern barrier that had killed many a careless pilot.

Head down, Gault returned to the office. When he looked up, he caught sight of his reflection in the glass door. Jesus, what a difference a phone call made. He ran his hand over the gray stubble on his chin.

"How old are you the moment you wake up?" he asked the reflection. *Forever twenty-one*. But that was before his body told him better.

"How old are you right now?" Now wasn't worth thinking about.

He fished a wad of keys from his pocket and fitted one of them into the lock. But he didn't turn it. He knew he wasn't going into the office yet. He had to talk with the *Lady-A* first.

The office building was flanked by two matching hangars. The one on the left belonged to her, to Annie—the *Lady-A*. The fact that she often had to share it with transient aircraft made no difference. It would always be hers.

Gault bypassed the sliding door out front and entered through the small mechanic's door at the side. The moment he switched on the work lights he felt calmer.

She was as beautiful as ever. She was a B-24, the World War Two bomber known as the Liberator. In 1943, she and her sisters had flown the big raid against the Ploiesti oil fields in Rumania. They'd taken off from Benghazi, Libya, a hundred seventy-eight of them. Only eighty-eight had returned to base. Of those, only thirty-three were still fit to fly, the *Lady-A* among them.

Gault stroked her aluminum skin. She still wore her original olive drab. Her twin vertical stabilizers were painted red with a diagonal white stripe. In the center of that stripe was a red letter N. It stood for Norfolk, England, the *Lady-A*'s last base of wartime operations. Her serial number, though faded, was still readable: 5440.

Five-pointed stars, the insignia of the Army Air Corps, embellished her fuselage and wings. Her turrets were in place, though without their .50-caliber machine guns.

She was faster than the more famous B-17; she could fly higher and carry a heavier bomb load, too, though she'd never gotten the press coverage of the B-17s, the Memphis Belles of this world.

By contrast to the sleeker B-17, the B-24 Liberator had a thick, stubby fuselage. Some called her the crate the B-17 came in. Others nicknamed her "the Flying Boxcar," and said she flew like one, too. German fighter pilots had called her and her kind flying coffins. But she'd brought Gault through twenty-five missions, the only plane in his squadron to survive the mandatory count.

She'd survived, he believed, because she'd been named after his wife.

His vision blurred as he moved to her Plexiglas nose turret. Leaning his forehead against the glass, he half-expected to see his bombardier, Vic Campbell, hunched over the Norden bombsight. But there was only Gault's own haggard reflection; it forced him away from the nose and along the port side, where he stopped to admire the bomber's nose art. A bright green serpent had its coils wrapped around a swastika, while its wide-open mouth held an orange bomb. Its faded red eyes still glinted evilly.

Right after the emblem had been painted, Gault had sent his wife, Annie, a snapshot. By return post, she'd answered, "That's a female serpent if I've ever seen one. I've got my coils wrapped around you the same way." From that moment on, the B-24's nickname had been the *Lady-A*.

"Annie," he said softly, "we've lost our grandson."

They'd raised Matt together after their son, Michael, and his wife had been killed in a car crash.

Gault pressed his palm against the plane's aluminum skin. "I should have listened to you, Annie. You begged me not to teach him to fly."

After his wife's death, Gault had tried talking to her at the cemetery. But when he sat beside her tombstone on the adjoining plot that he'd reserved for himself, the words wouldn't come. Only here with her namesake, did he feel truly connected.

He moved beneath her wing, absently testing the play in the supercharger's turbine wheel. He'd done the same thing before every mission, walking through the preflight with his crew chief.

He still did the check once a week, part of his promise to preserve the *Lady-A*. Only last year he'd replaced her control cables and linkage. He'd even rewired some of her key electrical systems, a sentimental gesture but one that had satisfied him greatly.

"If flying had killed me, Annie, that would have been fair. My share of luck was spent a long time ago. Twenty thousand hours of flight time. All that luck used up. So why did it have to be Matt?"

He sank to his knees next to the port side landing gear. The tires, changed whenever their rubber cracked too badly, were almost new.

"I kept my promise, old girl," he said, now addressing the plane. "When I saw you mothballed out in the middle of that damned desert, I knew it was fate. You'd saved me, so it was my turn to return the favor."

She'd looked like a derelict then, covered with dust and full of spiders and scorpions. During the war, B-24s were flown until they were either shot down or scrapped. But the *Lady-A*, like her crew, had been rotated home to participate in war bond rallies.

Buying her for five thousand dollars, one-seventieth of her production cost, had set Gault Aviation back a year. Once purchased, the *Lady-A* had to be partially disassembled before being transported to her hangar. Over the years, he'd slowly, lovingly reassembled her himself. More than anything he wanted to fly her one more time, but that was still just a dream. The cost of bringing her engines up to specs would have bankrupted him. Matt had shared his dream, of one more flight aboard the *Lady-A*. Gault closed his eyes, imagining the two of them sitting side by side in the cockpit, pilot and copilot. He should have spent the money. He should have made the dream come true.

Cartilage popped in Gault's knees as he moved beneath the fuselage and swung himself up into the plane through the open bomb-bay doors. He took a deep breath, inhaling her scent, a mixture of oil and dusty disuse, before working his way forward to the pilot's compartment.

Once in the left-hand seat, he found himself looking for Matt. But it was Brad Roberts, his old copilot, he saw, the same age as always, forever twenty-one. Even the dead were on board, Tim Lambert in his belly turret, Mark Tanner, the radio operator, and Perry Goddard, a waist gunner with two kills to his credit.

Gault looked down at his hands. On their own, they'd come to rest on the control yoke. In his mind he heard the *Lady-A*'s four Pratt and Whitney radial engines start up, all forty-eight hundred horsepower.

"Matt only had one engine," he told the *Lady-A*. "I wanted him to take the twin Cessna, but he knew we had a customer for her. He knew it would cost us money. And all because of some damned newspaper story. He was using his own vacation time because he was on the trail of a hot one. 'When I quit the paper to join the family business,' he'd said, 'I want to go out in a blaze of glory.' "

Clenching his teeth, Gault pushed the pain aside and left the plane, heading for the office. It was time to file a flight plan. After that, he'd call that archaeologist in Arizona.

4

Nick awoke to find two deputies standing outside her tent like guards, one on either side of the flap. She was asked to accompany them to the Emporium, where she was to be interviewed by the NTSB.

After delivering the message, they averted their eyes while she pulled on her jeans, shirt, and work boots. Then they marched her to the Emporium. The door was open, coffee was made, but there was no NTSB investigator inside, only Zeke Moyle.

"You're to wait," one of the deputies told her over folded arms, watching her every move. His partner left.

"Why get me here this early if there's no one to interview me?" she asked.

The deputy shrugged. "I do what they tell me."

Moyle offered Nick a cup of coffee and tried to start a conversation. She accepted the coffee but not the conversation. She pointedly kept her back toward him and stared at the deputy, who finally moved outside onto the porch, where he stood with his back to the screen door.

After a half-hour wait and too much coffee, she was on the verge of revolt. Five more minutes, she told herself, and she'd walk out the door and assemble her students. But before she got the chance, the phone rang.

Zeke Moyle answered, listened for a moment, then pointed at Nick. "It's for you, from Salt Lake City."

She took the receiver and said warily, "Yes, hello."

"Excuse me," a man said. "I asked to speak to Nick Scott."

"You are."

"The archaeologist?"

She sighed. The man's reaction was common. "It's short for Nicolette. And this is . . . ?"

"John Gault. That was my plane you found. My grandson, Matthew Gault, was flying it."

"I'm sorry," Nick said, aware of the inadequacy of her response, yet unable to come up with anything more appropriate.

"I understand you found the plane?" he said.

"That's right."

"Could you tell me what happened? Was the plane out of control? Was its engine out? What?"

"The NTSB investigator should be here any minute. Maybe you should speak with him."

"Please," he said. "The last thing I need is a second-hand report. Or worse yet, red tape."

Nick sighed sympathetically. "All right, Mr. Gault.

I'll tell you what I can. I didn't actually see the Cessna come down. But I heard it."

"How close were you?"

It practically landed on my head, she thought, but didn't say so. "I can't say exactly. I was in one of those canyons full of switchbacks, the kind where you can't see too far ahead. But once I heard the plane come down, it couldn't have taken me more than two or three minutes to get to the site."

"Was it already burning?" he asked.

"No, but there was gas everywhere."

"And my grandson?"

"I'm sorry. The plane exploded before I could get him out."

"Was he conscious?"

Nick took a deep breath. "He was dead."

"Thank God."

She knew exactly how he felt. Being alive inside the kind of fireball she'd witnessed didn't bear thinking about.

"What did the engine sound like before the crash?"

Nick hesitated. She didn't want to sound like a lunatic. On the other hand, she knew what she'd heard. "It sounded like a helicopter."

"That doesn't make sense."

"The sheriff's man said the same thing."

Gault didn't respond immediately, but she could hear his heavy breathing on the other end of the phone line. Finally he said, "What kind of archaeologist are you?"

Nick snorted. "I know what you're really asking, Mr. Gault. Do I know what I'm talking about? Airplanes are one of my passions."

"I see. What was the weather like?"

"Clear."

"And the terrain?"

"It's a flat plateau to the west. The narrow, red-rock canyon where your plane went down is in the Mescalero

Mountains. We're in a larger canyon about a mile west of the crash site."

"I'm looking at a map," Gault said, "and I don't see any place called Ophir."

"It's a ghost town, or almost anyway."

"Look. I'll be flying into Mescalero. How far is that from where you are?"

"About fifty miles," she told him. "But it's a good two-hour drive because of the bad roads."

"I need to see the site for myself and to talk to you face-to-face. I'll be taking off as soon as my twin-engine is serviced. Could you meet me in Mescalero?"

"I'm working on a dig here in Ophir, Mr. Gault."

"My airport guide shows no rental cars in Mescalero."

Nick closed her eyes.

"My grandson had been flying a long time. I have to know what happened."

Nick shook her head, remembering the state of the body even before the fire.

"Please," he implored.

She didn't like the idea of being away from her students that long. Still, she could put them to work on a new trench, and pray to God they didn't destroy an artifact because she wasn't there to preserve it.

"How soon will you be in Mescalero?" she asked.

"It's nearly nine. Let's say six hours from now. Three o'clock."

That meant she'd have to leave by one to get there on time. Half a day lost on her dig, with only one more day to go. She'd have to make up her absence with an evening lecture. On the other hand, her students might welcome an afternoon without her slave-driving.

"All right," Nick said. "I'll see you at the airport."

She hung up and glared at the deputy. "I have students waiting. The only way you're going to keep me here is to arrest me."

She walked out the door. He didn't try to stop her.

• • •

Nick was laying out the new dig site near the ruins of the old Ophir church when an NTSB investigator caught up with her. After introducing himself as Walt Kohler from the Phoenix office, he asked to speak to her privately. She got her students started on an exploratory trench, then joined him on the sagging porch of a miner's shack across from the Emporium.

"According to the sheriff's initial report," Kohler began, "you heard the airplane before it crashed."

"What I told them was, I heard a helicopter. I saw its shadow."

"The plane's?"

"The helicopter's."

He eyed her skeptically. "Are you sure it wasn't a UFO?"

"The last time I heard, Area fifty-one was in Nevada, not Arizona," she said. "But then, being with the government, you'd know more about that."

"Touché, Ms. Scott. But the fact remains, we found a Cessna, or what's left of it, not a chopper. What you saw could have been a trick of light."

"Maybe, but I had the impression that the helicopter was carrying something."

"You said you didn't see it."

"Like I said, I saw a shadow."

Kohler threw up his hands in disgust.

"I know airplanes," she said calmly. "On occasion, I've dug them up as part of my work as an archaeologist. They're also my hobby. I'm telling you what I saw. What you do with the information is up to you."

He humored her with a smile. She'd seen that look before, mostly on the faces of people who'd underestimated her.

"Airplanes are an unusual pastime for a woman," he said.

It was her turn to smile. Airplanes had been her

Land of Oz when she was growing up, her escape from her mother's black depression. But that was none of Kohler's business.

"Are you a pilot?" he asked.

"No."

"What about helicopters? Are you an expert in those too?"

"I prefer vintage aircraft."

From his clipboard, he removed a pilot's navigational map that had been folded to reveal only the immediate area. Even so, she recognized the corner of a no-fly zone.

"I don't see where a helicopter could have come from," he said.

"What about that no-fly zone?" she asked.

"It was a desert bombing range during World War Two."

"And now?"

"Are you kidding, out here in the middle of nowhere? It's abandoned."

"Why is it still on the map, then?" she pressed.

"It's still military property, for all I know. Now what else did you hear?"

"Nothing but the sound of the crash."

"There's nothing else to do, then, but thank you for your help, Ms. Scott."

"You didn't ask me about the body."

He referred to one of the papers on his clipboard. "You said he was dead when you got there. Or looked dead anyway."

"He was dead. I checked. But there's something else." She hesitated, wondering why she bothered to go on, but she knew she had to. "His skin was a funny color."

"Just how did he look?" Kohler asked, failing to hide his skepticism.

"Like he had a bad case of sunburn, and his face was slightly bloated."

"That could have been another trick of light. Those canyon walls are very red. A pale face might very well look reddish."

Nick shrugged. "You wanted my eyewitness report."

"I'll include your comments in *my* report."

"There were also plastic containers of gasoline in the back seat."

"I don't think so," Kohler said. "That, you must have been imagining."

Nick forced herself to remain calm. "I saw them."

Kohler shook his head. "It wouldn't be safe to fly that way."

"You can tell that to John Gault, the pilot's grandfather. I spoke with him a few minutes ago. He's a pilot, too, and he's flying here to see the crash for himself."

"Did he say how soon he'll be arriving?"

"Late this afternoon."

Kohler stood up. "I think it best that you not discuss our conversation with him. In fact, I'd appreciate it if you left Mr. Gault to me."

"The man has a right to know what I saw," Nick said.

"What you thought you saw, you mean. Besides, why upset him for nothing? Whether or not you saw shadows doesn't change the fact that the pilot is dead."

"I've already told Mr. Gault everything," Nick said, stretching the point. She was losing the battle to control her anger. "I think he's going to want to know what I'm wondering—are you people going to look for a helicopter or not?"

He smiled indulgently. "If there'd been a midair collision, we'd have the wreckage of a helicopter, wouldn't we?"

"I'm not the only one who's seen helicopters around here," she said angrily.

"So I've been told." His tone lumped her in with the UFO crowd.

She'd heard a chopper, though what it had to do with the crash of the Cessna she didn't know. As for the shadow, she'd seen that, too. Whether it had been carrying something was less certain.

5

Nick was about to leave for Mescalero when her father called from his office at the university in Albuquerque.

"I hear you've got yourself another airplane," Elliot said, dispensing with hello.

His tone grated. And the words were worse, mimicking one of her mother's favorite litanies. *Nick's got herself another airplane.* That was usually accompanied by a heavy sigh. Most days, Elaine had been incapable of accomplishing even the most simple of tasks. Instead, she stayed in bed, shades drawn, light forbidden, wrapped in one of her dark moods, leaving the chores to Nick, who wasn't old enough to cope with them.

"I'm fine," Nick said, "aside from the heat, the bugs, the food, and the body I saw incinerated. And how are you, Elliot?"

"Worried about my daughter, who never heeded my warnings about the life of an archaeologist."

"*Your* warnings!"

Don't ever follow in your father's footsteps, Elaine had said each time Elliot disappeared on one of his digs. *If you do, you'll be lost to all who love you. Never love dead people. They can't love you back. You spend all your time*

*hiding in your room with your model planes. Well, they can't
love you back either.*

But Nick would always think, yes they can, they help
me fly away.

"Okay, Nick," Elliot said, breaking the reverie. "You
win. Let's call a truce."

"I didn't know we were at war."

"Sometimes I speak without thinking. I'm sorry."

"Me too. The heat's got to me, and the condition of
that body didn't help much."

Her conversation with John Gault hadn't done much
for her mood either, because now she had a two-hour
drive ahead of her, across one of the most barren deserts
she'd ever seen.

"Which brings us back to my question," Elliot said.
"Tell me about this airplane that practically fell on you."

"Now I remember why I hated taking classes from
you. You're obsessive."

He snorted.

"Don't worry, Elliot. It's not one of mine."

"You've had a lot of them."

Shelves full, she remembered, plus bureau tops and
table tops, and even a squadron suspended from the ceiling. Over the years, she'd built just about every model
warplane from World War Two that had existed.

"This one's new," she assured him. "A Cessna. A
single-engine job, hardly worth collecting. No respect-
able historical archaeologist would want one."

"I remember you saying once you never met an airplane you didn't like."

"You didn't see this one." Or the pilot's dead, staring
eyes either, she thought, repressing a shudder.

"Okay, Nick, I know that tone of yours. Let's talk
about your dig."

"It's not bad as far as collectibles go," she said, deciding to withhold news of her latest discovery until he
could see it for himself. "The new site that we started

today looks promising, but time's running out. After my students leave, I may stay on here by myself for a while."

"It's a long shot anyway, Nick. Most personal artifacts don't survive a fire big enough to wipe out an entire town."

"Hold it, Elliot," Nick said, suddenly realizing that news of her involvement with an airplane had somehow crossed the state line into New Mexico. "Let's backtrack a moment. How the hell did you hear about the plane crash anyway?"

"It must have been on the radio, because it was relayed to me by one of your admiring colleagues. The one who loves you so dearly at Berkeley."

"You're joking. Ben Gilbert's supposed to be on sabbatical, though the word is he's really hiding out from the university's latest sexual harassment suit."

"Nevertheless, he called me. He said he couldn't get through to you."

Nick groaned.

"He reminded me that even when you're working for my department at the moment, you still belong to him."

"So?"

"He doesn't want you getting involved in anything that might discredit *his* department at Berkeley," he replied dryly.

"What about you, Elliot? How do you feel?"

"Hey, I'm only the messenger. But I know men like Gilbert. He likes to keep people under his thumb, so he can make them squirm. But all that squirming stops, of course, when they get tenure. Which means the longer he can stall your promotion, the happier he'll be."

"He'll have to give it to me when I publish my work on Ophir and the Benson sisters."

"I can get you tenure here in Albuquerque anytime you say the word."

As *the* recognized expert on the Anasazi Indian culture, Elliot's word was law in some places. His name on a paper lent instant credibility. And his last publication had included Nick's name as coauthor. That alone would have assured her tenure at most universities. But at Berkeley she had Ben Gilbert to contend with, and she wasn't about to give him the satisfaction of quitting.

"You only stay at Berkeley because you're so damned stubborn," Elliot said, reading her thoughts.

"Come on, Dad, you know how it would be. The moment I joined your staff, the screams of nepotism would start. The fact that I did all the dirty work on that last paper would be lost in the backbiting."

"I'll tell you what. I feel like getting my hands dirty right now. Why don't I join you out there in Arizona?"

"Swell," she said dryly. "I'm sure Ben Gilbert would love that. I can hear him saying, 'Nick's father had to come to her rescue.' "

"He won't even know I'm there. Besides, I'm bored stiff. I need some field work."

"One thing I'll say about this place, Elliot. It's your kind of country. Your Anasazi would have loved Ophir. It's surrounded by desert. There's virtually no water. There's only one road in, and that's little better than a rut."

"Is that a formal invitation?"

"My students are leaving the day after tomorrow anyway. After that, I could use some help."

"I'm on my way," he said. "In the meantime, I want your promise that you're not getting involved in anything extracurricular. Don't give a man like Gilbert any ammunition to use against you."

"I told you before, the airplane's a Cessna and so new it's boring."

"Remind me," Elliot said. "Was your mother right? Am I to blame for this obsession? Who bought you your first model plane?"

"You did. It was a 1926 Ford Trimotor."

"At least a plane that old comes under the heading of historical archaeology."

Sometimes Nick wondered if her father agreed with

those conservative archaeologists who considered her branch of the business little better than bin diving.

"Come to think of it," she said, unable to resist goading Elliot, "that Cessna I found could be a rare model. One of a kind maybe. In that case, maybe I ought to go back for another look. Maybe I've discovered a kind of elephant's graveyard for Cessnas."

"All right, Nick, you've made your point. I wouldn't have called if I didn't have your best interests at heart. Somebody has to look after you."

"I'm not my mother."

"Whoa. I never said you were."

Nick suddenly realized she was gripping the phone hard enough to make her arm shake.

"Me and my big mouth," Elliot said.

"Thank God I'm not one of your students anymore."

"You're right about that," he said. "I'd probably have to flunk you."

"I love you, too," she said.

As she hung up, Nick wondered if she should have mentioned that she was leaving the dig for an appointment with John Gault.

6

Nick was late. The new site had shown great promise, and it had been an effort of will to tear herself away from the dig.

She hit the brakes at the sight of the steel-haired stranger walking with his back to her on the highway shoulder. Her pickup truck fishtailed and showered the man with gravel, forcing him to jump clear.

"John Gault?" she asked.

"I used to be." He coughed as the dust settled. "Now I just might be dead."

"Sorry I didn't catch you at the airport. They said you'd started walking." She smiled at him. "I'm Nick Scott."

He rubbed his face. "I hope you're a better archaeologist than you are a driver. You scared the hell out of me."

"I missed you, didn't I? Now, get in and we'll grab something to eat before we start back to Ophir."

Once in the truck, he took a hard look at her with startling blue eyes. "My wife had red hair like yours," he said finally.

"And the rest of me?" she said rather tartly.

He squinted, creating a maze of crow's-feet that made him appear sad rather than old. "The rest of you is a lousy driver." He sighed and looked away, staring out at the bleak desert landscape.

"I really am an archaeologist, in case that's what you're wondering."

He turned back to her and his smile took twenty years off. "Friends," he said, offering his hand.

As soon as she shook it, his smile faded. Even so, she thought he looked remarkably calm for a man who'd just lost his grandson.

"Tell me about the crash," he said. "Has anything changed since we spoke on the phone?"

She'd been thinking about how to answer that question since the moment she left Ophir. Judging by the NTSB's reaction to her eyewitness account, she'd probably be better off censoring her comments to this man.

Nick shook her head without taking her eyes from the road. "Nothing's changed. The Feds are everywhere, and no one else is welcome."

"That sounds like standard procedure to me. Do they have any indication of what caused the crash?"

"Nothing's been said to me."

"Pilot error," he said. "That's the easy way out. It's also the usual ruling when nothing else shows up."

Two minutes later she pulled off the highway and into the Burger Barn's gravel parking lot. Half a dozen pickups were there ahead of them. In Berkeley, the place would have looked like a fashionable 1950s replica. Out here, its Formica counter and chrome stools showed the wear and tear of original equipment.

One of the locals moved down a stool to make room for them at the counter. As soon as they'd ordered burgers and drinks, Nick said, "Was that your Cessna 340 I saw landing a few minutes ago?"

Gault nodded. "I'm impressed. Most people don't know one plane from another."

"I used to build models as a kid. Mostly military, though. The older ones are my favorites."

"What war?"

"World War Two."

Gault sighed. "My war. Now tell me what's happening in Ophir."

"Do you know anything about the place?"

He shook his head.

"It's a ghost town," she explained, "or on the verge anyway. I'm on a dig there with some students from the University of New Mexico. The town is built at the mouth of a narrow canyon. Your grandson's plane went down about a mile inside that canyon. Bad luck really. There's plenty of flat desert country surrounding the Mescaleros. I was in that canyon looking for an Indian site when the plane came down."

"You got there before the fire?"

"That's right."

"And Matt was dead?"

"Yes."

"You're sure?"

"Absolutely," Nick said, then decided to hell with it, self-censorship wasn't for her. "There's was something strange about his body, though."

"What do you mean?"

"His skin was very red, and looked swollen."

"How close were you?"

"I touched him." She closed her eyes, seeing the cockpit again. "I suppose it could have been a reflection from the red gas cans."

He grabbed her wrist. "What the hell are you talking about?"

"The back seat was stacked full of red plastic gas containers."

"That can't be right." He shook his head. "Matt would never do something that stupid, or that dangerous."

Nick pulled free of his grasp. His grip was strong and left angry red marks on her skin.

"Sorry," he said when she gingerly rubbed her wrist.

"Nothing's broken," she replied tartly.

Gault dug into his wallet and extracted a photograph. "I want to make sure we're talking about my grandson."

Nick studied the snapshot of the young man carefully. He was handsome and had John Gault's startling blue eyes, though the last time she'd seen them, they'd been dull and flat. The Matt in the photo was lean, muscular, and tanned, a far cry from the body in the Cessna. Still, it was definitely the same man.

"I'm sorry," she said. "That's the man I saw in the cockpit."

Their food arrived, but Gault ignored it. "You said you saw gas cans, is there anything else?"

"Yes. Like I told you on the phone, I heard a helicopter."

"But not the engine of Matt's Cessna?"

"I heard only the helicopter," she said firmly, watching his face for signs of disbelief. When she saw nothing, she added, "I suppose you think I'm imagining things."

"I didn't say so, did I?"

"But are you thinking it?"

"I'll tell you when I am, Miss Scott."

"Why would a helicopter be anywhere near a ghost town?" he continued.

"I've seen them before, usually out near the mesa."

"I thought you said Ophir was in the Mescaleros?"

"It's called Mesa d'Oro. It's to the west of Ophir on the desert floor. It's kind of a landmark, the highest point in the area. I'm told there used to be some kind of military installation out there."

"I saw it flying in," he said. "I had to detour around it because it's in a no-fly zone."

"They tell me the restriction dates from World War Two, and that there's nothing out there now."

"Then why is it still on the map?"

She shrugged, took a bite of her burger, and chewed thoughtfully. Finally, she decided to push her credibility to the limits. "I saw a shadow pass over the cliff face just before the crash. I don't think it was the Cessna, however. There was something wrong about it."

He pretended to concentrate on his burger, but she caught him watching her in the mirror behind the counter. At best, he probably figured she'd been out in the sun too long. At worst, God knows what he thought. And she couldn't blame him for labeling her as a nut case. It made no sense, seeing shadows and hearing a helicopter when it was a single-engine Cessna she'd found.

"What kind of models did you make?" he said.

"Pardon?"

"The ones you built as a child."

"What you're really asking me is the same thing that ·agent was getting around to. Am I crazy? Well, Mr. Gault, if I remember correctly, a Cessna 182, the kind that crashed out in Sulphur Canyon, is also known as a

Skylane. It's powered by a two hundred and thirty horse-power Continental engine. A flat six, I believe."

His mouth dropped open wide enough to make her laugh. "To answer your question, World War Two models were my favorite. I built dozens of them."

"I flew one of them," he said. "A B-24 Liberator."

"When?"

"Early days, late forty-three and early forty-four."

"You don't look that old." She felt embarrassed as soon as the words left her mouth.

"I feel a hundred and six," he said and laughed.

"I've always wanted to fly in one of those bombers," she said.

"Would you settle for a guided tour on the ground when all this is over?"

"You mean you actually have one?" she asked, trying to contain her excitement.

He nodded. "Of course, the *Lady-A* doesn't fly these days, but she's as beautiful as ever, and she's in my hangar at the Salt Lake airport."

"I may just take you up on that offer. I'm researching life in Ophir at the moment, and I still need background material on a couple of its pioneering sisters. The best source of that information is at the Genealogy Library in your hometown."

He handed her his business card. "All you have to do is call me."

"In the meantime," Nick said, "I think we'd better get started. The road to Ophir's no picnic."

7

Nick sighed with relief the moment the turnoff to Ophir came into view. Road work on the narrow WPA bridge leading out of Mescalero had delayed them nearly an hour. Any longer and she and Gault would have been driving in the dark, not something to be taken lightly when tackling the last few miles of the rutted dirt track that led to the badlands around Ophir.

Her arms ached from fighting the pickup's suspension on the washboard road. Her head throbbed from squinting against the glare of the setting sun.

Road dust had seeped into every nook and cranny of the pickup. Her mouth felt gritty from it. Next to her, John Gault had acquired a patina as red as the dusty desert soil.

Nick squirmed, feeling sticky all over. More than anything, she longed for a shower and a cold beer. Probably Gault felt the same.

The man was impossible to read. His arms were folded across his chest, his eyes invisible behind dark aviator's glasses. He wore his leather flight jacket despite the heat and hadn't said a word for miles, not since they'd turned off the potholed asphalt that masqueraded as a state highway. After that, his gaze had locked on the great mesa to the west. Its red rock rose two thousand feet from the center of an arid plain like an inflamed, upthrust molar.

"Stop here," he commanded, suddenly breaking his silence as she negotiated the turn. He got out of the truck to stare at Mesa d'Oro.

"I've seen choppers out there a few times," she said.

He grunted. "Do you have any binoculars?"

"In the glove compartment."

He pocketed his dark glasses. Then, for the next few minutes, he stood beside the truck and focused the binoculars on the mesa barely visible in the fading light, while Nick slapped dust from her jeans and work shirt.

"Anything?" she asked when he finally returned the glasses to her.

He shook his head and got back in the truck. Surprisingly, Nick discovered that she was disappointed. They drove the rest of the way in silence.

The minute they parked in front of the Emporium, the screen door banged open and Zeke Moyle stepped out to greet them.

"You missed the excitement," he said as soon as he was within speaking range. "The Feds brought in a whirlybird to haul away some of the pieces, and the body too."

"I don't understand," Nick said. "They can't have finished their investigation so soon?"

"Yep. Pilot error, they told me."

Gault lunged forward and caught hold of Moyle's shirt with both hands. Gault's agility surprised her. She'd rarely seen a man move like that. Neither had Moyle, judging by the startled look on his face.

The force of Gault's assault had Moyle backing up on tiptoe.

"What else did they tell you?" Gault growled.

Wide-eyed, Moyle shook his head. It was still shaking when he banged into the Emporium's sun-blackened clapboard siding. Moyle had to be twenty years younger than Gault and a good twenty pounds heavier, but he made no attempt to escape the older man's grip. Instead, Moyle appeared to dangle there against the siding, like a bug pinned to a collection board.

Nick grabbed one of Gault's arms but couldn't budge it.

"I asked you a question," Gault said through clenched teeth. His tone sent a shiver down Nick's spine.

Moyle shook his head in denial. "They didn't tell me anything else. Ask them, if you don't believe me. They're still out in the canyon poking around in the ashes."

"Please," Nick said. "Let him go."

Slowly, Gault's head turned toward her. His eyes, the ones Moyle had been looking into, staggered her. In that instant, she knew he wasn't a man to be underestimated. She knew the look of obsession well; she'd seen it often enough on her father's face when he was homing in on some new discovery involving his beloved Anasazi Indians. Her mother, too, had worn such a look during her darker moods.

"Please," she repeated. "I'll take you out there myself."

Gault released Moyle so quickly the man staggered back.

Nick set a quick pace, with Gault staying right with her. Since there were only a few minutes of good visibility left, she stopped at her tent long enough to retrieve a pair of battery-powered lanterns and her canteen.

"This time of evening," she explained, "it will be pitch black by the time we're deep into Sulphur Canyon."

But she needn't have worried about the light, because they got no farther than a barricade of yellow plastic tape that had been strung across the canyon's narrow mouth. The flimsy deadline was enforced by two bulky sheriff's deputies standing on either side of Walt Kohler, the NTSB investigator, and a short plump man whom Nick had never seen before.

"This is John Gault," she told Kohler. "That's his airplane out there."

"And my grandson who was flying it," Gault added.

Kohler offered his hand.

Gault accepted it warily.

"This is Mr. Odell," Kohler said, indicating the

plump man next to him. "Frank Odell. He's a consultant on our accident response team."

Odell nodded without looking up from his clipboard.

Gault said, "The man at the store tells me you're already calling the crash pilot error."

The two Feds exchanged glances, but it was Kohler who spoke. "I don't know where he got that idea, Mr. Gault. We're professionals. We don't make judgments until our investigation is complete. Even then, as you know, there are times when causes are never fully understood."

"The man also said you've airlifted my grandson's body."

"That, he got right. We wanted formal identification as quickly as possible, for your sake as much as anything else, Mr. Gault. In fact, it would help if you could supply the name of your grandson's dentist."

"Dr. Patrick Keeley. His office is in the old Walker Bank building in Salt Lake."

"Thank you."

Odell made a note on his clipboard.

"There's something else," Gault said. "Dr. Scott tells me that my grandson looked like he'd suffered from exposure before the gasoline caught fire."

Kohler shook his head, frowning at Nick. "That doesn't seem likely," he said. "What do you say, Odell."

"Out of the question," he answered, not meeting their eyes.

Gault's eyes narrowed as looked from one man to the other. "She also saw extra gas cans in the back seat."

"I hope not," Kohler said. "That would be a clear-cut safety violation."

"I know that," Gault said. "And so did Matt. He would never have done something that stupid."

Kohler spread his hands. "There you have it, then. Ms. Scott must have misunderstood what she saw. Probably they were extra cans for water. Who knows?"

"I know what I saw and I could smell gasoline," Nick insisted.

"From the plane's fuel tanks," Odell interjected.

Gault stepped forward so that he was face-to-face with Kohler. "I want to see the crash site for myself."

"There's nothing to be gained by that, Mr. Gault. You know that as well as I do. You're a pilot, but we're the professionals when it comes to a plane in pieces."

"So am I," Nick said. "I've excavated several crash sites, one of them for the government so that aviators listed as missing in action for more than fifty years could be identified."

Kohler smiled condescendingly. "Stick to the past, Ms. Scott."

"The longer dead the better," Odell added.

Gault stepped away from Kohler to confront Odell, who was sweating profusely in the cool evening air. No doubt he was a desk jockey, Nick thought, not a field man.

"I'm going into that canyon," Gault announced. "The only way you're going to stop me is by having these deputies arrest me."

To Nick's surprise, Odell gave way.

"Suit yourself. We'll even go with you so you'll have some better light." He signaled to the deputies, who fired up a pair of kerosene lanterns.

Once inside the narrow canyon, the temperature seemed to drop suddenly. Or maybe it was Nick's imagination, or the dancing shadows that their lanterns cast on the sandstone walls that made her flesh crawl. Whatever the reason, she was shivering by the time they reached the wreckage. Very little was left of the airplane now, only small pieces of scattered debris.

"We'll be doing a final sweep of the area tomorrow morning," Kohler said.

Gault came to a stop at the edge of the charred area and began casting the beam from his lantern back and forth. As far as Nick could see, there was nothing left worth salvaging.

"Now that you've had your look, Mr. Gault," Odell said, "don't you think it's time you left this to us?"

Gault looked up from the ground, staring at the man, but Nick had the feeling that he was seeing nothing but his own inner thoughts.

"There will be paperwork for you later on," Odell added, "but that can be forwarded to you in Salt Lake."

Gault gave a curt nod and walked out of the canyon. Nick followed him.

By the time they returned to Ophir it was dinner-time. Nick's students had fended for themselves, coming up with cheese sandwiches and lukewarm Cokes. Nick invited Gault to join them for dinner. He insisted on providing dessert, Twinkies and Hostess cupcakes from the Emporium. She was touched by his consideration.

Between bites, Nick said, "Will you be flying back tomorrow?"

"Maybe. Matt was about to be married, you know. After the honeymoon, he was coming into business with me. A third generation of Gault Aviation."

"I'm sorry," she said quietly.

"Sorry enough to grant me a favor?"

"Let's hear it."

"I'd like to borrow your truck." He smiled crookedly. "To sleep in tonight, and then to take a trip into the desert."

Nick took a deep breath. "Looking for what?"

"I've been thinking over what you said. Matt could have landed somewhere else and got himself sunburned. If so, maybe I can find out where. And *where* might lead me to *why*."

"This is hard country," Nick said. "I've spent a lot of time in the desert, so I know what I'm talking about."

"I can't just walk away yet," Gault insisted. "I have to see the ground for myself. You said you heard a chop-per. Well, maybe there's a base nearby. Maybe the chopper pilot saw something. Maybe he can tell me why Matt's Cessna went down."

She stared at him. When they first met in Mescalero, she'd thought he looked no more than sixty. Now he looked exhausted.

"All right, you can use the truck tonight."

"And tomorrow?"

By then she hoped he'd change his mind. Challenging the badlands around Ophir could kill you just as easily as an airplane, though probably not as quickly.

8

Frank Odell hesitated to use his cell phone, despite assurances that it was secure. Still, he'd been told to keep in touch. And his cell phone was sure as hell safer than anything else in Ophir.

He'd had to drive halfway to Mescalero in order to get line-of-sight to the satellite. At that point, there was nothing but sand and a few scrubby-looking weeds. But it was a welcome change from the ramshackle buildings that clung to the sides of the played-out mines in Ophir.

Shaking his head, Odell scanned the landscape one more time to make certain he was alone, then hit the redial button.

A voice answered immediately. "Odell?"

"Yes, sir."

"No complications, I hope."

"Just one, the archaeologist."

"I thought everything burned."

"She got a quick look first," Odell said carefully.

"And?"

"She knows planes. She's an expert."

"For Christ's sake, you just said she was an archaeologist."

"Not the kind you think."

"So what difference does it make?"

"She's tenacious as hell."

"How do you know that?"

"Just talking to her was enough. I did a quick search on the net and her name turned up. She has a reputation for sticking to these things like ticks on a dog."

"You keep an eye on her, then," the voice warned. "I don't want any more mistakes."

Odell grimaced. The mistake hadn't been his, but he wasn't about to say so.

The connection was cut. He felt a chill; his hands were ice-cold.

9

Nick thought Gault looked worse the next morning. Sleeping in the truck had left him sore and tired. Gray stubble covered his cheeks. His eyes were red-rimmed and sunken.

One look at him and Nick knew what she had to do.

"If you still insist on driving into the desert, I'm going with you," she said.

"And your students?"

"This is their last day anyway. Most of it will be used for cleaning up the site and packing their supplies. They'll be glad to be rid of me."

He stared hard enough to make her blush.

"Matt would have liked you," he said finally.

"I'm sure I would have liked him. I already like you." She noticed that it was his turn to look embarrassed.

He turned his head away and said, "We'd better get going."

"I wish you'd reconsider, Mr. Gault."

"Call me John, and there's no need for you to come along. It's not going to be a picnic out there."

"You're on my ground now, *John*. I know how to survive out here. Do you?"

"I survived a war."

"There, you could see your enemies. Here . . ." Nick nodded in the direction of her truck. "Take a look at the water cans belted to the side of my pickup. That's twenty gallons' worth. I've taken courses on desert survival. I could find my own water if I had to. But it's always best to carry your own."

He squinted at her for a moment, then looked out toward the desert. "Is there water out there?"

"Not much. Someone might survive for a day or two."

"Christ. It must be a hundred degrees already. It feels like sunburn alone could kill you."

"That's possible."

She knew what he was thinking, that maybe Matt had landed in this same relentless heat. But why would a pilot take such a risk? Nothing plausible occurred to her.

Gault rubbed his face. He was obviously shaken, but she remembered how he'd looked yesterday when he'd grabbed Moyle. He'd been determined and fearless.

With visible effort he set his shoulders and clenched his jaw. His determination was obvious.

"I don't see how you can stop me from coming along," she said. "I've got the keys. Now, how about some breakfast?"

Fifteen minutes later, keeping the pickup in four-wheel drive, Nick left the dirt road behind and headed west toward the mesa, following two ruts that looked narrow enough to have been made by pioneer wagons.

She drove slowly while Gault stood in the back of the truck, his elbows on the cab roof, the binoculars to his eyes. To communicate, they'd opened both side windows and the sliding vent directly behind the driver's seat.

"Where does this trail lead?" he shouted.

"Nowhere, according to Moyle," she shouted back.

"Slow down," he instructed.

"Any slower and we'll stall."

"Stop then."

Nick eased the truck to a stop and got out. She joined him in the back.

"You said you've seen choppers out here before, is that right?" He took his eyes from the binoculars long enough to point at Mesa d'Oro.

"In that general direction, yes."

"It looks flat enough to land on top."

"The last time I saw one was a week before your Cessna crashed, and it was a long way off."

"Look for yourself." He handed her the glasses. A quick scan showed the bright blue sky to be empty.

"For the last time," she said, annoyed, "I don't imagine things."

Gault shrugged. "I spoke with one of the locals last night, a man named Dobbs. He's seen them, too. He also told me he's done some prospecting out by the mesa. Mesa d'Oro means mesa of gold, he told me."

"Zeke Moyle claims Dobbs sees things when he's drinking." Sarcastically, she added, "Moyle probably says the same thing about me behind my back."

"Dobbs claims he was chased out of there once by soldiers."

Nick shook her head. "I haven't seen anyone on the ground."

Gault took back the binoculars. "Did he tell you the choppers he saw were black, like shadows?"

"No."

"Mr. Dobbs is a regular fountain of information. He says there's an abandoned army base out here somewhere. But it can't be abandoned if that's where the soldiers he saw came from."

"So let's see if we can find it."

A base would explain a lot, Nick thought. It might even explain the NTSB investigators' attitude toward her.

Nodding, Gault lowered the binoculars and rubbed his eyes. "I'm not a fool. I don't expect to find all the answers out here. But Matt was no fool either. If he was here looking for a story, then I'd like to know what the hell it was."

She started to respond, but he spoke first. "And no, Nick, I don't think you're a fool either. If you tell me you heard a helicopter in that canyon before the crash, I believe you. And if you say my grandson's body looked strange, I'll believe that, too. But the fact remains, if a helicopter had anything to do with the crash of my Cessna, then it should have gone down. Since there was no sign of a chopper, in pieces or otherwise, I'd say an old army base is a good place to start looking for one."

Nick studied the trail ahead. It ran straight toward the mesa until it disappeared into the heat waves rising from the horizon.

"Help me watch for flood gullies," she said before vaulting from the truck bed and climbing back behind the wheel.

She set the odometer and crept ahead at five miles an hour. A mile later the track widened into a single-lane dirt road. It looked recently traveled.

Gault banged on the cab and shouted, "I see dust up ahead."

Squinting at the blazing landscape had her seeing spots. "I don't see anything."

"Stop."

When she did he handed her the binoculars through

the sliding window. Nick had to wipe the sweat from her eyes before she could get the glasses properly focused. Then she wished she hadn't.

"My God," she said, stunned. "It looks like a tank."

"Definitely military," he said, "probably a humvee. Do you see any markings?"

She wiped her eyes again, then the eyepieces. "I can't see anything but dust. Whatever it is, it sure as hell is coming straight at us."

She surrendered the binoculars, switched off the engine, and climbed out of the cab. Gault took another long look through the binoculars before joining her in front of the truck.

"It's painted in desert camouflage," he said.

"And?"

"I don't know, but it's always best to keep your hands in plain sight."

"There's a .30-.30 under the seat," she said.

He nodded toward the approaching vehicle, now close. "And they've got a machine gun mounted on top."

"Shit."

"Exactly," Gault said. "Put up your hands and don't make any sudden moves."

The humvee stopped twenty yards short of them, and two men got out, both carrying M-16s.

Nick shouted, "We're not armed."

The men, wearing camouflage fatigues that matched their humvee, approached carefully. They had no military insignia, as far as Nick could see. Neither did their humvee. Dark glasses hid their eyes. In uniform, they looked interchangeable.

"This is private property," one of them said.

"It's not posted," Nick answered.

"We stopped you short of the fence. But you've been on restricted land for the last half mile."

"And you are?" Gault asked.

"We're here to turn you around." He gestured with his M-16. His counterpart added, "Please."

"A plane went down near Ophir," Nick said. "We think a helicopter may have been involved."

"This land is closely patrolled. At the moment, you two are the only unauthorized personnel in our area."

"That plane belonged to me," Gault said. "And my grandson was flying it."

"I'm sorry, but you'll still have to turn around." Both men backed up a step and brought their rifles to the ready.

Nick glanced at Gault and couldn't believe her eyes. The weary man who'd started out with her that morning seemed transformed. His startling blue eyes had taken on a dangerous glint and his slouch was disappearing as he repositioned his weight. He looked ready to spring at the two men.

She laid a restraining hand on his arm.

"Are you army?" Gault demanded.

"We're not authorized to give out that information."

"And who is?"

Nick tightened her grip. "Come on, John, we'll look somewhere else. There are half a dozen roads east of here. With luck we can drive them all before dark."

Ignoring her, Gault pointed a finger at the nearest rifleman. "Do you use helicopters to patrol this area?"

His only answer was a repeated gesture for a U-turn.

Suddenly, Nick felt Gault's arm relax. She led him back to the truck, watched him get into the passenger's seat, then climbed in and drove as fast as she could. Dust clouds billowed behind them worthy of a warship laying down a smoke screen.

When the odometer said they were well beyond the pair's imposed property line, she slowed enough to be able to talk. "If they were military, they should have had insignia."

"Could be we ran into one of those right-wing militia groups," he answered. "Only I don't buy it. And don't forget, that mesa's smack in the middle of a no-fly zone. Crackpot militias don't rate that kind of treatment."

"How the hell did they find us, anyway?"

"I'd say it depends on what they're guarding. A missile base or something like that might have seismic sensors planted along the perimeter. Of course, you put a telescope on top of that mesa, and you could see for twenty miles in any direction. And we weren't exactly trying to hide, though the next time maybe we should."

She braked to a hard stop. "Hold it. Next time we might get ourselves shot."

"So you stay out of it."

"You're not taking my truck back there, if that's what you have in mind." She was sorry she'd tried to help. It was safer to stick to archaeology, she reminded herself.

"Nighttime would be best," Gault mused. "Of course a truck wouldn't be any use then. Its headlights would show for miles."

Nick pretended not to hear.

"In a plane," Gault went on, "I could come in at dusk."

"If they have sensors, they'll have radar," she pointed out.

"I'll fly under it."

"And do what? There's no place to land."

"A good pilot, flying the right plane, could set down on this road."

Open-mouthed, Nick stared at him, looking for any sign that he might be joking. But when he smiled at her, she knew he meant every word.

10

Nick and Gault returned to Ophir well after dark. By then, they'd driven every back road for miles, without spotting so much as a buzzard, let alone a helicopter. Or any place a Cessna could have landed safely, either.

The two Feds, Kohler and Odell, were waiting for them when they entered the Emporium. Both looked uncomfortable. Nick sensed bad news immediately. So did Gault, judging by the sudden set of his shoulders.

The one-room shack, hot and airless as she crossed the threshold, seemed abruptly dank.

Kohler spoke first. "As you know, Mr. Gault, we sent your grandson's body to Phoenix. Dental records were transmitted by fax first thing this morning. Identification has been confirmed. That was your grandson in the Cessna. I'm sorry."

Nick was about to offer Gault moral support when she saw his face. His jaw was set. He looked more angry than anything else.

"What we have to do now," Odell put in, consulting his ever present clipboard, "is to take care of the formalities. We need your approval for disposition of the remains. We can have them sent to a funeral home in Salt Lake City, if that's convenient."

"I'll pick them up myself, if you don't mind," Gault said, his voice taut. "I'll fly to Phoenix myself."

An immediate sense of relief flooded over her. If Gault was flying to Phoenix, he might forget his crazy plan to attempt a night landing in the desert.

Odell tapped his clipboard. "As for the wreckage . . ."

"You can keep it, as far as I'm concerned," Gault said tonelessly.

"Your insurance company might have something to say about that."

Gault opened his mouth to respond, then suddenly seemed to think better of it. His teeth snapped together and he hurried from the room.

Nick stared after him for a moment. When she turned back to the Feds she felt she had interrupted some secret conversation.

"By the way, Ms. Scott," Kohler said, "your father arrived while you were gone. We understand he's an archaeologist too."

"We figured he was worried about your students," Odell added, "the ones you've been neglecting."

Nick bristled at the implied criticism and wondered what business it was of theirs. But she decided to keep her mouth shut. Odell reminded her of Ben Gilbert, her unctuous department head at Berkeley. There was something essentially insincere about them both. Besides, her students would be on their way tomorrow, and that would be the end of that complication.

"Your father filled in for you," Odell continued. "He got your students digging another trench while he lectured them on the Anasazi Indians. He's a hell of a speaker, if I do say so myself. I damn near joined in when he said the Anasazi could have been right here in Ophir."

Teeth clenched, Nick left the Emporium without another word. Gault was waiting for her just outside.

"They're covering up something," he said, shaking his head. "I feel it in my gut."

What Nick was feeling was anger. Thank God her father hadn't arrived any sooner. His reputation was worldwide. His presence alone would be enough to eclipse her and undermine her authority if the dig were to continue. He wouldn't interfere intentionally, of course, but her students would look to him, not her. And she couldn't blame them. After all, Elliot Scott was the grand old man of southwestern archaeology.

"Most Feds are idiots," Nick said. "What they usually cover up is their own incompetence."

Gault snorted. "I'd agree with you except for the soldiers in the humvee. Matt was looking for a story. Those armed men may be part of it. Though they could be a coincidence. I don't know yet. But armed men patrolling a perimeter means something big's going on."

"And my helicopter?" Nick said.

"That's part of it probably. That and the gas cans you saw in the back seat, though as evidence it's burned and gone forever. I don't like any of it, but I don't know what the hell I can do about it."

"I hope that means you've given up your plan to land in the desert."

He ducked his head sheepishly. "I was angry when I said that. That's never a good time to make a decision. A night landing in that wasteland would be foolhardy. We both know that. Even so, I'd do it if it would help Matt. But getting myself killed won't change anything. Still . . ." He gestured helplessly.

"It's the right decision," Nick said. "Even if something funny is going on, I can't see what it would have to do with Matt's crash."

"I just can't believe that he would take the risk of loading gas into the back seat of his plane."

Before Nick could reply, he shook his head and walked away.

"You'll need something to eat," she called after him.

He raised a hand, acknowledging the comment, but kept on going.

Suddenly, she realized he was heading back toward the pickup. She slapped the pocket of her jeans. The keys were there all right, so he wasn't going anywhere for the moment.

She sighed. She'd catch up with John Gault later. Right now, she had to deal with her father.

• • • •

Elliot took one look at her and said, "Show my daughter an airplane and all else is forgotten."

He was seated in front of a campfire with Nick's students in attendance. An iron kettle hung over the flames. Since the cooking cauldron was her father's, a permanent resident of his four-wheel-drive Jeep, she knew he'd driven all night to get there, a three hundred fifty mile trip from Albuquerque. She also knew the next words out of his mouth.

"The famous Scott stew," he said, confirming her instincts. "I promised your students a real treat instead of that canned food you've been foisting on them. A sort of farewell feast."

Taking his time about it, her father looked around the circle of novice archaeologists. "I was only awaiting your arrival before adding the finishing touches." His eyes glinted with firelight.

With a groan, Nick sat down and closed her eyes. A day of driving in the desert sun had left her limp and exhausted, but that didn't stop her from feeling like a supplicant again. In an instant, ten years of hard work fell away. Once more she was a student, there to study at the feet of the great man. But then her father had always had that effect on her. Even a Ph.D., earned on her own at another university to avoid all possibility of nepotism charges, had failed to dispel her awe of his reputation. God alone knew what her students were feeling at the moment, probably awe tempered by the prospect of a decent meal.

With a dramatic gesture, Elliot rose to stir the pot. Standing in the firelight, casting a long shadow, his six-foot-three frame made him more imposing than ever. Cut him down to our size, Nick's mother had liked to say, and he wouldn't be half so formidable.

"This is an old family recipe," Elliot said, "created by my wife, Elaine, so that I could turn canned food into something as good as homemade while on my digs. I'm surprised Nick hasn't introduced you to it before now."

Because Elaine's cooking wasn't to be trusted, Nick thought. Eating directly from a can or a freeze-dried pack was safer. Nick had learned that after a disastrous Thanksgiving dinner when she was nine years old.

"Catsup's the secret," Elliot went on.

Sure. It covers up the salmonella.

But her unsuspecting, wide-eyed students couldn't take their eyes off Elliot. He had them mesmerized over catsup, for God's sake. If they'd been using their brains, they'd have caught on to his shenanigans by now and started laughing.

Nick broke the spell. "Do you remember the food poisoning?"

"That had nothing to do with one of my stews," Elliot protested.

Around the circle gazes faltered. Adoration gave way to hesitation.

"At least there was a hospital close by where we could get our stomachs pumped."

Elliot raised a hand, requesting a truce. "My daughter—your professor—loves her jokes."

Nick grinned to let him off the hook. "So let's eat. I'm starved."

Elliot began dishing out the stew. Nick took the first serving and dug in. Whatever he'd done to the canned goods, the result tasted like ambrosia after a day in the badlands with only PowerBars to gnaw on.

Once everyone was served, Elliot sat beside her. Pointed stares on Nick's part sent students edging away until she and her father could talk privately, as long as they kept their voices down.

Between bites, she said, "I hear you put my students to work digging one last trench."

"I wanted to make sure they got their money's worth."

"Look at them. They're exhausted."

"Wait till I bring out the marshmallows. There's nothing like sitting around an open bonfire roasting marshmallows to raise your spirits." He took a deep breath. "Smell that smoke. Doesn't that remind you of those digs I took you on as a child?"

There hadn't been that many. Elaine wouldn't allow it. *I'll be alone*, she'd worry. *Without even my daughter for comfort.*

"I really do have marshmallows," Elliot went on. "I picked them up on the way here." He winked, and suddenly she realized the glint in his eye was more than firelight.

"All right, Elliot, out with it. What the hell are you up to?"

"Remember what I used to tell you when you'd ask me why I love digging so much?"

" 'The next turn of the spade might be the one to reveal an undiscovered world,' " she quoted by rote.

He spread his arms as if congratulating her memory. The students picked up on his gesture and began applauding.

"You found something."

He reached under his seat and came up with a brown octagonal bottle. The brand name, Duffy's Apple Juice, was in raised glass lettering, as was the 1842 trademark.

"Does that help?" Elliot asked.

She hugged him. For her students' benefit, she said, "This had to belong to the Benson sisters. Throughout their diaries, there are constant references to their mother, who was a great believer in brand names. Duffy's was one of her favorites."

"You'll need more proof than that," her father said. "The neighbors could have been using the same brand."

"Just you wait," she said and hurried to her tent.

When she returned she proudly showed him what she'd found two days before. She noticed that the students were quiet, awaiting the great man's verdict. Carefully, he removed the object from its protective wrapping and held it up so that it reflected dully in the firelight.

"I'd say a late nineteenth-century pearl-handled implement of some sort. One end corroded due to oxidation. You can see the start of a curve here. Ah, a buttonhook. A lady's buttonhook." Elliot bowed to imaginary applause.

Nick remembered how much he liked to perform.

Two could play that game, she thought, and quoted an excerpt from Lillian Benson's diary from memory. " 'The fire took most everything we had. But what we miss most are the few treasures mother passed on to us. Our favorite was her pearl-handled buttonhook. But it's gone forever now, and when we're gone nothing will remain of our dear mother. It will be as if she never lived.' "

Nick took back the buttonhook. "This will be the highlight of my monograph, but now I can add the bottle."

And because of it, she knew, the Bensons would be remembered.

Elliot put an arm around her. "I taught you well, daughter. The trouble is, I'm only your department head for the summer. Your real boss just happened to give me another call."

"Dammit, Elliot. That's the last straw!" Nick spoke loud enough to send students fleeing for their tents. "If Ben Gilbert has something to say, he should have the guts to do it to my face."

As department chair at Berkeley, Gilbert had never forgiven Nick for having Elliot as a father, or for locating a long-lost World War Two airplane whose discovery made her an instant celebrity, not to mention the subject of a lead article in *National Geographic*. The fact that he had tried to get her fired as a publicity seeker, and failed, didn't help matters.

"You'd think he'd have better things to do," she said,

"considering the sexual harassment lawsuits the university is paying off these days."

"He's always sniffing around. Even the fact that my department's sponsoring this dig doesn't stop him. Oh, no. Ben Gilbert has his nose to the ground whenever it's not up somebody's ass. The trouble is, sooner or later, he's going to pin something on you. So forget Berkeley. I have an opening in my department right now. Tenure is yours the moment you sign the contract," Elliot offered.

"I wouldn't give Gilbert the satisfaction of leaving."

"If it weren't for him, you'd have tenure on your own."

"Just tell me what he said exactly."

" 'Tell her we have to talk soon,' were his words. It's what he didn't say that bothers me."

"Such as?"

Elliot shrugged. "I don't know for sure, but I don't like him any better than you do. So it's a good thing I came. You need someone to cover your back when you're playing with your airplanes."

"I'm not your little girl anymore."

"I should have covered your back then, too."

She laid a hand on his arm. Nick's childhood with Elaine was something she'd never fully discussed with her father. For one thing, no one who hadn't been there day after day, coping with Elaine's violent mood swings, could understand what Nick had gone through. For another, Elaine had extracted promises of silence, blood oaths as she called them. *Cross your heart*, she'd say, *and hope to die if you don't keep our secrets.* Elaine had been cowering in dark places most of those times, hiding from demons only she could see.

"That airplane isn't one of mine, Dad," Nick said. "But I'm still glad you're here."

Nodding, Elliot stared into the fire. Maybe it was the flickering light, or the smoke, but her eyes began to water. His too, judging by the way he was wiping them.

"The plane's still bothering me, though," she said after a long silence.

"I thought you said it was a new one, not collectible at all."

"This has nothing to do with archaeology. I think something's going on."

She summarized her brief acquaintance with John Gault, their encounter with armed men in the desert, and the NTSB's reaction to her eyewitness account of the Cessna and the body inside it.

When she finished, Elliot paced in front of the fire for a while before speaking. "What is it about you and airplanes? The last one damn near got you killed."

"It wasn't my fault."

"Where is this man, Gault, now? Maybe I'd better meet him for myself."

She snorted. "You're going to like him, Elliot. He's just like you, obsessive."

"And you're not?"

" 'A good archaeologist has to be obsessive.' Your words, Elliot."

It was her motto too, Nick realized. She'd worked hard to get where she was, tenure or no tenure. She, like her father, was a recognized expert in her field. As such, she deserved better than the treatment she'd received at the hands of Kohler and Odell. They'd challenged her abilities. Well, by God, if she got the chance, she'd make them eat their words.

11

As usual, Nick's alarm clock woke her ten minutes before sunrise. Even so, Gault was waiting for her outside the wash area. She shooed him behind the modesty tarp.

"Your father paid me a call last night," Gault said.

"Mm," she said, splashing her face with cold water.

"He's a very perceptive man."

"Uh-huh."

"What did you tell him about me?"

She dried her face before responding. "That you're as obsessive as he is, and that I was worried about you doing something dangerous, like tackling that desert on your own."

"I told you I was flying to Phoenix to pick up Matt."

"I know what you told me. My father's told me things like that too, then goes on about his business anyway, even if it's the exact opposite."

"Look," he said calmly, "you've given me more help than I deserve. I'm not at my best right now, but I just think that you—"

Nick stopped him in mid-sentence. "What's a nice girl like you doing in a place like this?"

She could see that at first he was bewildered. Then a look of understanding showed on his face and he started to laugh.

He's not so lost after all, she thought, deciding that he looked almost boyish when he laughed.

"Are you asking to borrow my truck again?" she said.

"I'd feel better renting it."

"I wouldn't want it shot up by those two Neanderthals we met in the humvee yesterday."

"I don't intend to make that mistake again," Gault said.

Buttoning her fresh work shirt, she emerged from behind the tarp. "So why do you need the truck?"

"Have you forgotten? My plane's in Mescalero. It's a long walk. I need a ride."

"I'll ask my father to take you."

"I thought you might like to fly with me," he said. "We could take a look at the mesa from the air and see what the hell's going on up there."

Nick licked her dry lips. More than anything she wanted proof that her helicopter existed. At the same time, finding it might be the worst thing that could happen to Gault.

"That might not be such a good idea," she said. "It's still a no-fly zone on the map."

The look of disappointment on his face had her reaching out to him, but she stopped short of contact. It was better not to embarrass him, she thought, then realized that wasn't why she'd shied away. There was something very appealing about him.

Nick pulled her baseball cap hard down around her ears, flattening her hair. What the hell was wrong with her? She loved planes, so her interest in Gault had to be connected. It was as simple as that. After all, he was a pilot.

Suddenly, she caught herself staring at him. To break the silence, she said, "Aren't you forgetting something? You could lose your license for violating a no-fly zone."

"I can always claim I was off course. Besides, whatever happens, I'm taking a close look at the area around the mesa, starting with where we ran into that humvee."

Nick turned away to gaze toward the horizon. The desert sky was cloudless. Today's predicted high temperature was 105, plus or minus five degrees.

"I've never flown in a twin Cessna," she said.

"Does that mean you'll fly with me?" Gault asked.

Nick took a deep breath and nodded.

"What about your students?"

"I'm seeing them off right after breakfast. After that, my father and I are on our own."

"What's he going to say about you endangering yourself?"

"He'll grumble for a while. But he knows how I feel about airplanes. After a while, he'll calm down and be happy puttering around the dig, looking for buried treasure."

Nick watched Gault's movements during takeoff with admiration. They were concise, with no wasted effort. His eyes shifted constantly, checking the sky one moment, the instruments the next. His hands seemed to move independently, touching and adjusting the controls. He set their radio to the Mescalero airport frequency.

As the Cessna rose into the bright sky, Nick felt soaring excitement. The power of the twin engines vibrated through every fiber of her body. The speed of the plane seemed twice that of a commercial jet, though she knew it was an illusion because of their low altitude. They were hugging the ground at two hundred feet to stay under the detection of radar if there was any monitoring of the area.

They were heading northwest toward the great mesa, which was invisible for the moment in the purple haze of the horizon.

A few minutes later Gault tapped her knee. "Use the binoculars!" he shouted over the engine roar, though they both wore headsets. "Start looking for anything. Smoke, dust, anything unusual."

The binoculars brought the mesa into her field of vision. But at this distance, it looked as unreal as the shimmering mirage lake from which it rose.

She checked the map in her lap, then held it up in Gault's field of vision and tapped a finger against what she thought to be their position, Sulphur Flats.

He took a quick look, compared it to the ground, and nodded. Sulphur Flats extended another thirty miles, all the way to the foothills of the Mescalero Mountains.

"Hell must look like this," he yelled.

His comment had her nodding. Seen through the foreshortening of the binocular's magnification, the desert floor looked like a thin veneer. Peel it away and the fiery pit beneath would be instantly revealed.

The unremitting glare had her seeing spots. She rubbed her eyes, making matters worse. Tears ran down her cheeks.

"Rest your eyes for a while," he said.

Even with her eyes closed, the bright desert sun shown through her lids. She tried to relax, but the engine throb made her tingle with anticipation. She risked a peek at Gault. He could have been sitting in a rocking chair for all the emotion he showed.

She shifted her gaze and realized that the mesa was close now, filling the windshield and looming over them. Its height, according to the map, was just under two thousand feet.

"I'm going over the top!" he shouted. "Even if they don't have radar, they'll sure as hell hear us."

It was like riding a roller coaster. The mesa was coming at them as if jet-propelled. She loved it. The feeling was pure exhilaration, more exciting even than the carnival rides she'd treasured as a child. Then and there, she vowed to take flying lessons the first chance she got.

Light glinted from the top of the mesa. Gault pointed, but she'd already seen the flash.

She brought the binoculars to her eyes. The flash had been sunlight reflecting off windows sunk into the side of a squat concrete building painted the same red sandstone color as the rest of the mesa. A similarly camouflaged radar dish was mounted on the building's flat roof. In front of the building a large white X had been painted on a blacktopped courtyard.

"Landing pad!" Gault shouted.

Nick panned the horizon but saw no sign of helicopters.

The mesa swept beneath them and Gault put the plane into a shallow dive toward the desert floor.

"That place doesn't show on the map," she said. "Go around for another look."

He banked sharply. At the same time, two helicopters rose from behind the far side of the mesa.

Nick pointed them out, but Gault had already spotted them. Both were painted black and showed no military markings. Nick realized that their chin-mounted cannons seemed to be aimed right at them.

Gault shoved the throttles forward and dove. The helicopters followed.

"We're a little faster than they are," he shouted. "If they give us enough time."

Nick's headset crackled to life. "Cessna 340, identify yourself."

"This is November-three-four-seven-one-Zulu en route to Salt Lake City," Gault answered. "Over."

"You're off course and this is restricted airspace."

Gault banked the Cessna first one way, then the other, his eyes scanning the landscape below. Nick spotted the old army barracks the same time he did. Even from five hundred feet up, she could see the high chainlink fence that surrounded them. Seen through the binoculars, the fence was clearly topped with razor wire. Behind it stood half a dozen men, all looking up at her, none of them waving. A dirt road, probably the same one on which they'd encountered the humvee, ended at the fence's double gate.

"That looks like a detention camp," she told Gault.

"Out here in the middle of nowhere? It can't be. It must be military."

Nick wasn't so sure. Gault hadn't seen the barbed wire. It looked more like a holding pen than barracks. They weren't soldiers. Nick would have bet on that.

Gault triggered his microphone. "Is this a military reservation?"

"Leave the area immediately," came the answer from one of the helicopters. "Failure to do so will be considered felony trespass."

Gault banked again, more steeply. By now they were heading south again, back toward Mescalero.

"Four-seven-one-Zulu, Salt Lake is the other way."

"Go to hell," Gault answered. To Nick, he said, "We're out of cannon range now."

Nick realized she'd been holding her breath. She exhaled deeply. "One thing's for sure, there are helicopters around here. As to what they're doing in this place, I can't imagine. But that building on the mesa sure as hell looks expensive."

In fact, expensive was an understatement, she thought. The word fortune came to mind. Because of the mesa's vertical walls, all the building materials would have to have been flown in by chopper.

"Only the military has that kind of funding," she added.

They were silent for the rest of the flight. And as much as she loved planes, Nick was happy to be back on the ground when they landed.

As soon as Gault cut the engine, she asked, "What kind of story was Matt after?"

"I don't know. He was always closemouthed about his work. 'Keep it to yourself,' he liked to say, 'and nobody will beat you into print.' "

"What kind of stories had he done in the past?"

"Matt was a crusader. He said journalism was one of the few places the little guy, the guy without money or political clout, could get justice. That was his creed, that and his sense of history. He believed we'd better learn from it or we'll be condemned to relive the atrocities."

"He sounds like a hell of a reporter."

"He was. He was always being threatened. That's why I was relieved when he finally agreed to come into the business with me. His fiancée was joining us, too, eventually. She's an Air Force pilot."

"Maybe she'd know what's going on up on that mesa?" Nick said.

"I couldn't ask her, because whatever it is has to be classified. Otherwise, why the choppers?"

"There weren't any military markings on them," Nick pointed out.

"That doesn't surprise me. If they're testing some kind of secret weapons system, they'd want to keep a low profile. Maybe Mesa d'Oro is the Arizona version of Roswell, New Mexico."

Nick shook her head and smiled. "Complete with aliens and flying saucers, I suppose."

"Lady Luck, I know about. As for lights in the sky and the like, I've never seen them myself."

"Let's assume you're right about the testing. Would Matt go after a story if it was a military secret?"

"Not without a lot of careful thought."

Nick closed her eyes and saw the men in the compound again. What kind of military secret could they be hiding?

Together, they climbed out of the Cessna. The sunlight hammered Nick so hard her head began to throb instantly. Underfoot, the asphalt felt gooey.

"Jesus," Gault said. "It must be a hundred and ten." He scanned the desert landscape beyond the runway. "You said you were an expert in survival. How long could you last out there?"

"If I knew where I was, I could probably make it far enough to find help. With luck."

Gault nodded. "I know about luck. We pilots spend too much of it. Matt's ran out in the wrong place."

"I could have accepted my luck running out," he continued. "But Matt's . . ." His shoulders slumped. "God, I remember him sitting with me in the *Lady-A*'s cockpit when he was a little boy. He'd pretend he was flying. It became a ritual with us, sitting in that old B-24, talking. The last time . . . God, it was only two weeks ago . . . he told me he'd been dreaming about flying her for real as long as he could remember. He said he used to wish for it all the time." Gault sighed deeply. "Maybe I'll do that. Maybe I'll rebuild her engines and fly her one more time. No matter what the cost."

Looking at him, she knew he was a man capable of doing just that.

12

Atop Mesa d'Oro, Frank Odell spoke without taking the binoculars from his eyes. "Do you think Gault will come back?"

"My boys will shoot him down if he does," the Director said, abandoning his own binoculars to pat Odell on the back. "Chances are he got the message from my Blackbirds and went home with his tail between his legs."

Odell lowered his glasses and eyed the Director skeptically. "And the archaeologist? Your *boys* said they saw her in the cockpit. What do we do about her?"

"Look, Frank, I'm not happy about the overflight. This man Gault caught us napping today, that's for sure. But what's done is done. What we have to do now is to make sure it doesn't happen again. As for this lady archaeologist of yours, she needs an artifact to do her work, doesn't she? There's nothing left of that Cessna but ashes, so no artifact, no fuss. That's the end of it."

"Not quite," Odell said, trying to hide the malice he

felt. "I've done a deeper background check on her. Remember the Scorpion?"

The Director turned away and for a moment Odell thought he hadn't heard him.

"The B-17 near Cibola," Odell persisted, "the one that . . ." His voice trailed off. He cursed his own stupidity, remembering too late that the Director had been a close friend of the famous industrialist who had died trying to hush up the B-17's discovery.

The Director turned back with a faraway, almost dreamy expression on his face. Although he was now facing Odell, the public relations man wasn't sure that the Director was even aware of who he was talking to.

"They tell me that archaeology is a crowded field." The Director suddenly seemed to notice Odell. "Too crowded. Isn't that right, Frank?"

Odell gulped. "The woman's famous," he replied. "We've got to be careful. Even *National Geographic* has featured her. They did a full-color spread on her when she found that bomber that had been lost in the jungle since World War Two. She spent months tracking it down. She's not the kind to give up easily."

The Director's expression darkened. "My friend was famous. What would a man like you know about true power, true fame? She's had her fifteen minutes. My Blackbirds will see to it that her time is up."

Odell groaned inwardly. Blackbirds was the Director's euphemism for his rabid two-man security team, Voss and Wiley.

"Your expression tells me you don't like the idea," the Director said, smiling.

Odell was fully aware that if he went too far, the Blackbirds would be pecking out his eyes. "They've made one mistake already." He waited for the Director to explode.

But he merely nodded. "For once, Frank, you're right. *Mea culpa.* But who the hell could have foreseen that archaeologist of yours wandering into Sulphur Canyon like that? Plain bad luck, I call it."

Odell glanced at Voss and Wiley, who were standing near the edge of the mesa. He suspected they tempted fate that way, teetering on the edge, just to show how macho they were. Though why they bothered, he couldn't imagine. No one in their right mind would question their abilities.

The Director smiled at the pair of them. Both wore dark suits, white shirts and ties, and looked unruffled, despite the heat. Their eyes were invisible behind mirror-like dark glasses. They reminded Odell of FBI agents, or maybe even Mormon missionaries, until they took off those glasses and you saw their cold eyes.

"Stop worrying, Frank," the Director said. "My Blackbirds are a precaution only. They'll be keeping tabs on things, that's all. No big deal."

As far as Odell was concerned, Voss and Wiley were vultures. Certainly Voss had the mental markings, a redneck if ever he'd seen one. As for Wiley, his expression never changed; he never gave away his thoughts. And all he talked about, at least in Odell's presence, were the tools of his trade. Odell suppressed a grimace. Did assassin qualify as a trade?

"Are there any suggestions you'd like to pass on to my Blackbirds before I send them on their way?" The Director's smile grew as he kicked a rock over the precipice. Despite the smile, his dark eyes remained flinty.

"We don't want them overreacting," Odell cautioned.

"My very words to them exactly."

The Director raised his binoculars to his eyes and peered down in the direction of Ophir. "You know, Frank, there's overreaction and then there's proper precaution. Look where Ophir sits, at the base of that crumbling old cliff." He lowered his glasses and smiled at Odell. "It's an accident waiting to happen, Frank. An act of God, that's what we need."

Odell shook his head.

"Don't worry, Frank, I'm not playing God." The Director picked up a red rock and hurled it over the edge. "Not just yet anyway."

As always, Odell stood back from the edge. The mesa was an acrophobic nightmare come true. It was said to have been named by Coronado himself during his sixteenth-century quest for the fabled seven cities of gold. Access was by helicopter only, but Odell knew that the Director had once hired professional climbers to make the attempt. Halfway up the vertical face, they had triggered sensor alarms. A hundred feet later, they'd radioed for a rescue team. Odell had the impression that the Director would have preferred to watch fate take its course.

"Now, why don't you see Voss and Wiley on their way, Frank, while I get back to work. Otherwise, they might feel you didn't like them. Besides, I have something cooking right now."

Odell grimaced at the thought of what the Director meant by cooking.

"That's what I like about you, Frank. You're predictable."

With that, the Director turned on his heel and headed for the main building. As soon as he was out of sight, Voss and Wiley crossed the courtyard to the waiting helicopter, whose 20mm cannons were shrouded in canvas to make them look less deadly. Odell joined them, though he would have felt safer handling rattlesnakes.

"Do you understand your brief?" Odell said. "No action is to be taken without authorization from either me or the Director."

"Whatever you say, Frank," Voss said.

"Remember," he replied, "we don't want any more problems cropping up."

Wiley, the taller of the two, drew an automatic pistol from his shoulder holster and studied it closely. "A silenced .22 is always best, Frank. There's no fuss or muss, no splatter. A clean kill is the sign of a true professional. Wouldn't you agree?"

Voss shook his head. "Give me a .357." He drew out an enormous revolver. "The noise alone will keep by-standers from sticking their noses in where they don't belong. And the impact—by God, that's something to see."

Odell grit his teeth. They were goading him, he knew, running a con on him. But knowing that didn't help. Their love of their job was real enough. And he had no doubt whatsoever that if the Director gave the order, they'd use those guns on him.

The helicopter pilot, dressed in a one-piece khaki flight suit, appeared in the chopper's open doorway. He eyed their weapons, shook his head, and jerked a thumb toward the nose cannons. "Mine's bigger than both of yours."

Unsmiling, Voss and Wiley holstered their guns, and disappeared into the chopper, sliding the door closed behind them.

Christ, Odell thought, retreating out from under the whirling blades. Thank God his wife had left him and taken their son with her. Otherwise, he'd have to explain why he worked in a place like this.

13

Gault insisted on walking Nick to her pickup. When he opened the door for her, she had to hold back a smile. Being out here so long, she'd forgotten how nice common courtesies could be.

She took a long look at the man holding her door. In the past two days, he'd aged terribly. The strength she'd felt the first time she saw him had drained away.

To hell with it, she thought, and hugged him tightly. There was a good chance she'd never see this man again.

"I'd feel better if you got a night's rest before flying to Phoenix," she said.

"I couldn't sleep. I'd just lie there thinking about Matt being in the hands of strangers."

He hugged her back. The determination was still there in his eyes. No, it was more than determination. It burned too brightly for that.

"I've just made a decision," he said. "I'll have Matt cremated. We can drop his ashes from the *Lady-A* as soon as I've got her ready to fly one last mission. A nostalgic flight of fancy."

"You said *we*."

"You can fly with me anytime," he said. "I don't know how long it's going to take to get my Liberator ready, but you'll be welcome aboard. I mean that."

It seemed to her that the simple hug had changed into a mutual embrace. "I'll look forward to it."

"You said you were coming to Salt Lake for research at the Genealogy Library. When will that be?"

"A week, maybe two," she told him. "I'm going to have to pry my father away from Ophir first. That man has a one-track mind whenever he gets near a dig. Then there's the helicopters we saw at the mesa. I might try to do something about them."

Startled, Gault stared at her. "What the hell do you mean? Those were gunships, for God's sake. Don't mess with them."

"I'm not going to shoot at them, but I am going to report them to our NTSB friend, Kohler. He all but called me a liar when I told him I heard a chopper in that canyon."

"Forget it. Kohler's no different than any other bureaucrat. He's afraid of making waves."

"Why do I have the feeling that you'd have taken on those choppers if you'd been flying something with guns?"

Gault chuckled. "They pissed me off. I admit it. But you can't go around killing people. Or taking unnecessary chances either. If you get yourself hurt, you won't be able to fly with me and the *Lady-A*. So, do I have your promise to stay away from the top of that mesa and its black helicopters?"

"Absolutely," Nick said, smiling because she didn't have to cross her fingers. It wasn't the top of the mesa she had in mind at all, but what she'd seen at the bottom of it. Those men behind the wire still haunted her.

She shook his hand and climbed into the kiln-hot truck.

He smiled and handed her a badly creased business card. "Don't lose my number."

"Never."

He started to say something more, then smiled, and headed for the terminal building. She started the engine and drove slowly away, watching him in the rearview mirror until the door closed behind him.

Originally, she'd intended to spend the second half of the summer working on her paper about the Benson sisters and their pioneer life in a mining town. That had included a one-day side trip to the Genealogy Center.

Now, she'd have to rearrange her schedule to fit in the *Lady-A*, because she wasn't about to miss a chance to fly on a B-24 Liberator. Not only was the bomber a piece of history, it was a childhood fantasy come true. Night after night, she'd lay in her bed staring up at the models suspended from the bedroom ceiling. For years, a B-24 had hung directly above her head. How many times had she climbed into its cockpit and flown away? she wondered. A hundred times? A thousand?

She whooped excitedly. The next time would be for real.

First, though, there was Walt Kohler and his sidekick, Odell, to deal with. The thought of making them eat crow had her whistling all the way back to Ophir.

But they were gone by the time she got there, along with all their gear and their guard-dog deputies. She found her father, Zeke Moyle, and Dobbs, the old prospector, sitting on the Emporium's porch, drinking beer.

"We saw your plane go over," Elliot said as she joined them.

"We saw them choppers too," Dobbs added.

Moyle snorted but didn't say anything.

"What about Kohler and Odell?" Nick said, snapping up Elliot's beer. "What did they have to say when they saw them?"

"They packed up and left," Elliot answered. "A little too fast if you ask me."

Bastards, Nick thought. She'd wanted to confront them, to find out what the hell was happening out in the desert. She hoped Gault had been right, that it was a secret military base. But the nagging thought that it was some kind of detention facility wouldn't go away.

"Well, I've changed my mind about the Feds," Moyle piped up. "They spent good money while they were here, so they're welcome back anytime. Hell, they're the last people I'm likely to see now that your students are gone, Missy."

"I'll pay for another round of beers if you stop calling me that," Nick snapped back.

Moyle's eyes lit up like a neon sign as he hustled inside to fill the order. Dobbs trailed behind him.

"Well, Nick," Elliot said the moment they were alone, "has Gault gone home?"

"It's only temporary. He's invited me to fly in his B-24."

Elliot shook his head in disbelief. "Tell me I'm wrong. Tell me that isn't a fifty-year-old World War Two bomber you're talking about."

"You know damn well it is."

"Your mother was right. I should never have bought you that first model airplane."

Those models saved me, Nick started to say, then settled for a shake of her head. Now was not the time to rake up memories. Besides, flying in a B-24 might well be child's play compared to what else she had in mind. Chances were she was being foolish, that a trip into the desert at night wouldn't prove a thing. But then again, it might.

Nick waited for her father to fall asleep before making her move. A note explaining her intentions had already been pinned to her sleeping bag. With luck, she'd be back long before morning, so Elliot would never have to read it.

She'd left her truck parked outside the Emporium, so no one would hear her leaving. Even so, she drove as quietly as possible with the headlights off until she was well away from Ophir.

By the time Nick swung onto the dirt road heading toward the mesa, the moon was low. From that point on, she kept the pickup in first gear, raising as little dust as possible, and watching the odometer closely. The only way she could follow the ruts without using the headlights was to drive with the door open, watching the ground beside the truck instead of where she was going.

She stopped a mile short of where she and Gault had encountered the humvee, then turned the truck around so it was aiming back toward Ophir in case a quick retreat became necessary. After that, she waited in the cab to see if her arrival would provoke some kind of response.

Finally, she climbed out of the truck, slung two canteens over her shoulder, and grabbed her flashlight. The sinking moon was casting just enough light to make the road stand out from the surrounding desert.

Taking a deep breath, Nick started down the road toward the mesa, which was cutting a black hole in the star-filled night. For a while each step was a thrill. Maybe there were sensors planted in the road, or worse yet, mines. But that didn't make any sense. Deer or range cattle, if there were any, would be constantly creating false alarms.

Even so, the farther she went, the more spooked she became. Traveling at night was accepted procedure in desert trekking she reminded herself. She was also carrying water—rule of survival number one—plus a compass and a Swiss Army knife. Of course, none of those would be much use if she ran into the soldiers again.

Relying on her memory and distances judged from her one fly-over in the Cessna, Nick estimated her walking time to the foot of the mesa at a little over an hour. At the fifty-minute mark, she heard a dog barking. Or was it a coyote? Whatever it was, it sounded close by.

She stopped dead in her tracks. If there were humvees and armed soldiers, chances were there'd be guard dogs too.

The bark gave way to a howl. Nick sighed with relief. Guard dogs stalked silently. At least, she hoped they did.

Five minutes later, she saw a dim light in the distance and headed for it. After another minute, it took shape and became a shaded window. The barracks building had to be directly ahead, and so was the chain-link security fence she'd seen from the air.

She was starting to edge forward when a light flared not more than fifty feet away. It disappeared in an instant, as if someone were striking a match.

Keeping low, she homed in on it, her eyes searching frantically for the glow of a cigarette. If it was a soldier she was heading for, God help her.

She fought to breathe slowly, quietly. Finally, her lungs rebelled, and she had to take a deep breath. It brought with it the smell of tobacco.

She squatted, searching for the telltale cigarette. When she saw it, it looked close enough to touch.

"I heard you coming," a man said softly.

Nick held her breath.

"My dog heard you, too."

Nick stayed silent.

"You cannot be a guard," the man said. "You would make more noise."

He lit another match, shielding it with his hand. In the glow, she could make out the chain-link a foot away. On the other side of it, his face lit up, stood an old man. Even in the flickering light, his face showed a lifetime of outside work that had weathered his dark Indian skin until it stretched over his bones like shrink-wrap.

Cupping his hands, he held the flame out toward her.

For an instant, Nick hesitated, then decided she was committed. She moved close enough to the fence for him to see her.

"Dear God," he said, closing his hands to extinguish the light. "You're a woman. Please, for your life, leave before the soldiers come."

"Do they come often?" she asked quietly.

"Yes."

"I'm surprised they let you out here by yourself."

"The doors are not locked, *senorita*. There is no escape. Some have tried, but all have failed. Besides, the desert is vast and I'm an old man."

Nick took a deep breath. It was unnerving talking to a stranger in the dark, but she wasn't about to walk away yet. "I flew over here today," she said quietly. "Did you see my plane?"

"Yes," he whispered back.

"There was another plane two days ago. Did you see that one?"

"Yes, *senorita*, I did. But you must go. It is not safe here."

"That plane crashed."

"If you say so, *senorita*."

The ambiguity of his answer sent Nick's heart hammering. She didn't know if he was afraid to contradict her or afraid to admit to anything.

"What do you say?" she continued.

"I know nothing." The old man paused. "Others might say differently."

"What others?" she persisted.

"One hears things. The guards sometimes talk loudly. Sometimes they forget I speak English. They think we are all stupid here."

"And the guards, they know about the plane?"

"Perhaps it did crash, but they did not think so."

"Please tell me, what did they think?" Nick wished she could reach through the fence and shake the answers from him.

"They were very amused. They thought it was a good joke that the plane should have come here."

"Did you see the pilot?" she asked.

"You're the only one I've seen."

Nick sighed. Even if Gault had managed to land out here and talk to the old man, it would have been for nothing. The old man knew nothing about Gault's grandson.

Suddenly Nick realized she hadn't asked the obvious question. "Who are you and what are you doing out here?"

"My name is Luis Sanchez. They keep me here because I am the only one who speaks enough English. The others know only Spanish."

"I don't understand what you mean."

"We wait and then we are summoned. Those who are, never come back."

Nick shivered. "Where do you come from?"

"From the other side of the border. We come without permission. In my country I was a teacher. I came to this country for sanctuary." His laugh was like a cough in the night.

Hairs rose on the back of Nick's neck. The old man's tale sounded like some ghost story made up to scare children. But she believed him. The sadness, the sound of inevitability in his voice was all the corroboration she needed.

"Do you know what happens on the mesa?"

"The black helicopters go there. The black ones carry many things, people, great boxes. Maybe even the plane you asked about, but I am not certain. My eyes are not that good anymore."

A door opened, spilling light from the barracks.

"Go, *senorita*."

"What about you?"

"There is no help for me. Now go. Run before they catch you."

Nick knew better than to run in the desert, even at night. But that didn't stop her. The old man's tone of voice had unleashed her childhood demons, and they didn't go away until she was back in her truck, racing toward Ophir.

14

Nick stood in front of the Emporium, staring at the overhanging cliff and its abandoned mine shafts, trying to focus on John Gault's invitation to go aboard his B-24. An honest-to-God guided tour would be a first for her. Up to now she'd never been inside a Liberator that wasn't in pieces. But thoughts of Luis Sanchez kept getting in the way. What the hell was going on out there in the desert? Could it possibly be some kind of INS holding area for illegal aliens? If so, why the secrecy? And why the helicopter flights to the mesa?

Nick shook her head in frustration.

Beside her, Elliot whistled shrilly. "I'd offer you a penny for your thoughts, but the dazed look on your face tells me everything I need to know. You're up there in the sky in one of your airplanes, probably that B-24."

"I was thinking about helicopters."

"They're not safe either."

"You're forgetting that my last B-24 got me on the cover of *National Geographic*."

"It could have been worse," Elliot responded with a grin. "It could have been the *Enquirer*. My advice to you, daughter, is to concentrate on the work at hand. That last trench I started may have more treasures just waiting to be uncovered."

"Gault's going to rebuild his plane for one last flight. He says it will be as good as new."

"When you're my age you'll know nothing's ever as good as new."

Nick punched him playfully.

"All right. How does this sound?" he said, calling a

truce. "We'll work my new trench for all it's worth, then I'll go with you to see that plane."

She hugged him. "You won't be sorry. Going on board that Liberator will be like visiting history, like stepping into an undiscovered Anasazi cliff dwelling. It's a chance of a lifetime."

"Maybe," Elliot said. "Let's get a cold drink before we go to work on your trench."

Zeke Moyle must have seen them coming, because when they stepped inside the dim Emporium, he had open beer cans waiting on the counter next to the cash register.

"Now that your students are gone, I propose a farewell toast," he said. "That includes you, too, Dobbs," he told the old prospector, who was killing time pretending to examine the dry goods.

The beer was ice cold, which meant it came out of Ophir's one and only refrigerator.

"I was just telling my daughter that this site needs further exploration," Elliot said.

"I hear you're an expert on Indians," Moyle said.

Elliot raised his beer-free hand, a gesture of modest agreement.

Dobbs gave up on his beer long enough to say, "What about those old Indian ruins out in Sulphur Canyon?"

Elliot looked inquiringly in Nick's direction.

"Sorry," she said. "I forgot to tell you about it. I was out there looking for the site when the plane crashed. At the time, I half-suspected that Zeke was putting me on about it."

"They're out there, all right," Dobbs said. "Me and Zeke used it for target practice a couple of times."

Elliot shuddered. "What kind of Indians?"

Moyle and Dobbs shrugged in unison.

"Where is it exactly?" Elliot asked.

"Like I told Nick here, there's a cave with some ruins in it about a mile inside Sulphur Canyon. My canyon, by the way. On my land."

"We have a contract to work the entire area," Nick reminded him.

"Which expires today, in case you've forgotten. After that . . ." He smiled and made a slashing motion across his throat.

"I'd think you'd be happy to have our company, not to mention our business," Elliot said.

"When I signed up with the university, I thought you people were going to make my town famous."

Nick sighed. "He was hoping we'd find notorious outlaws buried in boot hill," she explained to her father.

Elliot had a faraway look in his eyes. "We're too far south for the Anasazi," he muttered.

"Hohokam?" Nick prompted, picking up his train of thought.

"Could be Salado. The Hohokam were mostly a riverine people." He paused, pursing his lips. "Of course there was Ventana Cave. That was Hohokam. But the only way we're going to find out is to take a look."

He turned to Moyle. "We might find something in that cave to make you famous after all."

"Sorry. I have other plans for Ophir."

Dobbs snorted. "Sure, you do. You sold out to the Feds, didn't you? I saw you huddling with the bastards before they took off."

Moyle glared at the prospector. "Wasn't there something else you were going to mention to our guests here?"

Dobbs looked blank.

"You know," Moyle prompted, "the drawings."

"Oh, yeah. Now I remember. There used to be Indian drawings all over the place. That was way back, of course, before they started mining around here. But old-timers have told me that the whole cliff was covered with them scratchings."

"Where exactly?" Elliot asked.

Dobbs waved toward the door. "Where the old mine shafts are now. Above boot hill mostly, between there and the entrance to Sulphur Canyon."

"Not a quarter of a mile from where we're standing," Moyle added.

Elliot glowered at Nick. "Did you know about this?"

She shook her head. "I did not, and I haven't seen any sign of them."

"You can still spot them," Moyle said, "but only if the light's just right. What's left of them anyway, cut right into the sandstone."

"Petroglyphs," Elliot said excitedly. "Show us."

So much for Elliot's trench, Nick thought.

Dobbs led the way outside and pointed at the cliff face that loomed over boot hill.

"You've got to be standing right underneath to see them," Moyle said. "And like I said, the light has to be just right."

"Lead the way," Elliot told him.

Dobbs started to step off the porch but Moyle held him back. "Me and Dobbs have beer to drink. We'll leave the Indians to you."

Dobbs looked at Elliot uncertainly.

"It's okay," Elliot said, stuffing a ten-dollar bill in the prospector's pocket. "We can find our own way. Why don't you have another beer on me."

Donning her Cubs cap, Nick stepped off the Emporium's shallow porch and into the dazzling sun. For a brief moment she imagined that a shadow had passed overhead, and she thought she could detect a rhythmic, almost dreamlike thump. The powakus, she thought, the Hopi trickster. She shivered.

"Can you hear that?" she asked her father, uncertain herself that she'd heard or seen anything at all.

Elliot looked around and shrugged his shoulders. "All I can hear is the call of an unexplored site. Quit dawdling."

Nick tried to shake off the feeling of unease. The sky was bright and clear, but the heat from the blazing sun had lost some of its warmth.

15

Wiley looked down at the desert floor thirty thousand feet below him and regretted that they had to leave before things got really interesting. But as it was, they'd barely made the plane after planting the explosive. What a sight it would be when the Director pushed the button.

Wiley sighed. As usual, he kept his seat in the upright position, as was his habit on flights long or short. Sit straight, don't move unnecessarily, and you didn't get off the plane looking wrinkled and disheveled. Next to him Voss slouched and kicked off his shoes.

They were flying first class, such as it was on the commuter airline that flew out of Tucson, with stopovers in Flagstaff and Las Vegas on its way to Salt Lake City.

"We could have made better time driving," Voss said, yawning.

Wiley said nothing. Cooped up in a car with Voss crossing that much desert didn't bear thinking about. Even with air-conditioning, it would have smelled like a gymnasium.

From his aisle seat, Voss leaned across him to peer out the window. Voss, whatever his drawbacks, was good at his work. Better a reliable slob covering your back, than someone who might get you killed.

"Look where they've sent us," Voss said, pointing at the window.

Below, the Utah landscape looked as bleak and uninhabitable as Ophir.

"I hear Brigham Young called this state the promised land," Wiley said.

"A man with all those wives," Voss answered, "probably never had time to look out the window."

Wiley only grunted.

"What do you think of that lady archaeologist?" Voss asked.

"I think we should keep our minds on the job."

Voss leaned close and whispered, "Please, let her turn out to be the job."

Wiley sighed.

Voss continued, "You know what I'd like to do with her, don't you, where I'd like to put my .357?"

"Don't get your hopes up. We may have to walk away from this one."

"What about your .22? How would you use it on her?"

Wiley shook his head. Rather than risk metal detectors and X-ray machines, they were traveling without weapons. Once on the ground, their contact at the airport would resupply them.

Maybe then Wiley could talk Voss into something more civilized. On second thought, why tempt fate? The man was a master with a .357. Put something else in his hand and he might hesitate at the wrong time, or maybe even miss when he was guarding Wiley's back.

Thirty minutes later, the outskirts of Salt Lake City came into view.

"That's what I like to see," Voss said. "A city in the wilderness. A ten-minute drive outside of town and you're in the middle of nowhere. You could bury an army in that desert and nobody would be the wiser."

16

Nick and Elliot, armed with canteens, trowels, and hand picks, walked along the base of the cliff, peering up at the overhanging rock.

"I thought I trained you better," Elliot said as they reached the base of boot hill. "An archaeologist should always examine the local landscape carefully for possible sites."

"Look up there," Nick retorted. "Do you see anything?"

Squinting, Elliot shook his head. "You told me you'd spent a lot of time out here."

"And I never saw anything to pique my curiosity."

"If you were one of my students, I'd flunk you for lack of interest."

"You said yourself, this isn't Anasazi country. So what's so exciting all of a sudden about this site?"

"If it's Salado, possibly nothing, except we are outside their generally accepted territory. If it's Hohokam, you realize, no remnants of the above-ground structures have ever been found."

He lowered his gaze from the cliff. "Let's try the canyon. I don't see anything here."

Nick shaded her eyes to stare up at the red-rock escarpment above them. Halfway up the hundred-foot face, two abandoned mine shafts reminded her of empty eye sockets in a skull. From those two openings had poured the tailings that created boot hill. Some part of her, that place in her brain where education and logic gave way to superstition, felt as if the eyes were watching her. The eyes of the powakus.

"Look at this place," Elliot said. "It just goes to show you that the white man will live anywhere when there's gold to be had."

"Archaeologists will do the same," Nick shot back, "and they don't have gold for an excuse. Why—" She blinked and rubbed her eyes. "There, just below the mine shaft on the left." She moved sideways to get a better angle. Elliot stayed right beside her.

"I can see a stick figure," he said suddenly. "Its head is gone but the rest is okay."

Nick said, "I see it, but I don't believe it. It looks like Basketmaker Two."

"It can't be, not this far south."

"What do you think it is, then?"

"I don't know yet, but it's a major find if we can place the Anasazi in this part of Arizona."

"How the hell did they get up there to carve it?" Nick wondered out loud. The Basketmaker II period of Anasazi culture, she remembered, ran all the way from 1200 B.C. to 500 A.D, with the great rock art tending to be early rather than late.

Elliot began pacing back and forth along the base of the cliff. "There has to be a way." He stopped dead. "Here, the handholds begin here."

Centuries of erosion had shallowed the handholds that had been cut into the rock by the ancient cliff dwellers. Here and there, bullet holes pockmarked the sandstone wall.

"The Anasazi were great climbers," Elliot said, studying the boulder-strewn area at the foot of the cliff. "But we tenderfeet had better clear a drop zone in case we lose our footing."

Nick shook her head. "That's a fifty-foot climb. We need a ladder."

"I'm going up there, Nick. You know that. Besides, there's a rock shelf just below the figure. I can stand on that."

"I see it," Nick said, sighing. The shelf couldn't have

been more than six inches deep, but few obstacles would stop Elliot. To be the first archaeologist onto a site, to touch a piece of history forgotten for centuries, was electrifying. Better than sex, her father often preached. Sometimes she agreed with him.

"I'll go first," Nick said.

"Like hell."

"I'm a hundred pounds lighter than you are, Elliot, and a hell of a lot younger. If the rock's too brittle, I'll have a better chance."

Once most of the sharp boulders were removed from the area directly below the handholds, Nick started climbing while her father stayed on the ground, grumbling under his breath. She enlarged each handhold as she went. About ten feet up, the holes weren't as shallow. After twenty feet, they were deep enough to make the climb possible without constant pick work, though it was still a tricky ascent. And there was no guarantee the rock ledge would hold once they got there. The heat wasn't helping any. Her sweatband was already leaking badly enough to half-blind her.

"I'm coming down," she called, then cautiously groped her way back down the cliff.

"The handholds aren't as bad as I thought," she told her father. "But I'd be a lot happier if we had a ladder."

"I don't think the Emporium runs to fifty-footers, do you?"

Nick shook her head.

"Now that you've tested the handholds, Nick, I assume you'll let me go up."

Nick knew better than to argue at this point. "Just take it slow, Dad. That's all I ask."

She admired his technique, which was precise and cautious despite the adrenaline that had to be surging through him. Her own adrenaline rush was enough to make her fingers tremble. And he was a big man, linebacker-size he liked to say, though that was stretching it.

She gave him a ten-foot lead before starting up the

cliff after him. By the time she was fifteen feet off the ground, Elliot was just above her, feeling for a fresh handhold. In that instant, a tremor moved through the sandstone.

Tightening her grip, she looked up to see a black shadow filling the sky. It hovered there, above the canyon rim. At first, Nick couldn't understand what she was looking at, then the shadow slowly resolved itself into a helicopter, its rotors kicking up dust and debris. Small rocks began raining down.

"Don't they see us?" Nick shouted.

Her father's answer was lost in the rotor roar as the chopper descended even lower. The increased downdraft beat at her. A dust devil swirled to life on boot hill, sandblasting Nick from head to foot.

"Get down!" she shouted at her father.

Panicked, she lowered one foot, searching for a hold.

The downdraft intensified. She clawed at the sandstone. Her loose foot scrabbled, unable to lock onto a hold. Then suddenly the gale dislodged her other foot. For an instant, she hung there by her hands, until finally the wind became too much. It sucked her from the cliff face. At the same time Elliot yelled, "Look out!"

Nick landed flat on her back. Elliot hit so close beside her that his elbow rammed into her stomach. The impact knocked the wind out of her. By the time she caught her breath, the helicopter was gone and the dust was settling.

She sat up and realized her father wasn't moving, wasn't conscious.

Just then the ground shook beneath her, a sharp jolt, followed by a muffled thump.

Nick searched the sky, expecting to see the helicopter returning.

There was another thump, louder this time. She could feel it through her entire body.

Above them, the entire cliff face shimmied, then suddenly disintegrated in a deafening roar.

She grabbed Elliot's ankles and began frantically dragging him away from the base of the cliff.

An instant later, Nick was hurled flat by flying debris. Instinctively, she wrapped her arms around her head and curled into a ball.

Pain blossomed everywhere, her arms, her legs, her head. Dirt filled her eyes, blinding her. Dust choked her. She couldn't breathe. She was being buried alive.

Abruptly the roaring stopped. She kicked out. Thank God. Her legs were free. She squirmed frantically with her legs. Her hands tore at the rock around her head and face. She broke free before her air ran out.

She had to find Elliot. She wiped the grit from her eyes and blinked painfully. There was nothing to be seen but rubble.

"Elliot!" she screamed.

Nothing.

Then she saw it, his foot protruding from among the red-rock debris.

17

In a frenzy, Nick tore at the rocks covering Elliot. Her nails broke. Her flesh tore, but she didn't care. The pain only spurred her on.

Over and over, she called his name. But the only response was the ringing in her own ears. Probably she had a concussion. To hell with that. To hell with anything but her father. By God, somebody was going to pay.

She found his other foot. The sight of it gave her

hope. Only a few seconds had gone by. At least, she hoped that was all, that she was thinking straight.

She hugged his ankles and pulled. For an instant, she thought Elliot's weight, plus that of the rubble still covering him, was too much for her. Christ, digging him out completely would take too long. Even now, maybe she was too late. Maybe . . .

Screaming through clenched teeth, she strained to pull him free. By now, her breath was coming in ragged gasps and her lungs were on fire. She was about to go back to digging, when suddenly his body moved. Straining until she shook, she tugged at him. Rocks fell away, and he was free. She dropped to her knees beside him. Dear God. He wasn't breathing.

Fighting to stay calm, she cleared his mouth and began CPR.

Goddammit, Elliot, don't leave me alone, she screamed silently.

He coughed.

"Talk to me," she shouted.

"You're kneeling on my broken arm."

"Sorry." She moved. "Can you feel your legs?"

"Unfortunately, yes. They hurt like hell."

"Pain's a good sign," she said, too brightly.

"That's comforting. Now, help me up."

Once he was sitting, he blurted, "My God, there's nothing left of the cliff." Or Ophir either.

Until that moment, Nick hadn't noticed. Where they had just been climbing, there was only a gigantic rockfall. If she and Elliot had been higher or lower, they'd both be dead.

"There was an explosion *after* we fell," Nick said. "Somebody tried to kill us."

"Don't start imagining things, Nick. Maybe all that noise from the chopper caused a mine shaft to collapse."

"I don't buy it, Elliot. And why was the chopper there anyway?"

"Coincidence?"

"You don't like that answer any more than I do."

Elliot shrugged. "Maybe we ought to look for Moyle and Dobbs."

"They're under twenty feet of rock." As soon as Nick stood up, her ankle buckled. It was twice normal size and throbbing painfully now that her adrenaline was starting to ebb.

"It's not broken," she said, accepting Elliot's help. "It just surprised me. I can walk."

They helped one another to the pickup.

Elliot took one look inside and said, "I see you did listen in class. You kept your artifacts out of harm's way. But those wall drawings are gone forever. We'll never know if the Basketmakers got this far."

"You have a one-track mind," Nick said. But then so did she. The box containing the results of her dig was safely stowed behind the seat. At least something of the Benson sisters would survive. She'd still be able to finish her research.

But first, she had to get Elliot to a doctor.

18

Nick's hands were still shaking as she punched Gault's number into the telephone outside the emergency room in Mescalero, where she'd stopped to get her father's broken arm set. She needed to talk to someone and John Gault was already on her mind.

"I didn't expect to hear from you so soon," he said the moment he heard her voice.

"I'm calling from Mescalero," Nick said breathlessly,

then hesitated, wondering how to explain the situation. Finally, she just blurted out, "I think someone tried to kill us."

"What? Are you all right?"

"A few cuts and bruises, that's all, but my father's arm is broken. We were lucky to walk away."

"Jesus," he muttered. "Tell me what happened."

She took a deep breath. "Zeke Moyle put us onto some Indian drawings on the cliff near Ophir. My father and I were climbing up to get a close look when one of those black helicopters appeared overhead. The damned thing blew us right off the side of the cliff. Funny when you think about it. That saved our lives, because a moment later half the mountain came down on us."

"My God. How the hell did it happen?"

"My father thinks one of the old mine shafts collapsed, but it sounded like an explosion to me. But I don't know how the hell I'm going to prove it. Any evidence is probably gone completely, buried under the rockfall."

"Why would anyone bother destroying old ruins?" Gault said.

"It must have something to do with the story Matt was after."

"I already talked to Matt's editor. He claims he doesn't know what Matt was up to. It's probably true. Matt always said, 'If you talk about your exclusive before it's in print, it won't be exclusive anymore.' "

Thank God for small favors, Wiley said to himself, as he listened in on the headset. He signaled Voss, who was perched at the top of the telephone pole, monitoring the conversation on a second headset after finishing their phone tap. The tap had been an added precaution, a backup for the high-tech bugs already planted at Gault Aviation, but worth its weight in gold, considering what Wiley was hearing at the moment.

"Are you still coming to Salt Lake?" Gault continued.

We're already there, Wiley answered to himself. He and Voss were working out of a genuine phone company truck parked on 22nd West, the eastern perimeter of Salt Lake's International Airport.

"As soon as I get my father settled in at home," the Scott woman replied.

"Don't be too long," Gault said. "I'm about ready to start work on the *Lady-A*."

"I won't. Did everything go all right in Phoenix?"

"I had them double-check the dental records. It was Matt, all right."

"I'm sorry."

"I brought him home. That's all that counts now."

"I'll call you as soon as I know when I'm arriving," she said.

"I'll look forward to it," Gault answered.

The moment the line went dead, Wiley could hear Voss singing at the top of his lungs. "I hear you singin' in the wires, I can hear you thru the whine." The tune was barely recognizable as "The Wichita Lineman" and Wiley didn't think it was particularly appropriate.

As soon as Voss hit the ground he stopped singing and said, "Shit! I told you we should stick to guns and not explosives."

"Sure, Voss," Wiley said. "We should have all listened to you."

Wiley eyed his own hands with disgust. God how he hated digging in the dirt. It was no job for a professional with standards. If you don't hold to your standards, you don't get the desired results, he thought. His expertise was guns and that egomaniac up on the mesa had made him go outside his area of expertise and look what it had got them, a botched job. The Scott woman was still alive.

"You heard the bit about the helicopter, didn't you?" Voss asked.

Wiley nodded. "That's the Director for you. The man couldn't leave well enough alone. He had to have one last look, a moment of triumph, before pushing the button. He blew that broad and her father right out of our kill zone." Wiley shook his head in disgust. "All our hard work for nothing."

Voss drew the new .357 their contact at the airport had supplied. "Maybe now we can really go to work. This baby's still untested."

19

John Gault had just hung up the phone when his mechanic, Theron Christensen, entered the office. Christensen, unshaven, looked as tired as Gault felt. In fact, Gault suspected that his mechanic hadn't shaved since Matt's plane crashed. The mechanic was haunted by the thought that the crash had been his fault, that mechanical error had brought down the Cessna.

"I saw you through the window talking on the phone," Christensen said. "Was it something about Matt?"

Gault shook his head. "I was talking to the archaeologist I told you about. Now stop second-guessing yourself. We have work to do. As of now, I want you to start work on the *Lady-A*. I want her rebuilt and ready to fly as fast as you can do it."

Christensen looked shocked. "For God's sake, John. The *Lady-A*'s an old woman. Her engines will have to be completely overhauled. Do you have any idea how much that's going to cost?"

"If anyone can make her young again, you can, Theron."

"You're not listening to me. Sure, Matt wanted to see her fly again. So do I. But—"

"Think about it, Theron. Think about bringing the Lady-A back to life."

"I don't know if I'm up to it," he said doubtfully.

"You're the best mechanic I know."

"It'll take me forever."

"Hire help, then."

"Jesus. You're talking big money." Shaking his head, Christensen began writing on a legal pad. "A hundred thousand dollars minimum, maybe more."

Gault nodded. If rebuilding the Lady-A took every cent he possessed, so be it. He couldn't take it with him, and there was no one to save it for now that Matt was gone.

"I'll mortgage the house," he said. "Sell it outright if I have to. The business too."

Christensen put down his pencil. "These figures are rough. It could go to a hundred and twenty thousand to get the Lady-A airborne. More, if we have to fabricate some of our own parts."

"We're going to take Matt on one last flight, so do whatever it takes."

"Even if I can bring her up to specs, we'll need help to fly her. It's sure as hell not a one-man job, and I'm no pilot."

Gault nodded. In a pinch, one man could handle a B-24 if all its systems were working. But you couldn't count on that in a bird as old as the Lady-A.

"I've been thinking about that," Gault said. "I'm going to invite the old crew to come along." Those who are still alive, he added to himself.

"You're all older than the Lady-A," Christensen pointed out.

Gault shrugged.

The mechanic threw up his hands. "They can't all be crazy like you."

"You'd be surprised."

Gault smiled, remembering Vic Campbell, his bombardier. Vic lived in Nevada and was the letter writer among the old crew, the professional journalist, the one who kept in touch with the others. He was the man to contact first.

20

Vic Campbell, who hadn't been drunk in years, was swaying so badly he lost his balance and spilled his drink.

"Shit!" Blaire Foster bellowed from the next bar stool. "You got that all over me. I'm going to smell like a drunk when I get back to work."

"Sorry," Campbell muttered. "My aim used to be better."

As a deputy sheriff of Ellsworth, Nevada, Foster wasn't a man to be messed with.

"Sorry," Foster mocked. "Not as sorry as that rag you publish."

"There was a time I could hit targets from twenty-five thousand feet."

"Sure you did, old-timer."

Campbell opened his mouth to explain, then thought better of it. Nobody, especially an asshole like Foster, was interested in ancient history. Or an old fart who still thought of himself as a bombardier in his more nostalgic moments. An old fart who'd kept his old uniform until last year, when he made the mistake of trying it on.

Of course, he'd be losing weight soon enough, considering the doc's prognosis, delivered only an hour ago, of terminal cancer. Until that moment, Campbell—survivor of twenty-five wartime missions, more than half of them over Germany without fighter cover—had thought he'd live forever.

Campbell smiled at his own stupidity.

"What's so fuckin' funny?" Foster demanded.

The fact that he'd been coming to a place like the Crazy Horse Bar for twenty years, Campbell answered to himself. His only excuse was location. The Crazy Horse was next door to his newspaper, the *Ellsworth Gazette*.

"I said I was sorry," Campbell repeated, concentrating to keep from slurring his words.

"You love pissin' on the rest of us, don't you? You and your kind, Mr. Editor. You think you're better than us. To you, me and my friends are just hick cops."

Without warning, the deputy punched Campbell in the stomach. Air exploded from his lungs. He couldn't catch his breath. His knees gave way, and he collapsed onto the barroom floor.

"Too bad you don't have any witnesses," Foster sneered, looking around the Crazy Horse to make his point, that everybody present had damn well better mind their own business. "Print anything about me and I'll finish the job."

Whiskey rushed up Campbell's throat. He swallowed it down again and sat up. He'd been wanting to print the truth about Foster for a long time. The man was the worst kind of bully, one in a position of power.

Campbell grabbed the bar with both hands and pulled himself to his feet. To hell with Foster. He was probably as drunk as Campbell was.

Which isn't drunk enough, Campbell decided. He intended to drink himself into oblivion. It was either that or cry on his ex-wife's shoulder. Certainly Frieda would do her best to comfort him. She always did. But Campbell didn't want her seeing him this way, wallowing in self-pity. During the war, getting drunk was the only time you weren't afraid.

He took a deep, painful breath.

"Hey, Vic," Foster said, "why don't I buy you a beer? Or are you too good to drink with the likes of me?"

Campbell looked around the bar. He knew most of the faces. Probably they hated Foster as much as he did, but they'd never back anyone against the deputy. Even Bob, the bartender, was looking the other way, pretending to be busy.

"I was drinking straight whiskey," Campbell said, "but what the hell! I might as well switch to boilermakers."

"That's the spirit." Foster pounded him on the back hard enough to hurt. "Come on, Bob, pour a couple of shots to go with the beer."

Bob poured Wild Turkey, which Campbell had been drinking for the past hour.

"That's too rich for my blood," Foster said.

Campbell nodded at the bartender. "Put it on my tab."

Foster shook his head. "I don't know. People might think you're trying to bribe me."

"Shee-yit," Campbell said, words forming inside his head and coming out of his mouth against his better judgment, "everybody in town knows you come cheaper than that."

Foster's eyes changed from mean to crazy.

Backing up, Campbell glanced side to side, looking for a weapon. Foster didn't need one. He had his fists.

Foster offered his chin. "Go on. Take the first shot. That'll make it self-defense when I beat the shit out of you."

To hell with caution, Campbell told himself. He was

a dead man anyway, and he'd always wanted to take a swing at Foster.

The punch took the deputy by surprise, catching him on the cheekbone.

The next thing Campbell knew, he was in an ambulance on the way to the emergency room.

21

Once Nick got her father settled at his house in Albuquerque, she had to endure one of his well-worn harangues on the incompetence of modern medicine.

"You'd think they could come up with something better than a plaster cast in this day and age," he said. "This thing weighs a ton."

"It's a bad break."

"Your driving didn't help it any."

"If I thought you meant that," she said with a smile, "I'd break your other arm."

The drive out of Ophir had been hellish. God knows what kind of pain Elliot must have endured before they got off the washboard road and onto a decent highway. All the while, he just sat there, belted in, teeth clenched, saying nothing. Then he'd had to wait in Mescalero while she reported the landslide to the authorities and endured their red tape.

Nick felt Elliot's forehead but couldn't tell if he was feverish or not. Certainly, he was full of enough antibiotics to take care of most complications. In addition, they'd both gotten tetanus boosters.

"Don't fuss over me," Elliot said.

"The doctor said you should get some sleep."

"I set my own broken arm once on a dig in southern Utah, and did a better job of it too."

Nick sighed. "You're full of painkillers, among other things."

"Is that your way of saying I'm out of my head?"

"You'll feel better when you've gotten some sleep."

"I'll feel better when you've given up airplanes and gotten yourself tenure somewhere."

"That refrain is getting tiresome. Could you humor me just this once?"

Elliot closed his eyes and pretended to snore. That was more like him, she thought. When his eyes opened again, they looked slightly glazed. Thank God. Maybe the painkillers were taking hold.

"I'll go fix something we can eat for dinner when you wake up."

"No you don't, Nick. You have work to do."

"You're not listening, Dad. I'm nursing you for a while."

"The Benson sisters will get you tenure."

"They can wait for a while."

Elliot smiled mischievously. "Did I forget to tell you that I found another hatbox in the basement at the university? It's labeled the same way as the others, in Lillian Benson's own hand."

"What's in it?"

"I took a quick peek, that's all." He was speaking more slowly now. "It's mostly newspaper clippings, some from the *Ophir Post* and the *Bisbee Sentinel*."

"And?"

"I know better than to rain on a colleague's parade. The box is sitting on the desk in my office, its contents unread, by me at least."

The moment Nick entered her father's office she felt like a child again. Elliot's rank and reputation could have commandeered something more grand, but he didn't care about trappings. As a result, his office was little more than a glorified cubicle crowded with shelves stacked with artifacts.

His desktop was relatively clean, with only a beautiful conical Anasazi basket made from willow so tightly woven that it would hold water, sharing space with Lillian Benson's hatbox. Classic Basketmaker II period, Nick thought as she reverently moved the fifteen-hundred-year-old basket back into its humidity-controlled glass case. She was touched that Elliot had rushed off to Ophir, leaving the precious artifact exposed.

She eagerly slid off the string holding the box together and lifted the lid. Just as Elliot had promised, Lillian had been a collector of newspaper clippings.

The first few stories out of the hatbox, each handled with care, were routine and didn't tell Nick anything she didn't know already.

Then she came across a story that started her pulse racing. One week after the 1922 fire that destroyed his town, Ophir's sheriff, Scott Robert Manlove, asked for help in seeking the whereabouts of Pearl Benson. His plea had been published in the *Bisbee Sentinel*, twenty miles away. Pearl hadn't been seen since the night of the fire, though her sister, Lillian, had assured friends that they'd both escaped unhurt from their burning house. "Pearl seemed dazed," her sister was quoted as saying, "and may have wandered off into the desert."

Nick checked her notes. Lillian's diaries covered the period up to 1934, but Pearl's had stopped in 1922. Yet Lillian had said long after the fire, "But what *we* miss most are the few treasures mother passed on to us." Nick had quoted that passage to Elliot when she'd shown him the buttonhook. Surely that meant that Pearl was alive after the destruction of Ophir? In fact, Lillian's habit of saying "we" had led Nick to presume that both sisters were still alive until 1934, at the very least.

Strange, Nick thought, she certainly didn't remember Lillian mentioning even a temporary disappearance on Pearl's part. She checked her notes one more time. Nothing. Diary life had gone on after the fire, a steady stream of comments on day-to-day events.

Nick had always assumed that Pearl was the younger sister, although there'd been no facts in the diaries to confirm her belief. Certainly the writing had led Nick to assume that Lillian was the stronger of the two, the more mature woman. So Nick had concluded that Pearl had outlived her sister. For that matter, she'd assumed that it had been Pearl who had donated the diaries to the University of New Mexico.

Eventually, Nick would have to go over the diaries again to make certain she'd hadn't missed some obscure reference to Pearl. Perhaps it had been too painful for Lillian to mention.

Nick continued reading until she'd gone through all of the yellowed newspaper clippings. According to the last one, Pearl was never found by the sheriff, or questioned. At one point, there was some speculation that Lillian had been mistaken about her sister's survival of the fire.

Nick shook her head at that. Lillian's diaries were proof that Pearl had survived, so what kind of reporter would write such crap? No doubt, the same kind who were writing for the tabloids these days.

Nick read every clipping, but no answers about Pearl were to be had. Frustrated, Nick began pacing her father's office. Had Pearl Benson been an arsonist? Had Lillian known about it and protected her?

Feeling suddenly weary, Nick settled into her father's chair and leaned back. Staring at the mementos that covered his office walls never failed to evoke memories of childhood. This office had been Nick's sanctuary, her destination each time she ran away from home. She didn't always reach it, but that had never stopped her from attempting the five-mile trek.

Had the Benson sisters found such a comforting sanctuary after the fire? The diaries really gave no clue.

Chances were, Nick might never discover the answer to that or any of the other puzzles surrounding the Bensons and their pioneer life.

Ophir, too, might remain a mystery. She might never know what really happened, whether or not the cliff had come down on its own or had help. And what about the old man fenced in out there in the desert? Or the black helicopters? Would she ever have answers?

Probably not, she decided. But then archaeology was no different. It was a hunt for answers that usually came down to educated guesses. Well, by God, that was her job, and she'd better get to it.

Nick left the office and walked out into Albuquerque's 100-degree afternoon. Ten minutes later she was at an air-conditioned carrel in the stacks of the university library in pursuit of the Bensons. But where to begin? Women's lives had been so circumscribed in the Benson's time, though Nick sometimes wondered how much had actually changed since then. Lillian Benson had lived to be at least eighty-six, but the diaries dealt with the minutiae of domestic existence, not the larger philosophical issues. Lillian hadn't even mentioned women being granted the right to vote. That was something Nick would have to check out, in addition to the mysteriously missing Pearl. Did Lillian even exercise her right to vote? Nick certainly wouldn't be able to tell that from a buttonhook.

The buttonhook! She mentally kicked herself for not remembering. Lillian had exulted when high-button shoes had gone out of style. "They confine a woman so," she'd written. Perhaps Nick could quickly put together something based on *The Buttonhook as Metaphor for the Restrictions on Women in Early Twentieth-Century Western America*. That ought to stick in Ben Gilbert's craw. It might also get her tenure.

Half an hour later, as Nick was scanning for articles on the history of the buttonhook, a title caught her eye. *The Destruction of Buttonhook Creek: Rape of the Environ-*

ment. The author was Matt Gault. Out of curiosity she requested the microfiche.

The article was depressing, outlining the systematic poisoning of one of the few water sources in the Four Corners area by unscrupulous mining practices. Matt must have made a lot of enemies, she thought to herself, but he wasn't afraid to tell the truth.

She panned the microfiche to the end of the article. The author's picture was there in black and white, but she could imagine the same startling blue eyes as John Gault, and the same smile that didn't come easily.

She reluctantly put the article aside and returned to her research, but she couldn't get rid of the image of Matt Gault's face. She wondered what John was doing.

With a self-condemning shake of her head, she forced her mind back to buttonhooks, pearl-handled buttonhooks. Pearl! Pearl Benson was the mystery, the invisible woman. When had she really died? How had she died and why had her only sister made no mention of it?

Nick sighed and thought, to hell with sitting here. As great as the university's library was, she was wasting her time. In Salt Lake, the most complete and extensive repository of birth, death, and other early-American records was administered by the Church of Jesus Christ of Latter-day Saints. If the mystery of Pearl was to be solved it would be there.

Nick smiled. Along with the Bensons, Salt Lake had a more certain attraction, a B-24 Liberator named the *Lady-A*, not to mention John Gault.

22

John Gault had trouble getting through to his old bombardier at first. Vic Campbell's home phone didn't answer and neither did his newspaper, though the answering machine at the *Gazette* took a message. The callback came twenty minutes later.

"Skipper," Campbell said, sounding out of breath, "how the hell are you?"

Gault grinned. Only his old wartime crew called him that.

"I need my bombardier again."

"Have we declared war?"

"The *Lady-A*'s going to fly again."

"I'll be damned. What's the occasion?" Campbell asked.

"Matt's dead," Gault said, surprised that he was able to sound so matter-of-fact. "His plane went down in Arizona."

"Oh, Jesus, I'm sorry."

"Matt always wanted to go up in the *Lady-A*, so I'm rebuilding her engines for one last flight. I intend to drop his ashes over the Great Salt Lake, and I'd like my old crew with me."

"Now you tell me."

"What's the matter?" Gault asked.

"I'm in the hospital. I got into a fight."

"At your age?"

"It's a long story, Skipper."

"How long will you be laid up?"

"Five minutes ago I didn't think I'd get as far as the bathroom. Now, I'm checking myself out of here."

"Is that wise?" Gault said.

"I wouldn't miss flying in the *Lady-A* again for anything."

"It's going to take a while to get her up to spec."

"Before you called I was feeling sorry for myself. Now . . ." Campbell's voice rose dramatically. "Now I'm raring to go."

"I never thought I'd see the day that you felt sorry for yourself, Vic."

"Let me tell you something, old friend. I felt sorry for myself throughout those twenty-five missions we flew together. Without you, I wouldn't have made it. None of the crew would. You were our luck, John. We all knew that the first time we laid eyes on you. All we had to do was stay close to you, we figured, and we'd make it through that damned war."

Gault snorted. He'd always considered Campbell to be his lucky charm. "Are you still keeping in touch with the rest of the crew?"

"You bet, through my newsletter, the *Lady-A Gazette*, circulation six."

"Seven," Gault corrected, remembering the last issue.

"No more. Lee Randall's gone, a heart attack. It was quick though. Just like that, the lucky bastard."

Gault shook his head. He should have known about Randall, their tail gunner, who'd saved all their lives on more than one occasion.

"Four of us down," Campbell said, "six to go. You know something, Skipper. I dream about those missions sometimes. In the dream everybody's still alive. Tim Lambert squeezing into his belly turret, Perry Goddard at his waist gun, Mark Tanner on the radio when he wasn't firing his .50-caliber, and Randall in his turret up top."

"I see them, too," Gault said quietly. "Even when I'm not asleep. Who else will want to come along, do you think?"

"We've only got two gunners left, Skipper, Russ Yar-

brough and Jack Hill. But Hill's out. He's got arthritis so
bad his wife has to write his letters."

Gault felt a stab of shame for not having kept closer
tabs on his old crew.

"So that leaves us with Yarbrough," Campbell went
on. "He'll come."

"What about Novak, our navigator?"

"No way, Skip. I can still see him down on his knees
after that last mission, kissing the ground and swearing
he'd never fly again."

"You're right. I forgot about that."

"That's a bad sign in a man your age," Campbell
quipped. "Hell, a man your age is going to need a copilot."

"I'm old enough to know better than to get into a
fight," Gault replied, dodging the issue.

Campbell groaned for effect. "Don't remind me. But
I'm not so old I don't remember asking you about a copilot."

"If push comes to shove, I can handle the *Lady-A* by
myself, but you don't have to worry. I was planning on
calling Brad next, though why a rich son of a bitch like
him would be interested, I don't know."

"Roberts was always crazy. He'll love this."

Brad Roberts braked his Ferrari to a stop smack in the
middle of Pebble Beach's Seventeen-Mile Drive. It was
dawn, shift-change time for the one sheriff's car that patrolled the area. His high beams picked out the first of a
dozen hairpin curves that would eventually lead into the
straightaway approach to the Pebble Beach Lodge.

The car trembled as he revved its 12-cylinder, 380
horsepower engine. The sound of it, the feel of it reso-
nating through his body, made life worth living. Everything else was no more than going through the motions.
His latest wife, his three children who wouldn't speak to
him, none of them would so much as miss a tennis lesson
if he killed himself on the first curve.

He popped the clutch and screamed into the turn. From now on, the real risk was meeting another car. So far, that had never happened. The day it did, he'd take a swan dive into the Pacific and make his heirs happy.

In the middle of a controlled skid, he caught a blinking light out of the corner of his eye. He was about to ignore it, then had second thoughts. Perhaps the well-bribed guard on the Carmel entrance gate was trying to warn him of oncoming traffic.

He stood on the brakes hard enough to fishtail onto the dirt shoulder. By then the engine had subsided enough for the phone's ring to be heard.

"This is Roberts," he said curtly.

"Brad, it's John Gault."

"For Christ's sake. Where are you?"

"I'm standing in my hangar in Salt Lake, looking up at the *Lady-A*."

Gault sounded just the same, rock-solid. His voice had never changed, even when German fighters were closing in.

"How does she look?"

"She's going to fly again, and I'm going to need a copilot."

Roberts smiled, remembering the feel of the B-24's yoke in his hands, better than a Ferrari any day. Liberators looked like boxcars, some said. Others called them flying trucks and said they flew like one, too. But that was the challenge. Anybody could handle one of those easy-flying B-17s. But a B-24 took guts, not to mention brains and muscle. "I'm on my way, Skipper."

There was silence for a moment and then Gault said, "You mean you'll actually come?"

Roberts smiled to himself. "I seem to remember we were a team, Skipper. Nothing that's happened since can ever change that. I'll call you when I arrive."

Whistling, Roberts drove sedately all the way to the Monterey airport.

23

Frank Odell took one look at the outside thermometer and shook his head. What was God thinking about when he created Mesa d'Oro? Here it was 107 degrees in the shade, only there wasn't any real shade, just man-made concrete overhangs. Only mad dogs would be dumb enough to live in a place like this.

Odell tapped the thermometer. The mercury didn't budge.

He crossed the compound to the research building, where his meeting with the Director was scheduled. Odell had chosen to take the sunny route, instead of one of the interconnected air-conditioned corridors that linked the mesa's three buildings—research, staff quarters, and the Director's residence. The sunshine, he'd hoped, would dispel the sense of uneasiness that had come over him since hearing of the latest developments in Salt Lake, not to mention Ophir.

But his mood hadn't changed by the time he reached the manned guard station, where Odell had his ID badge examined by the hard-eyed sentry.

"The Director's expecting me," he said evenly.

The sentry merely nodded before ushering him into the wide, carpeted corridor. At the end of it, the Director's assistant stood by the open door.

Odell knocked anyway.

"Enter," the Director said.

Light streaming through the wall of glass directly behind the Director's desk turned the man into a black silhouette. Odell squinted against the dazzling glare, but the Director's features remained unreadable. Maybe it was just as well. The window behind the Director opened onto the mesa's sheer cliff and its two-thousand-foot drop to the desert floor below.

Odell took a seat and waited for the Director to speak. He didn't wait long.

"Do you ever wonder about the work we do here?" the Director asked.

All the time, Odell answered to himself, but only shook his head.

"What we do here . . ." The Director paused, as if choosing his words carefully. "What we do here is necessary if we are to survive in the twenty-first century. Modern life has become so complex there are no longer clear choices, only necessary ones. Don't you agree, Frank?"

He continued without waiting for Odell to reply. "It's always a matter of what's necessary, Frank. That's what we have to focus on. History will say that we did what had to be done and we did it without flinching."

His fingers drummed on the desktop. "That's why we're here, Frank. To make hard choices. Never lose sight of that. If a few have to die now to save thousands later, so be it. Wouldn't you say that's a cheap enough price to pay?"

Odell stared at the Director's hands. The man was nervous. Maybe he was human after all.

"You don't have to answer, Frank. Those lives will be on my conscience."

The Director pointed a forefinger at Odell's midsection. "I understand the archaeologist and her father survived the accident in Ophir." His tone made the comment an accusation, though Odell hadn't been personally involved in the episode, or the decision that precipitated it.

"Her father suffered a broken arm, I believe," Odell said. "He's back in Albuquerque, along with his daughter."

"That was more than a week ago, Frank. Now my Blackbirds tell me she's on her way to Salt Lake."

"So I understand."

"What do you think should be done, then?"

"Nothing." Just like nothing should have been done before, Odell added to himself. They'd been very lucky that the local authorities had thought that the landslide had been caused by natural gases building up in the mine shafts. "Restoring that old plane will keep them busy and out of our hair. So let sleeping dogs lie."

"I thought you were the one who said she sticks to these things like gum to your shoe?"

Me and my big mouth. "Surveillance is all that's necessary."

"You mean my ever faithful Blackbirds. Without them, you know, we'd be working in the dark." The Director got up to pace. "I'm like you, Frank. I'm only a middleman. We both are. We do what we're told."

Swell, Odell thought, the Nuremberg defense.

"It's too late to have second thoughts," the Director added. "That reporter had to be interrogated. We had to know what he knew. After that . . ." The Director shrugged. "It wouldn't have been wise to let him walk away."

Odell sighed. No one walks away, not from a place like Mesa d'Oro.

24

Nick was having second thoughts as she waited for her baggage at the Salt Lake airport. By now Elliot had probably forgotten his vows to take it easy and give his broken arm a chance to heal. Most likely he was back in his Anasazi museum at the university, cataloguing his latest finds and thumbing his nose at the doctor's orders. Nick's, too, for that matter, after she'd spent a week fussing over him.

She was about to go phone hunting to check up on him when she spotted John Gault crossing the terminal toward her. Today there was a spring in his step and he carried himself with nonchalant grace. She hadn't seen him in nearly two weeks, but it seemed like only yesterday they'd flown over Mesa d'Oro together.

Unexpectedly, he grabbed her in a bear hug. Then just as quickly, Gault broke the contact saying, "Until I saw you, I wasn't really sure you'd come."

"I told you on the phone I had work to do here at the genealogy center."

"And the *Lady-A*?"

Nick smiled. "I wasn't planning to start my research until tomorrow."

"That's what I wanted to hear. Now tell me about your father. How is he?"

"Sorry he couldn't come. He's supposed to be taking it easy. Doctor's orders."

They were interrupted as luggage began tumbling down the chute onto the carousel. Her bag arrived reasonably intact. It was small enough to have fit under her seat, but she preferred to fly unencumbered. As usual, she'd packed one change of jeans in addition to the wrinkle-resistant skirt with the matching olive blouse that she was wearing at the moment. The bag also held her favorite T-shirt, a couple of pairs of panties, clean socks, and her desert boots.

Hefting the carryall, Gault said, "Most women carry purses bigger than this."

"Most women don't dig in the desert or get excited about old relics."

"I hope that doesn't refer to me."

"Maybe I should have said artifacts." Smiling at him, she wondered just how old he was. To have flown in World War Two, he had to be seventy at least. But today he didn't look it, despite everything he'd gone through.

"I don't want to hear you calling the *Lady-A* an artifact," he said. "Or a relic either, for that matter. Not in front of her, anyway. Now, come on. I'll introduce you to her, and some of the crew."

The moment the hangar door rolled open, Nick was in love. Even in pieces, the *Lady-A* looked majestic. All four of her engines were partially dismantled. Their parts lay in precise rows on separate tarpaulins spread beneath each of the engine nacelles.

Two men were sitting cross-legged on the hangar floor, examining the parts of the outboard port engine.

"This is Nicolette Scott," Gault called to them.

"Just Nick," she amended as the two men got up, wiping their hands on rags, and came forward to greet her.

"Meet Theron Christensen," Gault said, introducing the younger man first. "My chief mechanic."

"And this," Gault said, "is my copilot, Brad Roberts."

Roberts responded with a grin and an outstretched hand.

Once Nick shook their oily hands, they stepped aside so she could admire the *Lady-A*.

"She's named after John's wife," Christensen said. "The Lady Ann."

Nick nodded. "John told me."

"When she behaved, we called her the *Lady-A* for short," Roberts said. He pointed to her nose, where a painted green snake held a bright yellow bomb in its fangs. "When she didn't, we called her the Serpent."

"No war stories yet," Gault said as he took Nick by the elbow and led her forward until she was standing beside the nose. Hesitantly, Nick ran her hand along the turret's spotless Plexiglas. Her fingers tingled with excitement the same way they'd done when she'd uncovered her first airplane. It, too, was a B-24 bomber, one that had disappeared over New Guinea during World War Two. Until her archaeological expedition found the plane, its crew had still been listed officially as missing in action. That particular B-24, though, had been in so many pieces it hadn't been recognizable at first.

"The *Lady-A* brought us through twenty-five missions," Roberts said.

"The question is," Christensen put in, "does she have another one in her?"

"I'd say that's up to you."

The mechanic nodded. "That's what's worrying me."

"Hey, Vic," Gault called at the top of his voice, "come out of there and meet Nick Scott."

Legs appeared in the open bomb bay.

"The feet belong to Vic Campbell, our bombardier," Roberts said.

The feet dropped onto the hangar's cement floor. The man who went with them ducked under the fuselage and limped over to shake Nick's hand. He moved stiffly, as if suffering arthritis. One side of his face was bruised and swollen. Stitches showed along his upper lip.

"Don't ask him what happened," Roberts said. "You'll only embarrass him."

"Every crew needs a colorful character," Campbell shot back.

Roberts snorted.

"How's the Norden coming?" Gault asked.

Nick blinked in surprise. "Why would you need a bombsight?"

"I picked one up after the war," Campbell answered. "By then they were declassified and out-of-date like the rest of us."

"And?" Nick prompted.

The bombardier smiled sheepishly. "The *Lady-A* deserves to be whole again, one last time."

Nick eyed the empty turrets. "You'll need machine guns, then."

"We're going to bomb the Great Salt Lake," Gault said. "With Matt's ashes."

Nick didn't know what to say. Neither did anyone else. Finally Christensen broke the silence. "Don't encourage them, Nick. I have enough to worry about with the engines."

Nick gazed up at the bomber, imagining what it must have been like to fly her into combat. "I'd like to go with you when you take her up." The words were out of her mouth before she'd thought them through. Elliot would have a fit. She could hear him now. *I won't have you flying in an airplane that's older than you are.*

Gault raised an eyebrow. The look he got back from his copilot was crystal clear, no women allowed.

Nick glared. "I've seen the commercials. A bunch of guys drinking beer together and saying, 'It doesn't get any better than this.'"

"Hell," Christensen said, "chances are she'll never get off the ground anyway. Now, if you'll excuse me, I've got work to do."

"Me, too," Roberts said.

The two of them went back to the port outboard, while Campbell disappeared into the bomb bay again.

"My wife would have wanted to come along, too," Gault said.

He and Nick circled the B-24, keeping well clear of

the tarps. When they reached the bomb bay, Campbell was in the bombardier's seat in the forward turret.

"Let me give you the guided tour," Gault said. He climbed in first and led the way to the cockpit. There, clean sheets covered both the pilot's and copilot's seats. Every instrument gleamed, as did the windshield.

"I'm impressed," Nick said. "And I see that she was made by Consolidated." She leaned over and lovingly touched the small plaque by the pilot's yoke that identified the manufacturer. "The plane I found in New Guinea was built by Ford. That one was in pieces. The *Lady-A* looks in mint condition to me."

"I don't know how Theron does it. That man leaves nothing to chance. Order and precision, that's him. I wish he'd leave this kind of grunt work to the rest of us."

Sighing, he offered her the left-hand pilot's seat. Instead, she slid into the right-hand chair and took a deep breath. The clean smell of oil pervaded.

Tentatively, she touched the copilot's control yoke. "Do you really think she'll fly again?"

"What do you say to that, Annie?" Gault cocked his head to one side as if listening for an answer.

"You'll have to translate for me," Nick said.

"She's never let me down before. Hell, the first time I saw her, I knew I could trust her. She was waiting for me on the tarmac at Sioux City, Iowa. My group had just completed advanced flight training. Until then, we'd been cadets, outranked by everything and everybody. Now we had wings. We were second lieutenants. We were officers and gentlemen."

With a snort, he wrapped his fingers around the pilot's yoke. "You had to be an officer to sign for an expensive piece of equipment like a B-24 Liberator. Anyway, I took one look at her and it was love at first sight. Can you understand that?"

"Any archaeologist could. Each time we dig, each time we make a discovery, we fall in love." She caressed the yoke in front of her. "To touch something that's been hidden away, whether for centuries or just decades, is indescribable."

Gault released his grip to stare at her. "On our missions, Brad Roberts sat where you're sitting. We flew twenty-five of them together, more than half over Germany. After the disaster at Ploesti, they rotated us back to England."

My God, she thought. He was at Ploesti. She looked at him in awe. To have survived the Ploesti raid was a miracle in itself. It had been planned as a low-level surprise attack on the Nazi oil fields in Rumania. Poor intelligence and navigational screwups had ended all possibility of surprise and turned the raid into a massacre.

"In those days," Gault went on, "it was too early in the war for fighter cover all the way into Germany. That meant the Krauts had a lot of time to kill us on the longer runs. No one else in our squadron made it. They weren't all killed, you understand. A few managed to bail out and spend the war in prison camps. We were the only lucky ones. We had the *Lady-A*."

"How did you manage to bring her here to Salt Lake?"

"They sent us back home for war bond rallies. After the war I found her mothballed in the desert."

"It's no wonder you've kept her all these years. I think I'm jealous."

"In some ways, you remind me of her. You have her guts."

"Somehow, I get the feeling you're not comparing me to this airplane," Nick said.

"My wife actually. She sent me off to war and said, 'Women are stronger than you think, John. So don't worry about me. Just take care of yourself.'"

Before either could speak, someone called from the bomb bay. "John, are you there?"

"That's Paula, my grandson's fiancée," he explained to Nick. "She *was* his fiancée, I should say. Come on up, Paula," he called. "There's someone I want you to meet."

Paula Latham looked young in her Air Force uniform, barely out of her teens, Nick thought. But the captain's bars on her shoulders and pilot's wings over her breast pocket meant she had to be a good deal older.

Paula reached between the seats to shake Nick's hand. "John tells me you found Matt's airplane."

"Yes, I'm so sorry. I wish there had been something I could have done."

Paula looked at her clear-eyed, and replied, "John's told me how you went out to the mesa with him. You've done more than you had to."

Nick thought about mentioning her midnight trek and decided against it. There was no use causing more grief when she had so few answers.

"I understand there was a landslide that destroyed the area where you were working," Paula continued.

"Yes. Both my father and I were very lucky. In fact . . ." She stopped and thought about what she was going to say and the realization came to her. "In fact, we're only alive because the helicopter blew us off the cliff before it collapsed."

She heard a sharp intake of air from Paula, and Gault grabbed her arm.

"Do you think this could tie in with whatever Matt was after?" he asked.

"Do you know what that was?" Nick turned to Paula.

"Not exactly. John and I have tried to figure it out, but Matt never talked about his stories until they were in print."

Nick groaned inwardly. She hated the thought that she might never know what happened in Sulphur Canyon, or on the mesa either. "Did he say anything that might help? Anything at all?"

Paula shook her head regretfully. "I've been through all his things. John has gone through them too. There's nothing. But I'm not ready to give up, and I can tell by the look in your eyes, Nick, that you aren't, either." Paula checked her watch. "Sorry, guys. I can't stay. I've got a crew briefing in ten minutes, but I'll call you later after I've had the chance to go through Matt's things one more time."

"Paula's regular Air Force assigned to the National Guard," Gault explained for Nick's benefit. "She flies a Hercules transport."

"But I'm on the waiting list for fighters," Paula said as she left the cockpit.

Gault slumped in his seat. "She would have been a great wife for Matt. Now . . ."

Nick could read his mind. Now there'd be no children, no one to carry on the family business. She started to reach out to him, then held back. He didn't strike her as the kind of man who'd welcome any kind of pity. She suddenly felt ill at ease. The copilot's seat was set up for someone with longer legs and the temperature of the cockpit seemed to have dropped by ten degrees.

She was relieved when Gault got up from his seat without a word and showed her the rest of the plane. Ten minutes later, they were standing in the hangar doorway, admiring the *Lady-A* from a distance. Seen under Christensen's portable work lights, standing in the middle of an otherwise empty hangar, the Liberator seemed to Nick like some pagan idol that men worshiped with blood sacrifices. She shook off her disquiet. She loved old planes and this one was a honey.

"I just thought of something," Gault said. "You were the first civilian woman to go on board the *Lady-A*."

"Well, now that she's been initiated," Nick said, "maybe she'll let me fly with her, if your crew doesn't object."

Gault winked. "Now that they've all met you, how could they say no?"

Nick let out the breath she'd been holding. As far as she was concerned, flying in a B-24 was every bit the equal of finding the missing Benson sister, or even discovering an untouched Anasazi cliff dwelling. Whether such a moment was better than sex, as her father claimed, was yet to be determined.

"Let's get some dinner," Gault said, "then we'll drive over to Paula's and see if we can help jog her memory."

25

After a dinner at the airport restaurant, Nick accompanied Gault on the short drive to Paula's apartment. She lived in a two-story, pale green stucco that looked as if it had originally been designed as a chain motel. But as soon as Paula opened the door, the impersonal facade disappeared. The walls inside were bright mustard and covered with cheerful Matisse prints. Paula herself was wearing a sleeveless white blouse, flowered skirt, and open-toed sandals—a far cry from her Air Force uniform. Behind her the smell of baking cookies wafted into the night.

Nick smiled, realizing that she'd been expecting austere military quarters decorated with technical manuals.

"I'm so glad you came," Paula said. "I've been trying to call you. I've found something."

She led them across the room to a dining nook, where a glass-topped table-for-two was covered with greeting cards. "It's the strangest thing. All the time I've been going through Matt's stuff I've found nothing. Tonight I decided to go through my things, little things he's given me in the past. I was going to make up a scrapbook with them."

Her use of *was* struck Nick immediately. It implied

so many things lost forever. It had the same effect on Gault, judging by the way he clenched his teeth.

Paula selected a card featuring a sappy-looking hound dog on the front. When she held it out to Gault, he rubbed his eyes and said, "You'd better let Nick do the honors. My eyes are really tired."

Paula raised an eyebrow. No doubt she was thinking the same thing Nick was, that he had to have 20-20 vision or he wouldn't be flying.

Nick read the inscription. "I will love you always no matter how old you are."

"Sorry." For a moment Paula turned away. "There's another message on the back. Kind of a P.S."

"If anything ever happens to me," Nick read, "be sure to toss my cookies." She looked at Paula, then Gault. "Does that mean anything to either of you?"

Gault shook his head. Paula said, "Matt loved choc-olate-chip cookies. That's what I'm baking right now. I thought . . ." She sighed deeply. "I don't know what I thought."

"Was it some kind of joke between you?" Nick asked, wondering if it might have had a private connotation.

"No," Paula said, not looking the least bit self-conscious.

"You're both missing the point," Gault said impa-tiently. "Why would Matt write 'if anything ever hap-pens to me?' "

That did get a reaction out of Paula, who blinked hard enough to squeeze out tears. "Dad . . ." She reached out to touch Gault's arm. "You've had enough to worry about without me adding to your troubles. Besides, you know how Matt was. I got a few hints that he was onto something important, but never anything specific."

"If it concerns Matt, I have to know," Gault said.

Paula moved back to the living area, sat heavily on the sofa, and hugged herself. "He told me that he was onto something monstrous—and don't bother asking what. He didn't say, except that he'd been working on the story for a long time and wanted to make one last try at confirmation before getting out of the journalism business forever. Then he was going to fly as long as you'd have him."

Gault took her hand.

"You know something, Dad, it's funny when you think about it. Matt and I both thought flying was a lot more dangerous than writing for a newspaper."

"There is something we know," Nick blurted. "That mesa has to be involved. Otherwise, why chase us off with helicopters."

"You're probably right," Gault answered. "But what can we do?"

"There's something more," Nick stammered. "I couldn't make up my mind whether to tell you or not. That day we flew over the mesa. I went back that night."

"You what?" Gault demanded. He let go of Paula's hand and crossed the room to grab Nick. For a moment she thought he was going to shake her.

"Do you know how crazy that was?" he continued. "You could have been shot, you might have broken a leg in the dark."

"I know you're concerned," Nick said levelly, "but I took the responsibility on my own. I can take care of myself."

"Of course you can," he replied. "I've no right . . ." His voice trailed off and he let go of her.

"I talked to an old man. He said it was some kind of prison. He also said that the helicopters flew people to the mesa and that those people never came back."

"What the hell are you two talking about?" Paula asked.

For the next few minutes, Nick recounted her night-time journey into the desert, and the interview with an old man who was being held prisoner behind a security fence in the middle of nowhere.

"It gives me the willies," Paula responded. "But we

still don't know anything concrete. For all you know, Nick, that old man was crazy."

"In his situation, I think I would be. But I believed him. You would have too if you'd spoken with him face-to-face."

"How the hell did he and the others get there in the first place?" Gault asked.

"He said they were all illegals. So maybe the Border Patrol grabbed them, or the INS. One thing's for sure, nobody's going to do anything about it unless it's us."

"What do you have in mind?"

"We could go to Matt's paper and raise a stink. Publicity might flush out something."

"Don't you think going to the police would be better?" Paula asked.

Nick shook her head. "Judging by the way the NTSB treated us, I don't think the police would take us seriously."

Gault smiled for the first time since entering the apartment. "I know someone who will. His name's Bob Hanlan. He's a congressman, and he's in town to make a speech. Since I taught the man to fly, he owes me."

26

Nick was impressed. Here it was eight o'clock in the morning and Congressman Hanlan was greeting Gault like a long-lost brother. One late-night phone call was all it had taken to set up the meeting at his office on State Street in downtown Salt Lake City.

While the two of them pounded one another on the back, she shook her head in amazement.

"I owe this man my life," Hanlan said as soon as he'd been introduced to Nick. " 'Never trust your gauges,' he kept telling me. 'Always eyeball your fuel level.' I'm standing here because I took his advice."

"Some fool said Bob's gas tank had been topped off when it hadn't," Gault explained.

Hanlan nodded. "I would have been somewhere over the Great Salt Lake when the engine conked out."

Hanlan looked to be in his fifties. He was bald except for a fringe around the ears, jogger-thin, and immaculately dressed in knife-creased tan trousers and a short-sleeve blue shirt, freshly laundered with light starch by the looks of it. His smile saved him from looking too perfect. It was slightly lopsided, and he should have seen an orthodontist when he was young. It made her want to trust him, which meant it had probably gotten him elected.

He was also shrewd enough to assess Gault's mood. "All right, John. Out with it. A man like you doesn't call for help unless there's a damn serious reason."

"It's about my grandson, Matt."

"I thought it might be."

For the next few minutes, Gault and Nick took turns explaining the situation to the congressman. Even as she spoke, Nick couldn't help wondering if they both didn't sound crazy. When they finished, Hanlan didn't say anything for a while. He just paced. Finally, he started asking them questions, short and to the point. He kept at it, rephrasing them until she felt wrung dry. Only then did he nod, check his watch, and say, "It's not quite noon in Washington, so somebody ought to be on the job."

He called his secretary in from the outer office. "Liz, get me Dick Stone on the phone, would you?"

When she left, he said, "Dick's my executive assistant in my Washington office. He does all the hard work. He researches everything for me, and boils down each piece of legislation into understandable English. No mean task, I can assure you."

The phone rang.

"Dick," Hanlan said, "I have an old friend of mine here in the office, John Gault. With him is Dr. Nicolette Scott, an archaeologist who's working for the University of New Mexico at the moment. I'm going to switch to the speakerphone, so they can listen in."

"Good morning," Stone said from Washington.

"Dick," Hanlan plunged in, "John's been looking into the crash of his grandson's airplane near a place called Mesa d'Oro in Arizona. Apparently there's something unusual going on there. It's designated a U.S. military no-fly zone and non-military helicopters are enforcing it. I hope you're sitting in front of your computer."

"Where else, sir?"

"That's my boy. See what you can come up with in our database."

"Place names aren't my favorite with this new software, sir, but I'll give it a try."

"Dick's a wizard," Hanlan said. "Of course, you'd be surprised what kind of access a congressman has. We can link up with just about anybody's computer, except maybe the CIA's." He winked. "Though I wouldn't be surprised if they could tap into our system."

From Washington Stone said, "There is a listing for Mesa d'Oro, Arizona. It's the site for something called the National Research Institute for Behavioral Statistics."

"A government facility?" Hanlan asked.

"Absolutely."

"What else have you got, Dick?"

"Nothing. That's all it says."

"What do they do?"

"It doesn't say."

"Who's funding it?" Hanlan asked.

"I don't know, sir. Let me try the budget."

Hanlan shrugged at Gault and Nick. "That's Washington for you."

"Uh-oh," Stone said. "Black money."

"That means the funding is classified," Hanlan said. "Which probably means the institute does some kind of work for the Defense Department. Check the no-fly zone, Dick."

"It's already working, sir. Uh-oh. We've got another hit. All inquiries to be submitted through ISA."

"That's the Internal Security Agency," the congressman explained. "Very hush-hush."

"They're probably tracking our computer entry now," his aide added.

"Okay, Dick. If the trench coats show up, refer them to me. I'll take the heat."

"Yes, sir."

Hanlan broke the phone connection, then leaned back in his chair. "Do you know how many intelligence agencies this country has?"

He held up a hand to forestall guesses. "Neither do I. That's why we set up the ISA. It's supposed to keep track of all covert activity. Because of it, damn near everything they do is classified. Their existence is too, I think. So that's it, John. I've hit a wall."

"And if I went to Washington and tried the Defense Department myself?" Gault asked.

"From what you tell me, you were seen flying over the institute. That means they already know about you, John. If they had anything to say, you would have heard it by now."

"What about the illegals we told you about? The man named Sanchez Nick spoke to."

"That I can do something about. I'll contact the Immigration people and have them look into it. You'll hear from me in a day or two, I promise."

Hanlan stood up to shake hands with Gault.

"And if my grandson's death is tied in to that mesa?"

"You bring me concrete proof of that, and I'll go after them no matter how secret their classification."

27

Frank Odell entered his classified identification code into the phone scrambler and waited. He'd been sitting in his office for the last hour, since the moment the alert had come through to stand by for a priority call. During that time, he'd eaten two Twinkies, a Snickers bar, and a bag of potato chips.

"All the basic food groups," he muttered to himself. He might as well have added ice cream, and pizza, and be done with it. In the end, none of it mattered. His arteries wouldn't kill him. Stress would do that. Hypertension in spades dealing with the Director or, worse yet, Mr. Smith. Now there was a man who made even the Director weak in the knees. Smith, it was said, wasn't his real name, but a house name used by a succession of ISA chairmen.

The phone rang. Odell picked up the scrambler phone and said, "Yes, sir?"

"Do you recognize my voice?"

"Yes, Mr. Smith."

"Do you remember the ground rules we laid down when I hired you for this job?"

"Yes," Odell assured him, remembering the daylong

briefing. Right then, he should have gone into another line of work. He'd started in newspapers, for God's sake. He could always go back. Sure, and starve to death. Or worse yet, fall behind on his alimony.

"I'd like to hear rule number one."

"I work for you," Odell said. "I answer to you. No one else."

"What about the Director?"

"He only thinks I work for him."

"From now on, I want daily reports on the Director's activities."

I'll be damned, Odell thought, *mistakes were catching up with the Director after all.* "I don't have access to his daily logs." Until now, Smith had been satisfied with weekly status reports, gathered mostly from rumors and hearsay.

"A packet is on its way to you. It will arrive within the next four hours. It contains everything you need for continuous surveillance. And no, you don't have to worry about installation. The necessary equipment is already in place."

Odell rolled his eyes. Security was not his job, not specifically. So maybe this was nothing but an exercise, a test of Odell's loyalty. Then again, maybe the Director was testing him through Mr. Smith.

"Don't think," Smith said, mind reading. "Just follow instructions."

"Yes, sir."

"We'll start right now. Give me your report on all activities for the past two weeks."

As ordered, Odell proceeded to bring the ISA Chairman up to date, including the destruction of the cliffs near Ophir and the dispatching of the Director's Blackbird team.

"Yes, that verifies what I have," Smith said as soon as Odell concluded. "What I tell you now goes no farther. If it does, I'll know about it."

"Yes, sir."

"There's a possibility, only a possibility at this time, that the Director is becoming a liability. In that event, I may require independent action on your part."

Jesus. Odell didn't like the sound of that.

"Consider my position," Smith said. "One of ISA's special objectives is radiation containment. And yours is just one of the sites I have to worry about. I'm sure you can understand the problems that raises."

"Yes, sir," Odell said, though he didn't understand a damned thing. Why was Smith telling him this? He fingered his radiation badge. As usual, it showed no sign that he'd been overexposed. Then again, maybe it was nothing but a dummy. Maybe he was a guinea pig and didn't know it.

"The Director promised me solutions," Smith said.

"And has he delivered?" Odell ventured.

"If he had, we wouldn't be having this conversation."

"You mean it's all for nothing?"

"I'm not asking you to be an assassin. Not personally anyway." The phone in Frank Odell's hand went dead.

28

Outside the congressman's office, Gault straightened his shoulders and took a deep breath. He looked like a man who'd come to a decision, Nick thought. She was tempted to ask him about it, but figured he'd tell her when he was ready.

Smiling crookedly, he tossed his keys in the air with one hand, caught them in the other, and then opened the passenger's door for her. Furnace air flooded out, a good ten degrees hotter than the ninety-degree sidewalk temperature. Downtown Salt Lake, as clean as it was, with its wide streets and pioneer landmarks, seemed on the verge of spontaneous combustion.

No, Nick decided, correcting herself, her impression had nothing to do with the weather. It was how she felt inside.

Gault drove west toward the airport. Within a few blocks the air conditioner had the pickup's small cab cooled down.

"Bob Hanlan's a good man," he said. "He'll do what he can for those illegals, but that will take time."

"Are you suggesting something else?" Nick asked.

"We need more information."

That was an understatement, Nick thought, closing her eyes against the road glare. But where would they look? Paula had nothing more to give, and Matt's cookie-tossing reference didn't make any sense.

Nick's eyes popped open. "What about the newspaper? Somebody there ought to know something. Reporters keep notes, don't they? And files?"

"Do you know anything about computers?" Gault asked.

"Enough."

"Matt gave me a tour of his office once. It's all computerized. The reporters type in their stories and push a button. The story goes to the editor, who reads it, makes whatever changes are necessary, and pushes another button. And bang-go. The story is set in type and ready to roll. The thing is, each reporter has his own computer, so he can store his own stories and research."

"Lead me to it," Nick said.

"Why don't I drop you at the paper and then head to the airport to see if Theron needs any help with the *Lady-A*."

"You're Matt's family," Nick pointed out. "They

might give you access to his things. They don't know me."

"I thought you were going to the Genealogy Library this morning?"

"If you can give up the *Lady-A* for a while, I can do the same with my research."

He snorted. "I guess Theron can get along without me."

Gault pulled over to the curb and stopped. "Before we turn around and go back to the paper, there's something I'd like to do."

Without warning, he leaned across the seat and kissed her on the cheek. The kiss was chaste, merely a sign of affection, but Nick couldn't keep the surprise out of her voice as she asked, "What was that for?"

"For being such a good friend," he replied.

Nick laughed. "Let's hope the people at the newspaper agree. If there are any clues about Matt's story, they should be there."

29

Wiley slammed on the brakes. "Jesus Christ! Why don't they make up their minds."

Ahead of them, Gault's truck pulled a U-turn and headed back toward town.

"I told you you were following too close," Voss said.

"Bullshit. The man's a menace on the highway." Wiley started his own U-turn.

"Hold it. Not too soon, or he'll spot us."

"What do you want me to do, lose him?" Wiley said, though he knew there was no chance of that.

"Shee-yit!" Voss emphasized his comment by turning up the volume on their radio receiver. Via the carefully placed bug in Gault's pickup, the lady archaeologist was saying, "It would help if you knew the editor personally."

"I know his name," Gault replied. "Reese."

"Anything else?" she said.

"I've never been a fan of the *Herald*."

"Look it up!" Wiley snapped as he completed the U-turn and accelerated.

Voss fanned through the telephone book. Carrying it, along with the Yellow Pages, was standard procedure on any assignment.

"Second South and Main Street," Voss said. "If you speed up we can beat them there."

Wiley checked the rearview mirror. "We don't want to get a ticket."

Voss flashed his credential. "This sucker will get us through anything."

Wiley nodded. Voss was right. The credential, which was absolutely genuine, guaranteed a free ride through any local law enforcement problem.

"And if that doesn't work," Voss said, drawing his .357, "I'll let this speak for us."

Wiley smiled grimly. He loved his work. But then who could blame him? Working for the Director, he and Voss didn't have to answer to the same rules everyone else did. They had life and death in their hands. They were immune.

They were going to finish the job. But first, they'd pay a visit to the *Herald*.

30

As Nick got out of the truck, the asphalt felt sticky underfoot. The sign on the Walker Bank Building read 9:45 and 90 degrees. By the time she and Gault reached the *Herald* half a block away, she was soaked and longing for her Cubs cap to keep the sweat out of her eyes. But wearing a baseball cap was hardly the impression she wanted to create. She wanted to look professional and in control. The expression on Gault's face made him look like a force of nature.

She disliked the *Herald's* editor, George Reese, on sight. He reminded her of Ben Gilbert, her double-dealing department chair. She tried to keep an open mind but his eyes were evasive and shrouded by a perpetual squint. His condolences to Gault sounded rehearsed, if not perfunctory.

Gault dismissed the comments with a wave. "We've come about Matt's personal effects."

"Of course."

"We'd also like to take a look at his files."

Reese put his hands together in a gesture that was so reminiscent of Gilbert that Nick wanted to throttle him on the spot. She could almost predict what he was going to say next.

He cleared his throat and fixed his gaze somewhere above and behind Gault. "Technically, those aren't Matt's files. They're the property of this paper and I can see no benefit from your perusing them."

"I'd just like to understand what Matt was working on before he died. Maybe it would help me understand why the accident happened."

A look of alarm crossed Reese's face. "I hope you don't think the paper's responsible for Matt's accident. Our employment package includes life insurance for our employees, but that's the extent of our liability. We never put our people in harm's way if we can help it. Besides, as I understand it, he was flying a private plane, one of yours."

Nick thought that Reese was starting to resemble a ferret. Then, seeing Gault leaning forward in his chair clenching his fists, she nudged him with her foot, a signal to let her do the talking. For a moment, she thought he was going to ignore her, then he sighed and sat back.

"What we really need," she said, "is a little guidance from you, Mr. Reese."

"Do you mind if I ask what your relationship is with Matt Gault?" the editor asked.

"She's a friend of the family." Gault answered so softly Nick knew it had cost him not to react more violently.

"You see, Mr. Reese," Nick improvised, "Matt thought a great deal of you. I don't know how many times I've heard him say how much he respected your work."

The flattery was obvious, but the man seemed pleased by it nevertheless.

"Matt was our top investigative reporter," Reese said. "We gave him a lot of leeway. He wasn't on a daily deadline like most reporters, but he'd let us know when he was getting close."

"Was he close this time?"

"That's a good question." Reese seemed to preen. "Matt was very guarded when it came to his exclusives, but we went along with him because he never let us down. This last story, though, was giving him fits. I know that much. He said he had everything but a source who'd go on the record. That's what he was after in Arizona."

Nick nodded encouragement. "Matt said you were the best when it came to protecting sources."

Reese smiled with pleasure. "We had a working headline, War Criminals. That was Matt's angle. Home-grown American war criminals in peace time. That's how he sold me on the story."

"Do you think any of it is written down?"

"Matt didn't like to put anything down on paper until he had it all up here." Reese tapped the side of his head.

"Surely, there are files?" Nick said.

"If I know Matt, we lost most of the good stuff when that plane of his went down. We might find something in his computer, but it won't be anything we can publish. I can promise you that."

"Mr. Reese," Nick said, "we'd appreciate anything that might help us come to terms with our loss."

"You have to understand that whatever's in the computer belongs to the paper. That's company policy."

"Of course."

"Matt's personal items are yours to take, naturally."

The personal items were nothing more than a framed photograph of Paula, a good-luck charm in the shape of a B-24, and a cigarette lighter that looked as if it had never been used.

Reese switched on the computer, then called up a directory of Matt's files, which dealt exclusively with past stories that had already appeared in the *Herald*.

"He should have erased this stuff," Reese said. "It's eating up disk space."

"Could we read through them first?"

"I could find you some back issues, if you'd like."

"That would be great for a scrapbook," Nick said. Out of the corner of her eye, she saw Gault grimace. For an instant she thought he was going to lose control and say something that would kill her rapport with Reese. But all Gault did was fold his arms across his chest as he perched on the edge of the adjacent desk.

Oblivious, Reese helped Nick into what had been Matt's chair, taking the opportunity to run his fingers along the small of her back. She smiled, masking her urge to kick him in the balls.

Reaching around her, Reese showed her how to access the files, beginning with an article on water pollution in southern Utah. They were using WordPerfect, probably due to the Utah location, but it wasn't much different from the word processor she used at Berkeley.

Nick heard a buzz as he leaned over her. He pulled out a pager and checked it.

"Seems I'm wanted," he said. "Nobody can do a thing around here without my help. If you need anything else . . ." He smiled suavely. "I'll be in my office. Or ask Chet here. He can always give you a hand."

Chet was at the next desk, one in a line of five. All had computers.

"This is Nicolette Scott," Reese told him. "And Matt's grandfather."

"Chet Green," the reporter said, nodding sympathetically. "I'll be here for a while if you need help."

"I'll be right back," Reese called over his shoulder.

Nick hoped not and went to work, while Gault stood behind her, reading over her shoulder. One by one she sorted through the list of files on Matt's computer. Matt had written on a wide variety of subjects, but there was no mention of Mesa d'Oro, or Arizona either for that matter.

When she ran out of files, she sat back and stared at the screen.

"Is that it?" Gault asked.

"I guess so."

Chet rolled his chair around. "What are you looking for exactly?"

"We were hoping to find out what Matt was working on in Arizona."

"You're not going to find much there," Chet said. "Matt didn't write anything down until he had the story complete. He did a lot of background work on the Internet, but he kept that to himself too."

There were icons for e-mail and Internet access. She tried the browser to see if Matt had left any bookmarks behind, but there was nothing.

"That was Matt for you," Chet said. "He could keep a secret."

"How long have you had the desk next to him?" Gault asked.

"A long time. Matt and I were friends, but that doesn't change things. We reporters are very jealous when it comes to our stories. One thing, I do know. Whatever Matt was working on made him jumpy. In fact, if you ask me it scared him a little. I know the feeling. I had it when I was working on a drug bust. I—"

Gault interrupted him. "How did you know Matt was scared?"

"Because he was sitting right here one day, when he ups and says, 'You know something, Chet, I'm going to have to take some precautions this time. I'm going to have to leave some cookie crumbs behind, just like Hansel and Gretel.'"

"They were bread crumbs and I seem to remember the birds ate those," Nick pointed out.

Chet shrugged. "Whatever he left behind I don't know about it."

"Is there anything else you can tell us?" Nick asked.

"Matt was a hell of a reporter."

Gault laid a gentle hand on Nick's shoulder. When she looked up he was nodding toward Reese's office. On the other side of the glass wall, Reese was in an animated conversation with two men. Though they were at least a hundred feet away, with their backs to Nick, their dark suits made her think immediately of FBI. Or Feds, anyway.

Don't get paranoid, she told herself. Probably they were nothing more than accountants dressed up to commit downsizing or some other fiscal crime.

"I don't like the looks of that," Chet said.

Gault immediately began gathering up Matt's personal effects.

A moment later, a security guard, carrying a small cardboard box, arrived and escorted them from the building. He refused to answer their questions or even to speak until they were on the sidewalk outside. Then he said, "I'm sorry. The paper is off-limits from now on." He handed Nick the box. "Matthew Gault's personal things from his locker are in here. Everything else belongs to the *Herald*."

"Why are we being thrown out?"

He tipped his service hat and said, "Have a nice day." Then he did an about-face and retreated into the *Herald* building.

Nick was furious. Gault was too, judging by the muscle twitching along his jaw line.

"What the hell's going on?" he snapped.

"I think it has something to do with those two in black. What did you make of them?"

"I think we met their brothers in Arizona."

"The NTSB men?"

"I'd bet on it. Well, to hell with them all. I'm going home to the *Lady-A*." With that, he headed for the truck that was parked down the street.

They were about to drive away, when Chet came jogging up, carrying a laptop computer in one hand and waving at them with the other.

"Mr. Reese sent me," he said somewhat breathlessly. "It's Matt's personal laptop. It doesn't belong to the paper. I was using it until just before you arrived today." He paused to take a deep breath. "I guess I could have kept it, but you know, Matt really was my friend." He thrust the laptop into the car.

"When you were using it, did you notice if Matt left any crumbs behind?" Nick asked.

"Not a one that I could find," Chet said. "Mr. Reese had two experts take a look, but they couldn't find anything either."

Nick was still musing about bread crumb trails as they pulled into the parking lot at Gault Aviation. Inside the *Lady-A*'s hangar, two mechanics she'd never seen before were in the final stages of reassembling the inboard port engine. Theron Christensen was standing beneath the engine nacelle watching their every move.

"I see we're making progress," Gault said enthusiastically.

"Another week and she'll be like new," Christensen assured them.

"I wish somebody'd rebuild me," Gault said. "I've logged too many hours."

"Don't tell the *Lady-A* that," Christensen shot back. He pointed at the mechanics working the engine. "You know Marty and Ben, don't you? I stole them from Delta for the rest of the week."

"You bet," one of the men called down from his perch on a ladder. "It's not every day you get to work on a warbird."

"I'll leave you to it, then," Gault said and headed for the sliding doors with Nick right behind him.

Once they were out of the hangar, and beyond Christensen's sight, Gault's shoulders slumped. His pace slowed. When Nick reached out to him, he shrugged her off.

"I meant it, you know," he said. "I have logged too many hours. Flying the *Lady-A* again is nothing but a dream."

"You heard Theron. He said she's coming along fine."

"Did I ever tell you about Lady Luck?"

Nick shook her head. "Don't tell me you're superstitious."

"A pilot has just so much luck to spend," he said, coming to a stop in front of the office door. "In the war, you burn it up like gasoline. After that, you owe the Lady. Sometimes, when I close my eyes, I can see her waiting to collect."

Nick hesitated. Was he feeling sorry for himself, or merely expressing a pilot's credo? Or feeling his own mortality?

"You could always stop flying," she said.

"That won't change anything. Lady Luck can catch up with you on the ground too."

"What are you saying, then, that you're not going to take Matt on one last flight?"

Gault shook himself. "I must be tired, that's all. And if Lady Luck catches up with me aboard the *Lady-A*, I'll die happy."

"Wait a minute. What about me? I'm going to be up there with you."

"Sorry. You said you had a day or two's research, so I didn't think you'd be sticking around that long. I guess I didn't think you were serious about joining the crew."

"I think you know better than that."

He ducked his head self-consciously and opened the door for her. Inside, Brad Roberts was leaning against the customer counter eating a doughnut. A mustache of powdered sugar covered his upper lip.

"I hope you saved me one," Gault said.

"What are copilots for?" Roberts reached under the counter and came up with a plastic bag filled with doughnuts. "Theron won't let us eat them in the hangar, otherwise I'd be out there helping."

Gault fished out a jelly doughnut. Raspberry filling ran down his chin at the first bite. "You're like me," Gault said with his mouth full. "Good only for washing windshields, until it's time to fly."

Roberts sobered. "Theron tells me you're stripping yourself bankrupt to rebuild the *Lady-A*."

"They tell me antiques are a good investment."

"Don't kid yourself. We're the antiques around here, and I wouldn't pay much for any of us."

"Is that male bonding?" Nick asked sarcastically. "Or bullshit?"

Roberts snorted. "What I'm trying to do is offer my help."

"You can do that from the copilot's seat," Gault said.

"Since you have a copilot and bombardier," Nick said. "What does that leave for me?"

Roberts snapped his fingers. "That reminds me. I called Russ Yarbrough a few minutes ago."

"He was one of our gunners," Gault explained for Nick's benefit. "The best man with a .50-caliber I ever saw."

"I told him we had one more mission to fly," Roberts said. "Do you know what the old bastard said to that? 'What took you so long?' "

Gault started to say something, then turned away to stare out at the tarmac, where his twin-engine Cessna 340 was standing.

"There's something you ought to know," Roberts said. "Russ lost his wife last month."

Gault leaned his forehead against the window. "I should have kept in closer touch."

"That ranch of his in Oregon," Roberts went on. "It sounds pretty damn scratch to me, so I didn't want to ask him to spend money getting here."

"I'll wire it."

"There's no need. I told him you'd fly up to Medford this afternoon and get him."

Gault moved away from the window, his eyes shining with rekindled passion. "I should have thought of that. Call Yarbrough back and tell him I'm on my way."

In that moment, Nick envied them both their common bond. Experiencing combat had been the defining moment in their lives. Everything after that must have been anticlimactic. It was a truth she'd read on countless gravestones. *He fought in the Great War*, read the simple inscription. It was as if nothing after that had measured up, neither wife nor children, nor the work of a lifetime.

32

Wiley and Voss switched vehicles, trading their sedan for an electronic monitoring van they'd parked on the highway within camera range of Gault Aviation.

"What a bunch of losers," Voss said, momentarily taking his eye from the telephoto lens. "Imagine spending all that money on an old plane."

"Cheer up," Wiley answered. "They'll probably kill themselves if they ever get up in the air."

"Bite your tongue. Where's the fun in that?"

Wiley sighed. No matter how much Voss enjoyed his work, or how much Wiley himself did for that matter, there was always a chance that something could go wrong. A real accident was the safest.

"Take a look at this," Voss said.

"What's up?"

"The old geezer, the pilot, he's climbing into one of the planes."

"You heard them talking. He's flying to Oregon to pick up one of his old crew." Another dead man in the making, Wiley thought, but kept it to himself rather than spoil Voss's prospects.

"Don't you want to look? He's starting the engines."

"I can always watch the tape replay later."

"Suit yourself." Voss began to hum, slightly off-key.

Wiley clenched his teeth. He'd had partners with worse habits, so he kept any criticism to himself.

Then the cell phone beeped. Wiley switched on the scrambler and punched up the speaker so Voss could listen in.

"Do you know who this is?"

"Yes," Wiley said, mouthing *Odell* for his partner's benefit. Voss grimaced.

"I need a full report," Odell said.

"We usually deal with the Director," Wiley said.

"Are you challenging my authority?"

Wiley and Voss exchanged inquiring looks, followed by reluctant shrugs.

"No, sir," Wiley said, "we took care of the reporter's laptop computer as instructed."

"Did you get rid of the bookmarks?"

"We know what we're doing," Voss answered.

"What about the cookie file? Did you dump that, too?"

Voss opened his mouth but nothing came out, so Wiley spoke up. "What the hell's a cookie file?"

"Idiots!" Odell said. The phone went dead.

"I know what a cookie file means," Voss said dryly.

"I'm listening."

"It means we fucked up."

Nick stood on the tarmac admiring Gault's expertise as he swung the twin-engine Cessna onto the taxiway and headed for the airport's short runway. Once he was out of sight, she returned to the office. The others went back to the *Lady-A*.

Nick sat at Gault's desk, staring down at Matt's laptop. "You're welcome to use it for your research at the library," Gault had told her. He'd also left her the keys to his truck to save her the trouble of renting a car.

One thing was certain, she'd better check the computer first before using it. Even though all computers worked pretty much the same, there was always the chance of losing something on an unfamiliar machine.

She plugged it in to save the batteries, which she might need at the Genealogy Library, and ran through the Windows start-up. Nothing unusual there. Next, she looked for Matt's files. There were none.

Gault had said his grandson was closemouthed and secretive about his stories, but there was such a thing as paranoia.

"All right then," she told herself. "Check the Internet bookmarks." After all, Chet had said Matt loved surfing the net for background material.

A moment later, Nick blinked in disbelief. There were no bookmarks either. Matt had definitely been paranoid.

Shaking her head, Nick unplugged the laptop and carried it outside to the truck. Across the airport, jet engines roared as one of Delta's Boeing 727s took off. It was a sight she'd loved to watch since her first trip to the airport as a child. But jets were one thing, a B-24 Liberator's twelve-hundred horsepower Pratt and Whitneys quite another.

Stop procrastinating, and get to work she told herself. Track down the Benson sisters. Worry about the *Lady-A* later.

But even as she headed for the library, she couldn't get the old bomber out of her mind. Or was it Gault who kept intruding on her thoughts?

"It's a good thing he went to Oregon," she chastised herself, "or you'd never get anything done."

In Oregon, Russ Yarbrough knew it was time to see his wife. He'd known it since the moment Brad Roberts called. Roberts' news of Gault's loss had shamed Yarbrough into action. By God, the Skipper hadn't allowed the death of someone close to paralyze him. Instead, Gault was doing something, not sitting on his butt moping like Yarbrough had been doing for the last month. No, indeed. The Skipper was taking action. And what a genius idea it was! To fly the *Lady-A* one more time. That was better than any memorial service or headstone.

Well, by heaven, Yarbrough would make it Donna's memorial too.

He smiled wryly as he thought of the *Lady-A*'s bomb bay doors opening. Maybe he'd shout. "Bombs away," and jump out along with Matt Gault's ashes. He nodded. The thought of joining his wife in eternity was appealing.

He left the ranch house and crossed the yard toward the barn. Halfway there, he paused to look back at the one-story cedar house. Part of him, the dreamer refusing to accept reality, half-expected to see his wife standing at the kitchen window, waving to him as she always did when he went out to saddle one of the horses. The realist in him saw how dirty the windows had become, how abandoned the house looked. He felt abandoned, too.

He gritted his teeth. From the veranda, Donna's favorite place, there was a panoramic view of the ranch.

Not that it was really a ranch, more of a hideaway actually. There wasn't much grazing land. Instead, a second-growth forest of birch, pine, and aspen stretched in every direction, except west where the road ran into the state highway.

Donna's meadow was due north. Yarbrough hadn't been there in a week.

In the distance, a chicken clucked. Another answered it. Donna's chickens, taunting him as usual.

"They're smarter than we are," she'd say every time she came back empty-handed from one of her egg hunts.

"We should keep them in coops."

"Range chickens are better eating. Their eggs have less cholesterol."

Since neither eggs nor chickens ever found their way to a pot, the point had been moot.

Yarbrough entered the barn and filled a bucket with chicken feed. Because the birds were too smart to come anywhere near the barn or its adjacent corral, he carried the feed well into the trees before spreading it around. Donna had done the same thing twice every day.

Once that chore was taken care of, he wrote a note to his part-time hand and neighbor, Jerry Jacques, giving precise instructions on the daily distribution of chicken feed and horse fodder. On second thought, Yarbrough decided a note wasn't good enough, not if he was going to fly off in a fifty-year-old airplane. He'd call Jerry later and put him on a full-time basis for the next few weeks.

That decision made, he saddled Donna's horse, Janie, a black and white pinto. His horse had been ridden yesterday.

Janie seemed skittish as he took the meandering trail leading north. Overhead, the low cloud cover was showing signs of breaking up, and last night's wind had subsided to occasional gusts that had the aspens quaking.

When Janie tossed her head and snorted, he patted her neck reassuringly. "I know, girl. I know you miss Donna."

The horse snorted again and settled into a steady pace, picking her way among the boulders and fallen trees. All the while, overhanging branches did their best to sweep him off the horse's back. Finally, he got tired of ducking and rode low, hugging Janie's neck like a jockey.

On occasion Donna had accused him of being a jockey in another life. *How else could you make it look so easy,* she'd say, *while I'm bouncing myself black and blue?*

He was short enough to be a jockey, too. Being short had gotten him into gunnery school, since B-24s didn't have much headroom. Thank God he'd been an inch taller than Tim Lambert's five feet six. Otherwise, Yarbrough would have been the one crammed into the belly turret.

Tim was dead now, a heart attack. Ridiculous when you thought about it, since Messerschmitts, Focke-Wulfs, and flak hadn't so much as scratched him.

He'd been the one hit by shrapnel, right in the ass, when the *Lady-A* took a hit. A huge hole had opened in her side, but somehow her aluminum skin had deflected just enough shrapnel to keep Yarbrough and Perry Goddard, his brother waist gunner, from being killed.

But Perry was gone now, too. A car accident. God almighty! Twenty-five missions they'd spent together, standing back-to-back in the *Lady-A*'s waist. Sometimes as much as five and six hours without fighter cover, with the Luftwaffe trying to kill them. Flying at twenty thousand feet in an unpressurized plane, with the thirty-below-zero temperature a death sentence if you were seriously wounded. Then some drunk flattens him with a Buick. Christ.

Janie's whinny startled Yarbrough out of his reverie. Donna's meadow lay just ahead.

"Good girl."

It was time to lay flowers on Donna's grave, maybe for the last time.

34

Nick was startled when she reached the LDS Family History Library on West Temple Street. She'd been expecting something lavish, awe-inspiring even, not the gray slab two-story building in front of her. It had a gray slab twin next door, the Church Museum. Both were drab and utilitarian compared with the soaring, six-spired Gothic temple directly across the street.

As she looked up at the temple, she was overwhelmed by the faith it had taken to build such a structure. She knew that decades had been needed just to haul those massive granite stones from the mountain quarries twenty miles to the east.

But at least those pioneers had achieved their goal in the end. In archaeology, that wasn't always possible.

Still, you had to try, Nick told herself as she entered the library. Once inside, she sat through the fifteen-minute orientation program, then headed for the computer stations on the second floor, where records were kept for the United States and Canada.

As she began accessing data, she was awestruck. Here at her fingertips were more records than could be found anywhere else in the world. On top of that, the orientation session had included the information that duplicates of everything were stored in the Granite Mountain Records Vault that had been sunk deep into the Wasatch Mountains. There, they were said to be even safer than if they'd been buried inside the NORAD complex at Cheyenne Mountain in Colorado.

Nick took a deep breath and decided to look up her family history first to make certain she had the hang of things. She entered her own name. In the blink of an eye, the microfiche reference appeared on the screen. All she had to do was pull the film and settle down in front of one of the readers if she wanted a look at a copy of her birth certificate.

This was a researcher's paradise. Literally millions of man-hours had gone into assembling the vast genealogical archives. Thank God for the church doctrine that demanded it, she thought, for the belief that the dead must be identified in order to baptize them retroactively into the church.

Nick was lucky. Benson was a common name, and she already knew the full names of the sisters' parents and where the family had lived prior to moving to Ophir. Fortunately, Lillian had left her that clue by mourning the loss of her Ohio home.

Five minutes later, Nick fed microfiche into the optical reader and made a startling discovery. The sisters' birth certificates had been registered in Lancaster, Ohio, on the same day in 1888. That made Lillian and Pearl Benson twins! There'd been no hint of that in the diaries. Quite the contrary, in fact. Nick had been under the distinct impression that Lillian was older than Pearl. Was she the dominant twin? Or was the theory of one twin being dominant an old wives' tale? And were they identical twins? Nick wondered.

She searched for the death certificates. Lillian had died in 1936 in Las Cruces, New Mexico. Pearl's certificate gave Ophir, Arizona, as the place of death. The year was 1922, the year of the fire.

But if she'd died then, why had there been no mention of it in the newspaper clippings? And if she'd perished in the fire, why had Lillian pretended that it had never happened?

The obvious reason was that it was Pearl who had set the fire in the first place.

Nick shook her head. Don't start creating history,

she told herself. Research the facts, then put them together. Make no assumptions in advance.

So think! Nick closed her eyes and thought about the diaries. Lillian's entries had been rather sketchy immediately after the fire, but that could be considered normal after such a calamity.

With a sigh, Nick went back to the computers, looking for more Bensons. Maybe another branch of the family still existed.

When she found no other Bensons that she could relate directly to the sisters, she asked for help from one of the staff, an earnest young man who looked younger than most of her students. His name was Grant Kimball.

As soon as she identified herself as an archaeologist and explained what she was after, he smiled knowingly.

"Pioneer families can be tricky," he said. "Going back into the nineteenth century can give you fits. Some of the polygamists were cagey when it came to their wives' names. Then you have the problem of using the same name over and over again. It often happened that if a young child died, the same name was given to the next son or daughter.

"I don't think that's what I'm up against here," Nick told him. "Both Benson sisters lived in Ophir, Arizona. One of them died there, the other in New Mexico. I found their death certificates. What I need is surviving relatives."

"This may be your lucky day. One of our prophets was named Benson. It's an important name in church history and has been extensively researched."

Kimball ushered her into an office where a computer with a large screen dominated the room. He selected a CD from a stack next to the computer and slipped the disk into the disk drive.

Row after row of Bensons appeared on the screen. "I didn't know there were that many Bensons," Nick said.

"These are all the Bensons that ever were or are,"

Kimball replied. "Luckily I can cross-search either by first name or date of birth. Do you have a birth date?"

Nick gave him the date and the machine seemed to click in a self-satisfied way and two names appeared.

"Here we are." Kimball pointed. "You've got two Bensons on that date, Pearl and Lillian. Let's see, now that I have an index number I can move backwards and forwards in time. What'll it be, parents or children?"

"Surviving relatives, if you can trace them," Nick replied.

"Can do," Kimball answered and busily started typing. Suddenly the computer made an indignant beep and a flashing message appeared on the screen. "Darn," Kimball exclaimed.

"What's wrong?" For a brief moment Nick imagined that they had triggered some kind of security violation and she almost expected to see armed guards rushing through the door.

Kimball turned toward her. "Our data's only as good as what we put in, you understand. Sometimes the database gets corrupted or our volunteers aren't as careful as they should be, although this shouldn't have happened with a Benson. In any case, I've got a cross-link here."

"Does that mean that you can't get the information?" Nick didn't recognize the software that Kimball was using and suspected that it was custom-made.

"Not exactly. This particular warning message indicates that links that we have set up to the name Pearl Benson may have gotten scrambled. Let's see how bad it is. I'll just dump all the links out."

Kimball activated the printer, which immediately started spewing paper, then pored over the printouts. "It seems we have an apparent contradiction here. We have two death certificates. Aha! We have a Pearl Benson with a death certificate issued on presumption from the town of Ophir."

"All formal records from that town went up in flames in 1922," Nick said.

"Some of these little towns were pretty slack about authenticating their documentation. We also have a Pearl Benson Taylor who died in Moroni, Utah, in 1946."

"Could it be a coincidence?" Nick asked. She tried not to feel excitement, but her intuition kept telling her that there was a hidden message in those diaries.

"Let's find out. Taylor is another prominent church name." Humming, Kimball inserted another disk into the computer. Within moments, he looked up from the screen and grinned. "That particular branch of the Taylor family, Pearl's husband to be exact, were schismatics."

"I'm afraid I don't understand," Nick said.

"Polygamy was renounced by the church in 1890, but there's always been a few splinter groups who have clung to the original teachings. This Taylor"—He tapped the screen—"was prominent in a group that settled in Arizona for a time. I told you this was your lucky day." He grinned. "It's kind of a hobby of mine, keeping track of all the misguided schisms."

"But this Pearl died in 1946," Nick pointed out. "Surely she couldn't still have been in a polygamous relationship."

Kimball smiled and shrugged. "Family life is very important to the Saints. Even now, divorce isn't that common."

"But a polygamous marriage isn't legal," Nick persisted.

"Oh, look"—Kimball again tapped the screen, diverting Nick—"they had a daughter, Lillian Taylor."

Lillian, Nick thought. She named her daughter Lillian. It was too much of a coincidence. This had to be the right Pearl.

"What can you tell me about Lillian Taylor?"

Kimball went through two more disks before he shouted, "Eureka!"

Lillian Taylor, married name Lillian Taylor Cowley, was now living only a few blocks away, in Salt Lake City.

Nick couldn't believe her luck. "You wouldn't have her address, would you?"

Kimball grinned. "Personal informational on the living isn't my area of expertise. For that, you need a phone book."

35

"Working late, are we?" Voss leaned over the back of the computer terminal and grinned at Chet.

The young reporter had been so intent on the story he was working on that he hadn't heard Voss and Wiley approach. He looked up and Wiley could see the dawning realization in his eyes that none of his coworkers were around in the *Herald*'s newsroom.

"Look at this place," Voss continued. "Nobody home but us chickens."

"Hi, guys. You startled me." Chet tried a weak grin, but Wiley could see his fear.

Voss pressed harder on the terminal, bending it forward on its stand until it was tilted toward Chet's lap.

"Uh, you're leaning on my computer," Chet pointed out.

"And now we're going to lean on you," Wiley said, moving to Chet's side. "We paid you five grand for that little erase job and you gave the computer back to the Scott woman."

"I can explain that," Chet replied eagerly. "It was a model 2000, see? With the money you paid me I could afford a model 3000. I've got it right here." He lifted a slender black laptop from under the desk.

"A model 3000. Wow!" Voss commented sarcastically.

"It's got an active matrix screen," Chet persisted. "Want to see it?"

"Do we want to see it?" Voss asked Wiley.

"I don't think we want to see it," Wiley answered. "I think we want to know how come you took our money and gave Gault's computer back with the cookies file intact."

The reporter looked confused. "Cookies file?" he repeated. "What's a cookies file?"

"You tell us, bright boy." Voss leaned over and grabbed a fistful of the reporter's shirt, half-lifting him up from his seat.

"Now let's not get hasty," Wiley intervened. "We should really go someplace quiet and talk this over."

"Look, guys. I did what you asked me, but if you're not happy you can have the computer. I mean I can't give you back the money. I spent it, you know, on the 3000." Chet's voice trailed off.

"Where can we go that's quiet, Chet?" Wiley asked.

"What's wrong with right here? There's nobody else around." Chet literally clung to his desk.

"Aren't you expecting anybody?" Voss asked. "Like the night watchman or somebody from the presses?"

"We're okay here, guys. That's why I like to work late. Nobody comes up here this time of night."

The killing blow came so fast the reporter was still smiling when Voss snapped his neck.

"Now we're going to have to carry him," Wiley said disgustedly. "I was going to sweet-talk him onto the roof."

"I got tired of listening to his bullshit." Voss grunted as he lifted the body in a fireman's carry. "You handle the elevator."

By the time they reached the roof, Voss was sweating badly. "Christ!" he complained. "It's even hot up here."

"If you had exhibited a little more self-control, you wouldn't have to be working so hard," Wiley pointed out.

"Seize the moment," Voss replied, balancing the body on the edge of the building's roof. "You ready?"

"Half a minute." Wiley opened up the laptop and quickly typed:

I can't take the low pay and lack of advancement anymore.

Sorry.

Chet

"Bombs away," he called out.

"That thing works on batteries, doesn't it?" Voss seemed reluctant to let go of his victim. "What if the batteries go dead before they get up here?"

Wiley pried Voss away and sent the body over the edge.

"Don't worry," Wiley said as they both headed for the exit. "The batteries will last. It's a model 3000, isn't it?"

36

The next morning Nick left her hotel armed with a street map of the city. The air was clear, the temperature sizzling as she headed uphill toward the avenues in search of a missing piece of Ophir's history.

Lillian Taylor Cowley lived on Eighth Avenue, high on the city's north bench. The house was one of those sturdy brick bungalows built to survive winters rather than please the eye. At the moment, the house was closed against the heat, with shades drawn at every window.

The woman who opened the door looked to be in her seventies, about the right age to be Pearl Benson's daughter. Her gray hair was pulled back into a tight bun, her glasses austere and rimless, and her housecoat old-fashioned. She could have been a face from one of those bleak pioneer daguerreotypes.

"Mrs. Cowley?" Nick asked.

The woman nodded.

"I'm Nick Scott. I called ahead."

"Of course you did, dear." Her smile changed her face completely, from reserved to motherly. She held open the screen door. "Call me Lily. Now come in before the heat does."

She led the way into a small, darkened living room dominated by a large sofa and two flanking overstuffed chairs. The smell of baking permeated the air.

"Whatever that is, it smells wonderful," Nick said, thinking that there must be something in the local water that encouraged everyone to bake.

"It's best to get your baking done early in this kind of heat," Lily said. "I'm making cookies for my great-grandchildren."

Nick breathed deeply. Something about the aroma intrigued her, a long-gone memory perhaps, though it wasn't memory of her mother's cooking. The only cookies Elaine had mastered came in packages.

"Come meet our guest," Lily called.

Another woman, a younger version of Lily, appeared in the kitchen doorway.

"This is my daughter, Pearl," Lily said. "It's her daughter's brood we're expecting to feed."

Nick shook hands, feeling triumphant. Lillian and Pearl. The search at the Genealogy Library had been on the money.

"She's named for my mother," Lily confirmed as if reading Nick's mind.

"And you are named for your aunt," Nick said.

"Before we get to that, dear," Lily said, "tell us again what this is all about."

She motioned Nick toward the sofa. As soon as Nick sank into the plump cushions, she went over the facts of her dig one more time, including the buttonhook find and Lillian's diaries that had been left to the university.

"I'd like to see that buttonhook one day," Lily said.

"I'll send you photos," Nick promised. "And a copy of my article as soon as I finish it."

"When will that be?" Lily's daughter asked.

"That depends on what you and your mother can tell me. At the moment, I'm having trouble piecing together exactly what happened after the great fire."

"Of course you are," Lily said, winking at her daughter. "It's a family secret."

Pearl beamed. "It's a story I loved hearing as a girl. It was so romantic and exciting. I always hoped something like that would happen to me." Her tone said her wish hadn't come true.

"I hope it's not so much of a family secret that you'll feel unable to tell me," Nick said.

"It depends on why you want to know," Lily replied.

"An archaeologist's job is to preserve the past. But Ophir's gone now, lost to time, and a cliff slide ruined my chances of understanding Lillian and Pearl Benson. If you don't help me, they'll be lost forever."

Lily smiled. "They've been baptized properly and raised to heaven."

Nick said, "Think of it this way. If I write their story, your great-great grandchildren will be able to read about them a hundred years from now."

Lily laughed. "At the rate we're going, there'll be a lot more generations than that in a hundred years. It might be nice, though, for the family."

"We should do it, Mother," Pearl added.

Lily nodded. "I think you're right. So many memories are lost when a person dies. Where would you like us to begin, dear?"

"Tell me about the fire in Ophir," Nick replied. "I found one death certificate that says Pearl died in that fire. But if that had happened, you wouldn't be here."

"Isn't that the truth." Lily smiled. "Well, dear, this is one time being old helps, because these days my memory works backwards. The stories my mother told me are fresher in my mind than what happened yesterday." She squeezed her eyes shut. "If I concentrate hard enough, I can still see my mother and hear her voice."

She paused to tuck stray hairs into the bun at the back of her head. "My mother and her sister were very close. Neither had married at the age most women were expected to. The plain fact was, both expected to die old maids. They expected to stay together to the end. Then came two things at once that changed everything. The fire and my father, Jedediah Taylor. Sometimes I wonder if he didn't set the fire to cover his tracks, but Mother always insisted that wasn't so."

Lily leaned back and smiled, as if she were enjoying her memories.

"Grandfather Jedediah," Pearl picked up, "was a rogue Mormon. Some called him that, anyway. But to me, he was like one of those heroes you see in western movies—misunderstood but willing to fight for his beliefs. He was a polygamist, you see. He stole grandmother away and made her his second wife."

"Don't mislead our guest," Lily admonished, wagging a finger at her daughter. "Mother was in love. He didn't have to steal her. She went willingly."

"How did they meet?" Nick asked softly.

"Polygamy was illegal in those days just like now, but my father didn't see it that way. He said what was good enough for Brigham Young was good enough for him. When the law came looking for him, he fled to Arizona until things cooled off a bit. For a while, he lived near Bisbee. When he finally got word that the law had stopped looking for him, he started back to Utah. On the way, he happened to camp outside Ophir. Pearl met him when he went into town to buy supplies. 'It was love at first sight,' my mother told me. 'One look at him and I was a goner.'"

A smile lit up Lily's face. "Jedediah was such a handsome man, mother didn't mind sharing him. She would have shared him with her sister too, but Lillian wouldn't hear of such a thing. It was a sin, Lillian said, and she threatened to have the sheriff run Jedediah out of town."

Lily leaned forward, rubbing her hands together. "I can see my mother now, saying, 'If love's a sin, so be it.'"

"Tell her about the fire," Pearl urged.

Lily shushed her daughter with a stern look. "The night Ophir went up in flames was the night my mother ran off. Whether Jedediah set the fire himself to keep the sheriff busy, we'll never know, I guess. Years later, mother heard that Lillian had told everybody she'd died in the fire."

Lily shook her head. "What a pity. My mother wrote to her sister many times, hoping for a reconciliation, but Lillian felt betrayed. She wrote back to my mother only once. In that letter she said, 'My sister's dead and buried.' In a way it was true, my mother told me once. She said the woman she'd been was gone forever."

Lily smiled at her daughter. "The cookies ought to be cool by now. I think our guest might like some."

"I've just had breakfast," Nick said.

"Take some with you, then, for later."

As soon as Pearl returned from the kitchen with a bag of cookies, Lily continued. "Years later, my mother decided to make one last try at reconciliation. She put everything down in a letter, but it came back unopened, stamped *address unknown*. My mother cried when she told me about it. I found that letter, still unopened, after she died. I expect you'll want to read it."

She took a polished wooden box off of the coffee

table and extracted a letter from it, handing it to Nick
without another word.

With trembling hands, Nick pulled the fragile paper
from the yellowing envelope and read.

My dearest sister,
Our lives have taken such different paths since that
dreadful fire that destroyed our home and yet I
dare ask, can we not meet again? My beloved
Jedediah has gone to his heavenly reward as has his
first wife, Rachel. Surely now there can be no
impediment to renewing that sisterly bond of love
and respect that nurtured us through the hardships
of youth?

Jedediah swore to me on his deathbed that he
had nothing to do with the fire and how could I
not believe him? He was such a good man and
what you held to be a sin, he counted as a sacred
duty.

You may think it strange that I would be
willing to share a man who meant so much to me
with another woman. In truth, Rachel became as
a sister to me and we were able to share the
burdens of a life that was full of joy, but held little
luxury. But Lillian, she was not you and never did
she displace you from my heart.

I've named my daughter after you, and I hope
someday that you will see her. She has Mother's
sweet face.

Do not be harsh with me for leaving you. I
was never as strong nor as independent as I know
you to be. I saw your heart break when that
young Latin teacher jilted you. I still remember the
handkerchief you embroidered for him with the
motto "omnia vincit amor." Don't you see, my
dear, love does conquer all. It certainly conquered
all I knew and made me leave family, friends, and
all society. But I have no regrets. Please give way

to that sisterly affection that once bound us so
closely. Let us be sisters again.

               In all affection, your loving sister,
               Pearl

A chill ran up Nick's spine, prompted by a remembered
passage from one of Lillian's diaries. *God has never seen fit
to provide a husband,* she'd written. *But sometimes I think it
was just as well. Judging from what I've seen, falling in love
seems a kind of madness. Or possibly an obsession I can well
live without.*

"Thank you," Nick said, returning the letter. "This
answers everything."

But she couldn't help thinking that Pearl's letter had
left too much unsaid. Whatever her motives had been,
one fact remained clear. She'd left Lillian behind to cope
with the fire and its aftermath on her own. To Nick, that
didn't sound like love. It sounded like obsession, a feeling
Nick knew well. For her, it was airplanes, for her father,
the Anasazi. And for her mother, despair had been an
obsession.

Or was obsession a kind of love? Nick didn't know,
and she suspected that Pearl Benson hadn't known
either.

By the time Nick drove back to the airport, Gault's two-man crew, Roberts and Campbell, were pacing back and forth on the tarmac in front of the *Lady-A*'s hangar.

"Why are you standing out here in the sun?" Nick said. "It must be a hundred degrees."

"John's overdue," Roberts replied. He looked ashen.

"How long?" she asked.

"Brad's just being an old lady," Campbell answered. "There's no need to worry."

To Nick, Campbell's good cheer seemed forced. His complexion, like Roberts', lacked color.

Roberts craned his neck, scanning the bright sky. "We should have heard from him by now."

Nick looked up too, but saw only empty sky marked with a few jet contrails.

"He said he'd start back from Oregon this morning," Campbell pointed out. "Well, it's only noon."

"Shouldn't we get out of the sun?" Nick said.

Theron Christensen, a mechanic's perpetual oily rag in his hands, emerged suddenly from the deep shade inside the hangar. "I've been telling them that for the past hour, Nick. Maybe they'll listen to you."

Campbell and Roberts shook their heads in unison.

"Mad dogs and bomber crews," Christensen snapped. "They're all the same."

"Cut the crap, Theron," Roberts said. "You're just as worried as we are."

Christensen winked at Nick. "I might be if I hadn't just spoken to John on the radio. He's on final approach right now."

"And Yarbrough?" Campbell asked.

"You've got yourself a gunner." The mechanic shook his head in disbelief. "You're all nuts."

"It takes one to know one," Campbell shot back.

My God, Nick thought. Another volunteer for the *Lady-A.* No, volunteer didn't say the half of it. Men who'd shared combat were forever linked. She knew that from friends who'd served in Vietnam. For them, war had been the definitive moment of their lives, one they kept living over and over again in their dreams. Or in this case, one they intended to live again aboard the *Lady-A.*

Five minutes later, the Cessna rolled to a stop in front of Gault Aviation. The moment Gault cut the engines, Campbell and Roberts, now looking their old selves, rushed forward.

Nick and Christensen hung back rather than intrude on the reunion.

A man Nick presumed to be Yarbrough came down the airstairs first with Gault right behind him.

"Jesus, Russ," Roberts shouted at Yarbrough. "You've gone bald, you old fart."

"That's what John's flying does to you. I had hair before we took off," he replied.

Laughing, the four of them pounded one another on the back. Finally, Yarbrough broke free and whooped, "Lead me to the *Lady-A.*"

As one, the four crewmen charged toward the hangar, scooping up Nick and Christensen on the way, making introductions on the go.

The moment they entered the hangar, Yarbrough's entire face lit up.

"Damn," he murmured. "She's still beautiful."

Nick thought the plane looked menacing, somehow. She couldn't put her finger on it, but the olive-drab surface of the B-24 seemed to devour the light. She shook off the feeling.

"How soon will she be ready to fly?" Yarbrough asked, pointing at the work in progress, which included two ladders rolled against the engines on the port side, each holding a freelance mechanic.

"That's up to Theron," Gault said. "He's our miracle worker."

"If we don't run into any snags," the mechanic said, "the engines will be ready one week from today. Of course there are other systems to be checked, too."

Yarbrough ran his hand along the wing. "I don't see any .50-calibers."

"A gunner to the end," Roberts said.

"That's enough reminiscing," Christensen said. "All sightseers out of my hangar so my boys can get their work done on time."

"It was the same in the war," Yarbrough mused. "Hurry up and wait."

"We'll be in the office if you need us," Gault said.

While the men reminisced and ate Lily's cookies, Nick used Matt's laptop to write up her notes on the Benson sisters. But even as she typed, she realized how frustrating archaeology could be at times. At best, her portrait of pioneer life in Ophir would only scratch the surface. True, she had found out what had happened to Pearl Benson after she fled Ophir. But she now knew how much had been omitted from Lillian's diaries, the cruel jilting, the elopement of Pearl. The more she found out, the more obvious it became that the diaries were like the mirrored surface of a deep and murky pool that gave no hint to the true nature of its depth. And going back to Ophir was now impossible. Her dig site was under half a mountainside. Still, she had enough material to publish a credible article, though not enough to satisfy her own curiosity.

Nick was checking her disk space when Gault waved at her. "Come on, Nick. There's only one cookie left. Chocolate chip. It has your name on it."

Nick froze. There it was, right in front of her, for anyone to see.

"I'll be damned," she shouted. "I know what Matt

meant in his note to Paula. "If anything happens to me, toss my cookies." It's a file, a computer file."

While Gault and his crew gathered around, Nick scrolled through the File Manager display and showed them the file nestled under the Internet browser directory. It was listed as cookies.txt.

"Some web sites actually write on your machine when you visit them. They leave a record of when you accessed them. Look, here they are," she said as she opened a file.

"Looks like gibberish to me," Campbell retorted.

"No, see for yourself. Here's nytimes.com and here's another site," she said, pointing to the site names interspersed with times, dates, and status codes.

Eagerly, Nick went to work, visiting one site after another, hoping they'd find out what story Matt had been researching in Arizona.

The first few sites were disappointing. They involved discontinued government projects mostly, though none had been in Arizona. One site referred to early weapons tests in Nevada and Utah.

"Does that mean anything to you?" Nick asked Gault. "Did Matt ever mention it?"

"Not that I can remember."

"Something must be here. Otherwise, Matt wouldn't have left the note."

Nick went onto the next web site, and the next. After an hour had gone by, the crew deserted her to watch Christensen at work on the *Lady-A*. Only Gault remained behind, his chair next to hers as they both peered at the computer screen.

Shaking off her growing sense of disappointment, Nick logged onto an American Medical Association site. What came up was biographical material on a Dr. Karl Maitland, a graduate of Harvard Medical School who'd done his internship at Massachusetts General Hospital. After that, he'd gone on to specialize in cancer research at several hospitals, including Sloan-Kettering and Johns

Hopkins. His articles had appeared in medical journals in this country and England. His most recent appointment was as Director of the National Research Institute for Behavioral Statistics. The bio included a photograph, showing a middle-aged man with a neatly trimmed black beard.

"Bingo!" Nick shouted, grabbing Gault's arm.

For a moment, he looked blank, then suddenly he broke into a wide grin. "Son of a bitch. That's the outfit Bob Hanlan came up with, the one on top of that damned mesa."

He hugged her. "You're a genius."

It was Gault who finally broke contact, saying, "What the hell do you think they're doing up on that mesa?"

"Let's see what else we can find on Matt's web sites," she said, missing the feel of him against her as she went on to the next site.

Three log-ons later a B-24 home page came up. Nick blinked in disbelief. The image downloading on the computer screen was a photograph of the *Lady-A*, obviously taken in her hangar.

"Matt took that shot himself," Gault said. "I have a copy of it on my desk." He left his chair to fetch the photograph.

As soon as he handed the silver-framed photograph to her, Nick held it up next to the screen. The shots were perfect matches.

She tapped a nail against the screen. "This has to be Matt's personal home page."

"He never said a word to me about it. I wonder why?"

Because, she thought to herself, Matt hadn't wanted to involve him in something that was obviously dangerous, what with black money and the government involved. At the same time, Matt wanted backup material in place. *In case something happened to him,* as his card to Paula had said. But what?

Hairs prickled on the back of her neck

"Hold it!" Gault said, leaning forward until his nose was close to the computer screen. "Look there." He pointed at the B-24's nose. "You see! The *Lady-A*'s nose art is different. Something's written on the serpent."

Nick squinted but couldn't make out the text.

"Keep your fingers crossed," she said and moved the cursor onto the serpent. "We're in luck. It's hot."

A double click of the mouse brought them a close-up. The serpent's coils contained the words *annie has james k. polk's number.*

"Does that mean anything to you?" Nick asked.

"Do you remember me telling you that Matt was a student of history? Well, presidents were a favorite of his. When James Polk was elected president his campaign motto was *fifty-four forty or fight.*"

"So?"

"That's the *Lady-A*'s serial number, fifty-four forty. She fought too. Matt called that serendipity."

Nick looked doubtful. "He went to a lot of trouble to put up this web page. Somehow, I don't think serendipity explains it. Can you think of anything else that it might mean?"

Before he could answer, the phone rang. Since Nick was closest she answered.

"Gault Aviation," she said.

"Is that Nick Scott?"

She recognized Congressman Bob Hanlan. "Yes, Congressman," she said for Gault's benefit. "Would you like to speak to John?"

"Is he there?"

"Yes, sir."

"I'm here at the airport, in the VIP suite at the main terminal building. My plane leaves for Washington in one hour. I'd like to see the two of you before then if possible."

38

"Shit!" Wiley blurted. "Did you hear that?"

Voss threw down his headset, a duplicate of Wiley's. "You're damn right. It shouldn't have gotten this far."

Wiley switched off the tape recorder and removed his own headset. They were sitting in their telephone truck, which had been carefully parked in line-of-sight of Gault Aviation. To avoid drawing unnecessary attention, the truck's engine was off, which meant no air-conditioning.

"I can't believe it," Wiley said with a shake of his head. "Now we've got a congressman in on the act."

"Whoa! Don't say *we*. They can't blame us for that."

"Don't count on it," Wiley said. "They've already tied that cookie file to our tails."

"What are we, mind readers? Nobody said a goddamned word about any kind of cookies."

Wiley grunted his agreement. "And now that busybody archaeologist has tied Maitland to the mesa. Jesus Christ, when he hears they've come up with his name he'll go ballistic."

"If it gets him off his ass, I'm all for it."

"Sometimes, I think it's Odell we ought to worry about, not the Director."

"I know what you mean. There's something sneaky about that bastard." Voss mopped his face. "It's like a furnace in here. The way I'm sweating all over the electronics, it's a wonder we haven't gone up in flames."

"For God's sake, be careful."

"Then start up the engine and cool things off for a while."

Wiley hated to risk it, but equipment failure was the last thing they could afford. Besides, they had credentials good enough to get them off just about any hook. Even so, he checked the perimeter for agents or sniffers before firing up the engine. Once the air conditioner was working, he and Voss positioned themselves in front of the vents and basked in the breeze.

After a while, Voss sighed contentedly and said, "We're the professionals, by God. Odell and the Director should get out of the way and let us do our job."

With a nod, Wiley picked up the litany. "First they're in a hurry to blow up that damn cliff, then they decide to wait and watch and pussyfoot around. Well, look what that's got us, a congressman, for Christ's sake."

"And what was all the chitchat about fifty-four forty?"

"You heard them. It's the plane's number or some damned thing."

"Maybe they're onto our bug and are trying to confuse us," Voss suggested.

Wiley thought that over. Discovery seemed unlikely, especially by amateurs. "You know something, Voss, that woman is starting to piss me off."

Voss pumped his fist. "That's what I like to hear. Let's rig for satellite transmission to the mesa. Maybe when they hear what's going on, they'll get off the dime."

"Don't get your hopes up," Wiley said as he began aligning the satellite dish. "Knowing Maitland's name doesn't prove anything. And even if it did, what are they going to do about it?"

Voss looked crestfallen.

Wiley relented. "I'll tell you what. If they recall us before you have your fun, I'll give you the archaeologist. After all, who's to know. One accident looks much like another."

39

Congressman Hanlan opened the door to the VIP suite, took one look at Nick, grinned, and said, "I can read your mind, Ms. Scott. 'Your tax dollars at work.' Am I right?"

Her response was to critically eye the lavish room. It was large enough for two back-to-back desks, a massive conference table, and an extravagantly appointed wet bar. "Close," she said.

"The airline keeps this available for a few select friends. Thank God, I'm not on the Transportation Committee, or there might be a conflict of interest."

The conference table, she noticed, held nothing but a speakerphone.

Hanlan nodded at his aide, who was hovering nearby. "Ken, stand guard for us outside in the hall, will you? No interruptions."

"Yes, sir."

As soon as the door closed behind him, Hanlan motioned Nick and Gault to sit down at the table. Once they were all clustered around the phone, the congressman got down to business. "After you spoke with me, I contacted a friend at the Justice Department. Even he got the runaround because of the black money funding. I was about to drop the matter when I remembered that somebody at the INS owed me a favor. They agreed to send in a team on the pretext that they'd been tipped off about illegal aliens in the area."

"And?" Gault said.

"There's someone I want you to talk to. After you

do, you'd better walk away, John. Because that's what I'm going to do. I don't have any choice."

Hanlan laid a hand on the phone. "You have my word that you'll be speaking to a federal agent whom I trust, but he has to remain anonymous. So, if you're ready, he's waiting at an outside phone right now. He'll sound strange, but that's a necessity to avoid voice printing."

Gault glanced at Nick. She looked as impressed as he was.

The congressman pressed the redial button. The moment the call was answered, he said, "This is Hanlan. The friends I told you about are here with me now. Why don't you tell them what you told me?"

"At your request a team was sent to the area at the base of Mesa d'Oro in Arizona," the agent said, sounding more like Donald Duck than a human being. "The place was deserted. But there was no doubt that it had been used as a detention center. Unfortunately, the entire area was sanitized before we got there."

"Explain," Hanlan said.

"It was far too clean to have been abandoned for more than a few days. Even the ground inside the fenced compound had been raked."

"Did you speak with anyone on the mesa? Were any reasons given?"

"It never got that far. Another agency arrived on the scene and intervened. Officially, the mesa doesn't exist. Neither do the barracks, nor anything else in the area. As of now, everything has been sanitized, including me."

"That sounds like they knew you were coming," Gault said.

"They could be listening right now," the agent replied.

Nick tensed. Her pulse pounded in her ears. She felt short of breath. Another question had to be asked, though she was afraid of the answer and the personal guilt that it would carry. "Why would they rake the compound?" she said.

"If there were people being held there against their will," the agent replied, "then killing them would be one way of getting rid of the evidence. It would also require an extensive cleanup."

Dear God, Nick thought. Had she been responsible for the old man's death, just by talking to him?

"Somebody has to pay for this," she muttered, as much to herself as anyone else.

"I didn't hear that," the agent said. "As of now, Congressman, we've never met. And I've never heard of Mesa d'Oro either."

The phone went dead.

Hanlan stood up. "That's the end of it, then. Some things are better left unknown. I'm sorry, John."

As he reached out to shake Gault's hand, Hanlan froze. His eyes, like Nick's, had locked on Gault's face. Never before had Nick seen such a look. It was pure anger, yet worse, because there was something inevitable about it, like a force of nature. Then suddenly it was gone, replaced by a calm resolve.

"Matt was onto something important," Gault said. "I think you know that as well as I do."

"I don't *know* anything, John. I may suspect things. I may have hunches, but I can't afford to act on such things."

"I can," he said in a self-possessed tone that was even more chilling than his anger.

The congressman took Nick's hand. "Do me a favor, Ms. Scott. Look after this old buzzard. Now, if you'll excuse me, I've got a plane to catch."

40

As Nick watched Gault climb into the *Lady-A*'s bomb bay and disappear, she had the sense that he was being swallowed by the past. It was the one place she could never join him. Only his crew had that privilege.

What was he thinking? she wondered. Was he reliving the war, or the telephone conversation with an agent so concerned with his own security that he'd disguised his voice electronically?

She couldn't get the conversation out of her mind. Maybe she never would. Maybe it would haunt her like one of Elaine's demons. For Nick, her demon would be the old man behind the chain-link fence.

The trouble was, the congressman had been right. There was nothing they could do. They had no answers, only suspicions. She'd said as much to Gault on the walk back from the passenger terminal. And she thought he agreed until they'd reached the hangar. It was then he said, "Let's see what Annie has to say before we decide anything."

She crossed the hangar floor to stare up at the B-24's cockpit. Gault was already in the pilot's seat. Beside him sat Theron Christensen.

Gault slid open the side window. "Stand clear, Nick, we're going to start one of the engines."

She answered with a thumbs-up and backed away. So it hadn't been the past Gault was reliving after all.

An inboard propeller turned, slowly at first, then picked up speed as the engine caught hold. The entire hangar vibrated with the roar.

After less than a minute, the power was cut and

Christensen and Gault dropped out of the bomb bay. Together, they pushed a roll-away ladder against the nacelle and climbed high enough to check for oil or coolant leaks.

The phone on the hangar wall rang.

"Get that for me, will you?" Gault called down to her.

"Sure." She caught it on the next ring. "Hello."

"Nick, is that you?"

"Elliot, how did you track me here?"

"Where else would a bomber-obsessed daughter of mine be hanging out?" he said, reproach in his voice.

For Gault's benefit, she shouted, "It's for me, my father."

"People will think I'm checking up on you if you say things like that," Elliot said.

"Aren't you?"

"I've been doing sums, Nick. That plane's over fifty years old. You're not thinking of flying in it, are you?"

"Its engines are being overhauled even as we speak."

"And the rest of it?"

Nick laughed. She knew her father only too well. "I'm fine, Elliot. You don't have to worry about me. I don't need baby-sitting. So stay home and take care of your broken arm."

"Listen to me, Nick. Airplanes are fine as a hobby. I encouraged you as a child because I knew you needed something to help you cope with your mother's moods."

"You're damn right I did."

"I should have been there more often."

Nick said nothing. When Elliot wasn't teaching, he'd been off on one of his digs. At the time, she hadn't understood that he was only doing his job. Yet even now, that knowledge didn't help much. The feelings of abandonment were still painful. Probably, they always would be.

"Do you know why I built model planes?" Nick ventured.

"I'm listening."

"Because I dreamed of flying away in one of them."

"You were never that gullible as a child," Elliot said. "You knew reality from fantasy."

"That didn't stop me from running away."

"A lot of children go through that stage."

She'd run to Elliot that first time, a seven-year-old fleeing one of her mother's impenetrable moods. By day, when Elliot was at work, Elaine had refused to leave her bed. Making lunch, cleaning up, everything fell on Nick's shoulders. She even tried to vacuum the house, mimicking Elaine on her better days, but Nick was too small. Finally, in desperation, she'd hoped to motivate Elaine by grabbing the blankets from her bed and dragging them into the living room. Elaine had followed, but only far enough to curl up next to a heat register behind the sofa, which was too heavy for Nick to move.

"I'm running away," Nick had told her.

No answer came from the darkness behind the sofa.

"I'm nòt coming back, ever."

"Hide for me," Elaine managed to say.

Nick had packed a sandwich and started walking toward the university where her father taught. She remembered the way, because Elliot had driven her there several times.

Nick shook her head at the memory and spoke into the phone. "You found me that first time I ran away," she reminded Elliot.

"You'd fallen asleep outside the archaeology museum. God knows how you made it that far. Sometimes, Nick, I think you're still trying to run away."

"I suppose that's a reference to the *Lady-A?*"

"Just promise me one thing," he said.

"Stop worrying, Elliot. John Gault's no fool. He won't fly an unsafe plane, and his mechanic sure as hell wouldn't let him take off in one either."

Elliot groaned for effect. "Just call me when you land and tell me you're safe. That's all I ask."

"It's a good thing your students don't know you like I do, Elliot. You're a softy and all bluff."

"Stop the flattery and tell me about your plane before I flunk you."

By the time she'd hung up, Gault was descending the ladder. Christensen was right behind him, wiping his hands on a grimy cloth.

"Well?" Nick said.

"That engine's tip-top," Christensen told her, "and clean enough to eat off. Not so much as a leak, even under full throttle."

"So why the long face?"

"I ran into a problem earlier. While you two were talking to the congressman, I was running tests. The bomb bay doors stuck halfway open during one of them."

Nick looked for herself. The bomb doors were open, as they always were when a Liberator was on the ground.

"Sure, they look fine now," he said. "That's the trouble. They worked four times in a row before hanging up on me. Then I toggled a couple of switches and bang, they opened right up again. At the moment they're working like new."

"Does it matter?" Nick asked.

"In an emergency, the bomb bay's the best way out," Theron said.

"We can always crank them open if we have to," Gault said.

Christensen shook his head. "Intermittent failures are a mechanic's worst nightmare. It could happen again anytime, or never. That's the problem. It's like playing Russian roulette. Besides, our crank handle is missing."

"Can't you rig something?" Gault asked.

Christensen mopped his sweating brow. The temperature inside the corrugated metal hangar had to be well over a hundred degrees. "I've tried a socket wrench, but it's not the same. In a crisis, it would take forever to get those doors open that way. It's a matter of leverage." He squinted at the B-24. "I wouldn't feel right sending the *Lady-A* out to fly equipped like that."

Gault patted his mechanic on the back. "Relax. We're not going to war."

"Maybe so, John. But if I make a mistake, someone dies."

Nick nodded sympathetically. Thank God she didn't have his job. Better to be an archaeologist and deal with the dead. *The longer dead the better*, her father liked to say. *That way no one can question your theories—no matter how stupid they sound.*

"What you both need is a few hours' sleep," she said.

"Maybe you're right, Nick. But there's something I want to check first. Ben, one of my freelance mechanics, spotted something he didn't like. If you don't mind, I could use both your help."

With the three of them working together, they rolled the platform ladder—which could also be used as boarding stairs—into place against the rear of the fuselage. After locking the wheels, Christensen went up first, stopping halfway to get a top view of the elevator planes.

"They look okay to me," he said, as if expecting someone to confirm his assessment. "But I think I'll replace the hinges just to be on the safe side. We can do that first thing tomorrow."

At the top of the ladder, with Nick and Gault right behind him, Christensen began shaking his head. "Shit! There goes our timetable. Ben was right. It's the beginning of a rudder stress fracture."

"Can she fly with it?" Gault asked.

"Sure, until it gives way. The trouble is, there's no telling when that might happen."

Christensen collapsed onto the platform. "This liberator was built by Consolidated, and they're long gone. Which means any spare parts needed will have to be handmade, and God knows how long that will take."

"What about scrounging a rudder?" Nick said.

"Where? The closest air museum is the one down in

California, and they're so desperate for spare parts they tried to buy the *Lady-A* last year. All they wanted her for was scrap."

Nick descended the ladder and paced, racking her memory. Where was that collector who'd contacted her after the discovery of a B-24 in New Guinea? Stopping in her tracks, she snapped her fingers. "How far is Malad, Idaho?"

"A three-hour drive, maybe. Why?"

"There's an airplane collector who lives there. His name's Kitar, if I remember correctly. He tried to buy a chunk of plane from me once, a B-24 that had gone down in New Guinea during the war. But it wasn't mine to sell, not that I would have anyway."

"I know the place," Christensen said. "Kitar's not really a collector, more like a poacher. He's got a tourist trap he calls a museum."

"You've been there?"

"Yep, and I remember one thing distinctly. He's got a rudder from a Liberator."

"So why are we standing here?" Gault said, charging down the ladder with Christensen right behind him.

Nick stared at Gault. He answered her gaze with a forced smile. Exhaustion had dulled his eyes and drained his face of color.

"Look at you, John. You're dead on your feet. Theron and I will go."

For a moment, she thought he was going to argue. Then he nodded and walked back along the fuselage, disappearing once again into the *Lady-A*.

41

Kitar's combination bar, grill, and air museum was just outside Malad City, about a hundred and twenty miles north of Salt Lake on Interstate 15. From a distance the place looked like a hangar. As Nick got closer, she realized it was a converted barn.

She pulled into the gravel parking lot next to the yellow shell of an ancient biplane, whose fabric was pocked with fake bullet holes. With a sigh, she switched off the engine of Christensen's camper-shelled pickup truck and tapped him on the shoulder.

He twitched. "I wasn't sleeping, just resting."

His snoring had been triggering sympathetic yawns from her for the last fifty miles. Only the potholes' occasional jarring had kept her alert.

"I hope this trip is worth it," she said. "Otherwise we're going to have to steal a rudder somewhere."

"John was right about you," Christensen said. "You're both alike when it comes to airplanes."

"What else did he say about me?"

"Not on your life." Grinning, he got out of the truck. "Women always ask that question. And whatever you answer, it's always wrong."

Nick stopped to admire the biplane, which also had FINE FOOD stenciled along its fuselage. A fake bullet hole dotted the i in FINE.

"Don't eat the hamburgers," Christensen advised. "Or anything else that can spoil."

She followed him inside. Stickers and logos from squadrons and bomb groups dating back to World War One covered the front of the bar and the mirror behind it. Pieces of airplanes decorated the walls: the canopy from a P-51 Mustang, a P-38's wingtip, the snout of a P-47, complete with Flying Tiger teeth. More importantly, the tail section and rudder from a B-24 Liberator hung over the door to the rest rooms.

The man behind the bar squinted at Christensen, did a theatrical double take, and said, "Jesus, Theron, you look like the walking wounded. How long's it been, for Christ's sake?"

"The air show—two years ago at Hill Field."

"That's right. Too bad about Matt Gault. I read about him in the paper. Let's drink to his memory."

Christensen turned to Nick. "This here's Nick Scott, the archaeologist who found his plane."

"Jack Kitar," the man said, reaching across the bar to shake her hand. "It's a pleasure, ma'am."

Nick smiled and shook his hand.

Without being asked, Kitar set up two beers. There was no one else at the bar, and only one of the half-dozen tables was occupied.

"You give John my condolences," Kitar said. "If I can do anything, all he has to do is say the word."

"Now that you mention it, there is something," Nick said.

Kitar winked at Nick. "I remember you now. You're that lady archaeologist who wouldn't sell me parts of that plane you found in the jungle."

"That was a long time ago," she said.

He tapped the side of his head. "I've got a memory like an elephant."

"The plane didn't belong to me."

"That figures. Goddamn government red tape. I'll bet she's still out there in the jungle, rotting, and doing nobody any good."

"You're probably right."

"What the hell. I forgive you. Besides, any friend of Theron's is okay by me. In case you didn't know, he's the best damn airplane mechanic in Utah, but he's got an obsession about Liberators."

"Me, too," she said.

"I'll be damned."

Christensen said, "We're getting the *Lady-A* ready to fly again."

"Now there's something I'd like to see."

"We can offer you a ringside seat."

Kitar snorted. "You hear that, ma'am? I learned a long time ago that you've got to keep your eyes on these mechanics. Ticket, indeed. Why is it I have the feeling that my piece of B-24 is the price for that ticket?"

He came out from behind the bar to eyeball the tail rudder hanging on brackets over the men's room.

"Do you know how long I've had this piece of history?" Kitar said, winking at Nick.

Christensen raised an eyebrow but kept quiet.

"Since the day I opened this place," Kitar said. "It's part of me and my museum. Heart and soul."

"I wouldn't ask if it wasn't important. Gault has his mind set on flying the *Lady-A* as a last tribute to Matt's memory. And I've got myself a case of metal fatigue."

"My tail isn't any younger than yours."

Christensen pulled a chair from one of the empty tables and stood on it to take a closer look at the tail section. "It's in better shape than mine, I'll say that for it. The *Lady-A* saw combat, you know. My guess is yours didn't. I'll tell you what. I'll swap you the *Lady-A*'s rudder for yours."

"Has she still got her combat markings?" Kitar said.

"Absolutely."

"I'd have to see it first."

Nick laughed. "He's got you there, Mr. Kitar. It's outside in the truck."

Kitar fetched himself a chair and joined Christensen. Then, almost reverently, he ran his hand along his rudder's edge. "Combat or no combat, I've had her a long time and would hate to part with her."

"The *Lady-A* flew twenty-five missions," Christensen pointed out. "She was her squadron's only survivor. You can put up a plaque to that effect."

"Enough, already."

"I just wanted you to know what you were getting."

"I'll want a signed affidavit from Gault testifying to those missions."

"You'll have it before we take off."

"You've got a deal," Kitar said. "But I'm surprised Gault didn't come himself."

"He wasn't fit. The fact is, he hasn't had a decent night's sleep since the Cessna crashed."

And he probably wasn't getting any sleep now, Nick thought, remembering the look on his face as he'd climbed aboard the *Lady-A*.

"Now what about a crank for the bomb bay doors?" Christensen asked. "I saw one the last time I was here."

"Why would you need one?"

"Like I said, this is a memorial flight." He lowered his voice as if there was someone to hear. "We're going to drop Matt's ashes over the lake."

"Cranks are hard to come by," Kitar said, mugging at Nick to show he was joking, though the gleam in his eyes said profit was at stake.

"Before we talk business, I want to see it," Christensen said.

The crank, brought up from the basement after much searching, looked a lot like the tire jack that had come with Nick's last car. In her case, the jack had been useless, as she'd learned the hard way trying to change a flat in the middle of a rainstorm.

But Christensen seemed satisfied. "All right, Kitar, how much?"

"I don't want money. It's got to be trade, something I can put up on the wall."

"Do you have anything in mind?"

"What else do you have in that truck of yours?" Kitar asked.

Christensen looked at Nick and spread his hands. "Did you see me put anything in the truck besides the tail?"

She shook her head.

"Don't give me that crap, Theron. I know you."

The mechanic grinned, reached into his pocket, and brought out a small case.

"What kind of medal is it?" Kitar asked immediately.

"It's John Gault's Distinguished Flying Cross."

42

Wiley and Voss had switched positions for the drive back from Idaho. Voss monitored the transmissions from the bug they'd installed inside the pickup's radio while Wiley, behind the wheel, stayed well back from the truck. At the moment, the only thing audible was engine noise and snoring.

"They ought to be ashamed of themselves, calling this an Interstate," Wiley complained. "Look at the potholes, for Christ's sake."

"Maybe you should try to miss them once in a while," Voss suggested.

"I didn't see you doing any better on the drive out. And it was light then. Now it's dark and—"

Voss cut him off with a slashing motion.

"Theron, are you awake?" the woman was saying.

"I am now."

"I'm still trying to figure out what Matt was after. Did you see him before he took off?"

"Of course. We went through the preflight together. That plane was sound. I know it."

"John knows that, Theron."

There was silence for a moment, then the woman asked, "Did Matt say anything to you about his flight or his destination?"

"What we talked about mostly was his coming into the business. He was looking forward to it. Matt was a good pilot, you know. Not as good as John, but someone I'd fly with."

"Did he ever mention anything about his story?" she asked.

"Never."

"What about names, then?"

"I don't think so."

"How about Maitland, Dr. Karl Maitland?"

"I think he said something about seeing a doctor. No, that's not right. We were standing in front of the *Lady-A*'s hangar when Matt looked up at her and said, "She's just what the doctor ordered.""

"Anything else?"

"No. After that, he climbed into the Cessna and took off."

"I'm sorry I bothered you. Go back to sleep," the woman said.

When the snoring resumed a few minutes later, Voss spoke up. "She's like a dog with a bone, isn't she?"

Wiley nodded as he activated the scrambler system on their cell phone. Almost instantaneously their call came through one of the ISA satellites.

The Director answered.

"She's still asking questions about you," Wiley advised him.

"By name?"

"Yes, sir."

"Do you have any reason to believe that she knows anything about our project?"

"No," Wiley said, "not yet."

"We shouldn't take the chance," Voss interjected.

"I don't want either of you overreacting," the Director answered forcefully. "Since she and her father managed to escape that unfortunate earthslide at Ophir, we must be prudent. Another attempt may be too soon. Besides, how could she possibly know what we're doing? Everything's classified."

"Maybe the old man in the desert told her?" Voss suggested, nudging Wiley to show he was trying to get them some action.

"Impossible. We wrung Sanchez dry before it was over. He and everybody else in that camp. The only thing they knew for sure was that they were scared to death of us."

"What about the reporter?" Voss insisted. "He found out, didn't he?"

There was a sharp expletive at the other end of the line.

Voss and Wiley exchanged grins. The Director seldom swore. When he did, he usually let them go to work.

"Where are you two now?"

"Following the woman on the Interstate, north of Salt Lake," Wiley answered.

"All right," the Director said. "Let's put a stop to her. But remember she's a prominent archaeologist, so it has to look like an accident. I don't want any more complications."

"Yes, sir," Wiley said, terminating the satellite connection.

"It's a good thing you're driving," Voss said immediately. "I'm a better shot."

"Who said anything about guns?"

"Think about it. Now's the perfect time. She's doing damn near seventy. We shoot out one of her tires and that's it. Highway splatter."

Wiley thought that over. A blowout, even one caused by a bullet, ought to be safe enough. There'd be nothing left of the slug, no evidence.

"Get me close enough," Voss said, "and I'll make the shot."

"You heard the Director. No more complications."

"We may never get another chance like this. The road's practically deserted."

"All right, but you'd better use my .22," Wiley said as soon as Voss drew his revolver. "A .357 slug is too big to risk."

"That thing of yours is a fuckin' peashooter," Voss objected, but he took the silenced .22 just the same.

Gradually, Wiley closed the distance. When they were in range, Voss lowered his window and waited for a break in oncoming traffic.

"When I say the word," Voss said, "hit the high beams so I can see what I'm doing."

One car to go, Wiley thought, after that the road ahead was empty. He glanced in the rearview mirror. There was nothing behind them but darkness.

"Now," Voss said a moment later.

Wiley switched on the high beams. The bright light caused the pickup to veer slightly.

"Steady," Voss commanded.

Wiley saw the pothole at the last instant. Before he could warn his partner, Voss shouted, "Shit! I missed. I hit the fucking tailgate."

Wiley stomped on the accelerator, passing the truck at ninety miles an hour. They'd fucked up. They'd left a bullet hole behind.

"We're going to have to get rid of the evidence before we do anything else," Wiley said through clenched teeth. "You heard the Director. No more complications."

"You saw the truck," Voss said. "They didn't even know they'd been shot at. Chances are they'll never see that hole."

"You're sitting in the passenger seat. Do you want to call the Director and tell him that?"

43

The *Lady-A* attracted a crowd as she rolled out of the hangar on her tricycle landing gear. One moment, Nick was standing there, alone with Paula, looking at the B-24. In the next, more than a dozen mechanics and pilots came running, most from the National Guard facility across the taxiway. They surrounded her and Paula as if sensing theirs was the best vantage point.

A week had passed since she and Christensen had driven to Idaho together. The new rudder was safely attached and had passed every test the mechanic could devise.

Gault and Roberts were already in the bomber's cockpit. Christensen was driving the tow tractor, while Yarbrough and Campbell acted as lookouts, checking for wing clearance and shooing bystanders out of the way when they got too close.

Despite the B-24's wingspan of 110 feet, its 66-foot fuselage, its four 1200-horsepower engines, and its twin vertical stabilizers, it looked small compared to the nearby jets.

When sunlight hit the nose, the serpent glowed, and Nick realized it had been repainted during the night. Now its eyes blazed malevolently; its fangs dripped red venom.

A shiver ran down her spine. For the first time she thought, *I do not like this plane*, but couldn't explain why. Perhaps because it was simply out of its time. It belonged in a museum or in pieces scattered across some godforsaken landscape. It didn't belong here, ready to fly again fifty years too late.

"Are you sure you want to go?" Paula asked.

"I'd pay if I had to," Nick replied and meant it.

Christensen got off the tractor to disengage the coupling.

"Gault looked tired this morning," Paula said. "Tired pilots make mistakes."

"If you ask me, he looked like a kid with a new toy."

"That, too." Paula snapped a salute toward the cockpit.

After stowing the tractor out of harm's way, Christensen set the wheel chocks. Then, one by one, he pulled the props through as a precaution against leftover fuel in the cylinders.

Nick offered to help, but the mechanic insisted on doing the pull-through himself. "The *Lady-A* knows my touch," he'd said. "And I know hers. If something's wrong, I'll feel it."

As soon as he finished, Christensen waved Paula over and handed her an extinguisher so she could stand by as a fire guard. Only then did he attach the external starter.

When that was done, the mechanic moved to the front of the plane and signaled thumbs-up to Gault. Gault answered in kind, then waved Nick on board. Until that moment, she'd held her breath, wondering if he'd actually live up to his promise that she could join the crew.

He'd kept reminding her that anything, even engine start-up, was dangerous in an old warbird like the *Lady-A*. But she'd been just as insistent that this was the chance of a lifetime for a historical archaeologist.

Paula gave Nick a thumbs-up, then waved her on her way.

Quickly, Nick trotted to the bomb bay and climbed into the plane, with Paula, Yarbrough and Campbell right behind her.

"Where do you want me?" Nick asked.

"Don't look at me," Yarbrough said. "I'm a waist gunner. I'm staying where I belong."

"You come forward with me," Campbell answered.

Yarbrough grabbed one of the newly purchased parachutes and headed toward the back of the plane. Gault Aviation, she'd been told, didn't normally stock chutes, since commercial flying was supposed to be safer than driving.

The box holding Matt's ashes had been secured to a bulkhead next to the chutes.

Crossing her fingers for luck, Nick moved forward to stand in the narrow opening directly behind Gault and Roberts. Both men acknowledged her arrival, showed her how to plug her headset into the intercom system, then went to work. Campbell had left her to crawl into the bombardier's compartment in the nose.

Through the windshield, she could see that the crowd of admirers had grown considerably. One of the mechanics was doing his best to herd them out of the bomber's path.

"By the book, Brad," Gault said.

Roberts nodded. "Master switch on. Brakes on."

"Hydraulic pressure?"

"Eight hundred."

"Carburetor filters?"

"On," Roberts said. "Throttles set for one thousand RPM."

"Primer pump on."

"Oil pressure at seventy."

Nick marveled at their efficiency. They checked everything, autopilot, fuel tanks, wing flap indicators, each dial and gauge. Nick took notes, hoping that one day she might get the chance to write a paper on bomber restoration.

"Everything's up to specs," Roberts said finally. "Theron's a genius."

Gault gave his copilot a thumbs-up. "Warp speed, Number One."

The engine coughed. Smoke belched from the exhaust before the engine caught hold with a deafening roar. Immediately, the whole plane shook. Nick felt the vibrations through the soles of her feet; she was filled with a sense of power that grew until it resonated throughout her entire body.

Once all four engines were turning over, Christensen crowded into the cockpit beside Nick and plugged in his headset.

"I hope everyone's got enough room to breathe," Gault said.

"If I get any closer to Nick," Christensen answered, "we'll be engaged."

Gault glanced over his shoulder, smiling at Nick. "Hold on." He nodded at his copilot and said, "Close bomb bay doors."

"Doors closed," Roberts responded. "Booster pumps on. Magnetos checked."

Gault adjusted the control tabs and set the rudder two degrees right to compensate for engine torque.

"Autopilot off. Fuel mixture to auto-rich," Roberts said.

Gault released the parking brakes and opened the throttles slowly. The *Lady-A*, all sixty thousand pounds of her, rolled onto the taxiway. They were third in line for takeoff, behind a pair of Boeing 727 commuter jets.

"What's the holdup?" Yarbrough asked from his waist position.

"The jet jockeys in front of us are playing tourist," Roberts answered. "They act like they've never seen a Liberator before."

Even as he spoke, the lead 727 started its takeoff run.

"One down, one to go," Gault reported.

"I feel naked back here without a .50-caliber," Yarbrough said.

Gault tapped Roberts on the arm. The copilot nodded.

"Stand by for takeoff," Gault said over the intercom.

As soon as the second of the 727s began rolling, he switched the radio to its command setting and asked the tower for clearance.

Once it was given, he stood on the brakes and eased the throttles forward.

"Manifold pressure at full military power," Roberts said a moment later.

Gault released the brakes and the *Lady-A* surged down the runway.

44

Wiley and Voss had joined the crowd of bystanders lining the security fence adjacent to Gault Aviation. Their work clothes, complete with Delta Airlines logo, kept them from standing out. Only their designer dark glasses clashed with their present personas.

As the B-24 started its takeoff run, they joined the applause.

Wiley jerked his head, giving his partner the high sign to move away from eavesdroppers. They ambled away slouch-shouldered and shuffle-footed, as they thought befitted Delta's rank-and-file union members. Only when they were beyond earshot did Wiley get down to business.

"Have you ever worked on anything that old?"

Voss shook his head.

"I was thinking about planting a bomb if it ever comes to that."

"An engine's always good, what with the wing tanks so close by."

Wiley nodded. He'd been thinking the same thing.

"It might be easier," Voss said, "if we requisitioned a missile."

"There are no handheld missiles in stock at the mesa," Wiley pointed out. "Which means we'd have to wait God knows how long before taking delivery."

Voss squinted southwest toward the Oquirrh Mountains, the direction the B-24 had taken. "The bastard's out of range now anyway."

"It doesn't matter. Chances are if we have to go to work, it will be a straightforward job. Take the woman out and the rest of them will be running around like chickens with their heads cut off."

"I thought that bullet would do it," Voss said. "With evidence like that, I figured they'd order us to kill everybody. But that damned truck is so beat-up the hole didn't even show. And nobody has any guts anyway." He shook his head. "I think they're underestimating her."

Wiley nodded grimly.

Six hundred and fifty miles away, in his office atop Mesa d'Oro, Frank Odell had his eyes on the Director's Blackbirds.

"Or a reasonable facsimile," Odell muttered to himself, since what he was watching was their transponder signals. Their electronic blips, relayed via satellite, placed the pair somewhere in or near the airport in Salt Lake City. The tracking system was just one of the new gadgets that had been provided by the ISA.

No doubt Chairman Smith was watching a similar blip on his screen in Washington, one representing Odell.

Christ! All this because the bomb on that Cessna had a delayed fuse so the chopper could get clear after dumping its load in the canyon. A minute either way and the archaeologist wouldn't have seen a damned thing. Sheer bad luck, that's what Odell called it.

Just then the secure phone rang. "This is Odell."

"Do you recognize my voice?"

It belongs to the devil himself, Odell thought, but said, "Yes, sir."

"I see the next forty-eight hours as critical."

If Odell lived so long.

"At the end of that time," Smith went on, "one of two things will have happened."

Here it comes, Odell thought. The proverbial shoe about to drop.

"In the meantime, I won't tolerate any further broken promises from anyone. I hope you understand that, Frank."

"Yes, sir."

"I've been too tolerant, that's the problem. As a result I've got four hundred thousand barrels of radioactive goo, and the Director's unfulfilled promise to find me a solution. You see that, don't you?"

"Yes, sir," Odell said.

"Very well. As I said, the next two days are critical. Consider yourself on continuous alert until then. After that, either the matter will be settled without repercussions, or you and I will have to see to it ourselves. In either case, I'm afraid there will be extensive casualties."

"Yes, sir."

"Are you up for it?"

"Yes, sir." Anything was better than being among the casualties.

45

Nick was surprised by the unrelenting noise. Flying by commercial jet was bad enough, but four twelve-hundred horsepower Pratt and Whitneys rattled every nut, bolt, joint, and hinge inside the Liberator. Communication was damn near impossible except on the intercom.

Only when Gault leveled off at four thousand feet and throttled back to cruising speed, two hundred miles an hour, did the racket subside somewhat.

"We'll circle the basin once," Gault said, "before heading over the lake."

He banked east toward the ten-thousand-foot Wasatch Mountains.

"Why don't we fly over them," Christensen said. "You know how Matt loved the view."

"Did you check our oxygen system?"

"You know better than to ask."

Gault half-turned in his seat to look at Nick. "What do you say? Are you game for a high-altitude run?"

She answered with a nod.

Gault wiggled the wings. On a jet Nick might have panicked, but here, flying a piece of history, she felt a sense of exhilaration. She felt like a pioneer. Modern planes were pressurized. The *Lady-A* was wide open. If they flew too high, they'd all be freezing without flight suits.

She yawned to ease the pressure building in her ears.

"You know something," Roberts said over the intercom, "I think she flies better now than in the old days."

Christensen, who had his head cocked to port as if

listening to the engines on that side, said, "Do they sound okay to you?"

"Like music," Gault answered.

Exhilaration or not, Nick hoped he was right. She had no means of comparison, but one thing seemed certain. The B-24 didn't so much soar as lumber along.

"On oxygen, everyone," Gault said a few moments later. "I want a full systems check."

By now the Wasatch Mountains looked very close.

Roberts, carrying a portable oxygen bottle, immediately rose from his seat. Before leaving the cockpit to check on Paula and the rest of the crew, he pointed Nick into the copilot's chair and plugged her into the oxygen supply. Then he and Christensen left the cockpit together.

Beside her, Gault pointed to his oxygen mask. "It's like the smell of an old friend."

To Nick, the smell of rubber was overpowering. The more she breathed, the queasier she got.

"Matt would have loved this," Gault went on. "He used to sit here in the cockpit and pretend to fly while I told him old war stories. Why don't you give her a try, Nick. Go ahead. Take the yoke."

Very gingerly, she touched the copilot's yoke in front of her.

"Come on. Hold it like you mean business."

Mimicking his grip, she wrapped her hands around the yoke. Gault let go of his immediately.

"Put your feet on the rudder pedals."

Nick held her breath and eased her feet into position.

"You use your heel for brakes, your toes for the rudder," he said. "But for the moment just hold her straight."

Nick's arms shook with the strain.

"Relax," he said, "the *Lady-A* practically flies herself."

Vibrations, almost electric in their intensity, flowed

through the yoke, into her arms, and through her body. The sensation triggered memories of the horror stories pilots told about the Liberator. It was nothing but a flying brick just waiting to fall out of the sky. It was an agony wagon, a pregnant cow. Its controls were sluggish and temperamental. Only maniacs volunteered to fly B-24s.

She risked a quick glance at Gault. He had a huge smile and his face glowed with pleasure. He was in love. No doubt about it. They all were, Roberts, Yarbrough, Campbell, and Christensen. To them the *Lady-A* was a beautiful woman.

The yoke bucked.

"It's only turbulence," Gault assured her.

But Nick had the uncanny feeling that it was the *Lady-A* who'd bucked, not some wind current. Probably she was jealous. Probably . . .

Come on, Nick thought, be logical. This was a piece of machinery. The yoke shuddered again.

Nick clenched her teeth. She was a scientist, a historian of artifacts. *So act like one*, she told herself. But her heart continued to pound. Her mind knew better but, like everyone else, superstitions persisted despite all her attempts at intellectual exorcism. This plane doesn't like me, she thought.

Christensen came on the intercom. "Try opening the bomb doors."

"You'd better let me take her back," Gault said.

She released the copilot's yoke as soon as he took hold of his. An instant later one of his hands seemed to move instinctively toward the control panel.

"Bomb bay doors coming open," he said.

"Again, please."

Gault glanced at Nick but spoke on the intercom. "Mechanics have to be humored."

"You won't be laughing if you have to land with them open," Christensen said.

Nick kept her fingers crossed as Gault went through the procedure one more time, again without failure.

"That's my girl," Gault said, his hand caressing the manufacturer's plaque, a small brass plate on the pilot's side of the instrument panel immediately left of the compass indicator.

Nick remembered him making the exact same gesture the first time he had shown her the plane. How many times had he stroked that plaque? she wondered. The manufacturer's name was almost worn away and she had to squint to make out the serial number, 5440.

"I'm satisfied for now," Christensen said.

Gault glanced at Nick, then swung the B-24 north, following the ridge of the Wasatch. From their present altitude, fifteen thousand feet, Nick could see the great salt desert to the west, a white plain spreading all the way to the horizon. Out there, she knew, the ill-fated Donner Party had lost all hope of reaching California before the winter set in.

Gault tapped her on the arm and pointed at the bleak landscape. "You told me you were an expert in desert survival. How would you do against that?"

"In the desert, any desert, you carry water with you. That's the first rule. You travel only at dusk and at night. You follow trails or roads if possible. If you know where water is, you head for it. And if you find water, even if it's not drinkable, you soak your clothes with it. That helps preserve your own body moisture."

Nick raised her hand, ticking off points finger by finger. "Protect yourself from the sun during the day. Find shade or create it. Drink water at the rate your body is sweating. Rationing it won't extend your life significantly. Without water, you'll live only two or two and a half days even if you stay in the shade and don't move. It's good to be armed, too, so you can shoot your own food."

"I seem to remember you telling me you were a good shot," Gault said.

"My father taught me as soon as I was old enough to go on one of his digs."

Christensen came on the intercom. "All systems are functioning."

"All right," Gault answered. "We fly the mission for Matt. You'd better get up here, Brad. Everybody else, take your stations."

As soon as Roberts was in his copilot's seat again, Campbell checked in from the bombardier's cubbyhole in the nose. Paula, Christensen, and Yarbrough were in the waist. Nick stayed put.

"This is the life," Roberts shouted at Nick, ignoring the intercom. "I feel like I'm home."

Looking at them calmly going through their checklist, Nick decided that men like Gault and his crew were a special breed. The hardships they had endured in the war were beyond belief. Imagine flying six hours in an airplane like this with Germans trying to kill you every minute of the way.

The intercom crackled to life.

"Theron, we've got a problem," Gault said. "Number three engine is overheating."

"I'm on my way," Christensen answered.

As soon as he edged past Nick and plugged into the intercom, the mechanic said, "I'm getting too old for this kind of thing."

"The temperature is still rising," Roberts said, tapping the gauge.

"What about cowl flaps?" Christensen asked.

"Open," Roberts said.

"Then we'd better shut her down," Christensen said. Gault nodded.

Roberts went to work. A moment later he said, "Number three feathered and secure."

Christensen leaned forward to get a closer look at the instrument panel. "You should have fired me a long time ago, John. I'm over the hill. Maybe we should abort now, before we lose another engine."

"Relax, Theron. The other three are rock steady."

"We made it through the Nordhausen mission after

they shot up one of our engines," Roberts said. "Once we start across the lake we'll be headed for the airport anyway. So I say we keep going."

Nick was dumbfounded. Here they were, flying a crippled plane over badlands the equal of anywhere on earth, and Gault and Roberts looked perfectly calm.

"Do I get a vote?" Paula asked over the intercom.

"Paula," Gault replied, and Nick could hear the tenderness in his voice, "you may not be crew but you are family."

"Then, let's finish what we started," she said.

Gault looked back at Nick.

"Paula couldn't have said it better," she told him.

Five minutes later, Gault announced, "Target dead ahead."

"I have it," Campbell answered.

"Engage the autopilot," Gault said.

The moment Roberts complied, the B-24 lurched. "She always did that on our missions," he said for Nick's benefit.

Gault released the yoke, though his hands continued to hover at the ready. Campbell and his Norden bombsight were flying the *Lady-A*.

Gault unbuckled his seat belt and stood up. "I'll help Paula."

Rather than intrude, Nick stayed where she was, peering over Roberts' shoulder.

"Ready," Gault reported a moment later.

"Opening bomb doors," Campbell answered.

No one said a word for the next few minutes as the *Lady*-A lumbered on with her bomb doors open.

Then Gault's voice came over the intercom. "Matt, you know I'm not good with words, you were the one for that. But I kept the poem you gave me. I know you've slipped the surly bonds of earth and are up there in the burning blue. May your wings be laughter-silvered and I know you've touched the face of God."

Nick felt rather than heard the bomb bay doors close and she imagined Matt's gray ashes made golden by the sun as they streamed across the burning blue of the desert air to fall as silent as tears on the face of the Great Salt Lake.

46

Nick took one look at Gault, his pale face and red-rimmed eyes, the gray stubble on his cheeks, and knew that Matt's farewell flight had taken a terrible toll.

Paula, quiet and withdrawn, had returned to duty. The rest of them—Gault, Roberts, Yarbrough, Campbell, and herself—were seated around a worktable in the *Lady-A*'s hangar. As if afraid to make eye contact, the four men focused intently on Theron Christensen, who was atop a roll-away ladder working on the number three engine. He'd been at it ever since they'd landed. At the moment, banks of work lights had the hangar bright as day, despite the midnight hour.

If the *Lady-A* had made her last flight, why bother? she wondered, but didn't ask. She knew the answer already, she thought. They needed the *Lady-A* whole again. If she was fit for combat, so were they. If Christensen could make her young again, they would be young again.

Nick shook her head. Someone had to be practical. "I think it's time everybody got some rest," she announced.

"That's the first sensible thing I've heard in hours," Christensen called down from his perch. "Besides, my work would go a lot faster if I didn't have so many kibitz-ers hanging around."

The mechanic wiped his hands on his overalls. "One thing's for sure. Except for an overheating engine, the *Lady-A* is in better shape than her crew."

Gault, who'd been gazing at the *Lady-A*, tried to smile but only succeeded in looking sad, so sad that Nick walked out of the hangar to escape it.

Gault caught up with her a few minutes later as she stood on the tarmac in front of the sliding doors.

"My father knows each star by name," she said, star-ing up at the sky.

"And you?"

"Enough to navigate at night if I have to."

He sighed. "I didn't learn much navigation until af-ter the war. In those days I trusted my navigator, Novak, to tell me where I was. You know what he'd say when I asked him where we were? 'Just east of Norfolk,' or 'south of Le Havre,' or Berlin, or wherever we were heading. Then he'd come back on the intercom a moment later and give me a more precise location. Swiss Novak, we called him, because he always ran an exact heading to neutral countries.

"When our twenty-five missions were over, he finally admitted the truth. 'In navigator school,' he said, 'they taught us to always give the pilot some answer, even if you had no idea where you were. That way, your pilot won't get nervous.' "

"Would you have been nervous?" she asked.

"Terrified is more like it, but then we always were, except on our weekends in London when we were blind drunk. The day after was okay, too, because then you were too hung over and sick to be scared."

She laid a hand on his arm. "How long since you've had any real sleep, and I don't mean on one of Theron's cots?"

"I get by on catnaps."

"You're not twenty-one, John, no matter what you think."

"Christ, Nick, I'm not up to driving home at the moment. I'll just flop here for a while."

"Give me the keys. I'll drive."

He directed her through town, ignoring the freeways, to an older section near the university. His house was a small-scale Victorian, more of a bungalow really, that reminded Nick of the student housing around Berkeley. Only in Berkeley this time of year, the fog would have everyone wearing sweaters. In Salt Lake, the one A.M. temperature was still hovering in the seventies.

"Would you like a cup of coffee?" he said, his face gray with fatigue.

"Don't bother. What I need is a shower."

"I've got two bathrooms. You're welcome to use one of them and the spare bedroom, too. I'd hate to think of you driving back to that airport hotel this time of night."

Her own feeling of exhaustion, plus the enticement of an immediate hot shower, overcame Nick's reservations. After all they were both adults.

Gault fetched clean towels. "If you want I can throw your dirty clothes in the washer," he said. "They'll be dry in an hour."

"They are a bit grubby."

"Just drop them outside the door. I'll leave you something to wear."

Nick stood under the shower, wondering about her intentions. The safe thing to do would be to tuck him in and be on her way. Only now she'd have to wait for her clothes to come out of the dryer.

She thrust her head under the spray. Thank God her hair was short enough to dry on its own.

Twenty minutes later, wrapped in a robe many sizes too big for her, she opened the bathroom door. Her dirty clothes were gone.

She found Gault in the kitchen, wearing a matching

robe. He was standing next to a rumbling washing machine, drinking coffee.

"You need sleep," she told him, "not caffeine."

"It's Postum actually, Mormon coffee we call it in Utah."

His hair, like hers, was still damp. A shower had changed his complexion from an exhausted pallor to ruddy, easing her concern somewhat.

She took a sip and shook her head. "The Mormons might have something to say about the brandy you've added."

"I needed the courage."

"You?" She shook her head. "I don't believe it."

He paused and silence between them grew. Finally, he said quietly, "I'd like you to stay."

Her blood heated, and she leaned forward to kiss him. A deep shudder ran through her and she found herself saying, "On the other hand, John, they say sex is the best kind of sleeping pill."

They were heading for the bedroom when the doorbell rang.

"Stay where you are," Gault said, "I'll get it."

Nick was about to abandon her robe and slip under the covers when she heard Christensen's voice. Figuring a visit this time of night meant trouble, she joined them in the living room.

Her appearance widened Christensen's smile.

"I was just telling John the good news," he said. "Number three's running like a clock. She never was overheating. It was a faulty thermostat, giving us a bad temperature reading. Of course, I'll run her up first thing tomorrow morning to double-check. I would have called but I couldn't get through."

Gault looked sheepish. Nick could see the reason for herself. The phone was off the hook.

"Sorry," Christensen said. "I should have waited for morning." He started for the door.

"You did the right thing," Gault called after him. "I would have worried all night about that engine."

Hesitating on the threshold, Christensen raised an eyebrow in Nick's direction. "I doubt that, somehow." Then he smiled and closed the door behind him.

"Christ," Gault said and collapsed onto the couch. "That's a load off my mind. I want the *Lady-A* to be perfect." He leaned back and closed his eyes. His entire body sagged with relief.

Nick felt the same way. No doubt for different reasons they'd both let their guard down the moment they heard that the *Lady-A* was airworthy again.

But Gault was anything but airworthy. Nick could see that for herself. If he didn't rest, it wouldn't matter how well the *Lady-A*'s engines were running. He'd be a danger to himself and everybody else if he tried to fly any kind of plane.

Suddenly she realized he was snoring.

"John?" she asked tentatively.

She could see he was completely out.

"I think we both need sleep," she said, grabbing his legs and swinging them onto the couch.

She took the single blanket off the bed and covered him. She'd make do with the sheet and bedspread.

"I'm not letting you off the hook, John," she said. "I hope you can hear me in your dreams."

She leaned over and kissed him.

He stirred, and for a moment Nick was afraid she had wakened him, but he turned over on his side and murmured, "Goodnight, Annie."

47

Nick lurched upright in bed. The morning sun blazed in her eyes. But the light that had awakened her was inside her head, its message in fiery letters, ANNIE HAS JAMES K. POLK'S NUMBER. She knew the meaning of the cryptic comment on Matt's laptop computer. Or at least she thought she did.

She dressed quickly and went looking for Gault. She found him in the kitchen pouring coffee into cups that had been set out on a serving tray along with a sprig of geranium. His thoughtfulness touched her. So much so, that she decided that her rush to see the *Lady-A* could wait. After all, maybe she was wrong. Maybe Matt, the history buff, hadn't left another message behind.

"I was going to serve you coffee in bed," he said as he handed her one of the brimming cups.

She accepted the offering shyly, aware that perceptions change in daylight, especially when you're sleeping in a man's house, albeit in separate beds.

He must have sensed her awkwardness, because he looked sheepish and said, "Maybe we'd better go. The *Lady-A* doesn't like to be kept waiting."

"I was thinking the same thing."

Gault looked at her quizzically.

"I think the *Lady-A* might have something to tell us," Nick said. "And no, I'm not going to explain myself here and now. You'll have to wait and see for yourself."

And so will I, she added to herself, then realized that someone else had the right to be there too, Paula Latham, Matt's fiancée.

Thirty minutes later, armed with doughnuts from the

office, she and Gault entered the *Lady-A*'s hangar. The huge sliding doors stood open, flooding the entire area with sunlight. Even so, Nick had the sense that the bomber stood in shadow. More than ever, its drab camouflage paint seemed to feed on light.

At Gault's insistence, they kept their distance from the plane while eating. But Nick no longer felt hungry. She forced a swallow, but the doughnut suddenly felt like a large lump. She gave up and handed the rest to Gault, who finished it off quickly. Then he dusted his hands free of crumbs and walked over to the plane.

"Well, old girl," he said, looking up into the airplane, "how do you feel this morning? Forever twenty-one?"

"Is that how you feel?" Nick asked, coming up behind him.

He kissed Nick gently. "I'm getting there."

"And the *Lady-A*?"

"You heard Theron. He ran up the engine again and she's as good as new and ready to go."

Nick stared up into the empty bomb racks and felt cold. Yet the temperature inside the hangar had to be well into the eighties already, on its way to a hundred and five, according to the weather report.

She wondered if she wasn't about to make a fool of herself. Maybe she'd misinterpreted the message on Matt's laptop.

Gault ducked under the open bomb doors and ran his hand along the fuselage. "I still love you, Annie. But you know that."

He beckoned Nick to follow as he worked his way toward the nose. "You don't have to be jealous of Nick."

When Nick caught up he whispered into her ear, "Not yet, anyway."

"Aren't you afraid she'll read your mind?" Nick asked.

"There were times during the war I had the feeling

she could do just that. She seemed to anticipate my every move"

Nick smiled. Her father often spoke to his Anasazi relics, but not quite like John Gault. There was always something in Elliot's tone of voice that said he was only half-serious when he communed with the long dead. In Gault's case, the connection seemed more personal. He treated the plane as if it were alive.

They'd come to a stop beside the newly painted serpent. Gault took Nick's hand. "You're something, do you know that?"

"Not in front of the *Lady-A*," Nick teased, though part of her felt distinctly uneasy.

Gault switched his hands from her to the B-24. "Never fear, Annie. No one will ever replace you. Nick knows that. She was with us yesterday. You must have felt her. She took your controls for a while."

And the *Lady-A* hadn't liked it one bit, Nick remembered. Hold it, she told herself. Don't start imagining things. An airplane was a machine, nothing more. It didn't think. It didn't hold grudges. It wasn't a she or a he, just an it. Still, Nick couldn't shake the sensation, even now, that the bomber had a jealous soul.

"Aren't you going to say something to her?" Gault asked.

"I'm not sure she likes me."

Gault snorted. "You haven't seen her mad. That's when you know who she likes and who she doesn't. Then she's no lady at all."

Nick said, "We're going to need a screwdriver for what I have in mind."

The anguished look on his face made her laugh. "Don't worry, John, I'm not going to harm your beloved airplane."

Shaking his head, he grabbed a small tool set from one of Christensen's work bench, and led the way into the bomb bay. Together, he and Nick worked their way forward to the cockpit and settled in, he in the left-hand seat, she in the copilot's position.

Before she could explain what she had in mind, he leaned forward to stare at number three, the inside engine on the starboard side.

"We lost that engine once before," he said, "during the Hamburg raid." He let out a long sigh. "If you couldn't keep up with the formation, you were like a stray sheep among *Focke-Wulfs*."

Nick repressed a shudder. Gault had too many ghosts haunting him as it was, so why add more? Because, she told herself, he deserved to know the truth. Besides, there was always the chance that she was imagining things. But she didn't think so, not since the moment she'd entered the cockpit and checked the instrument panel.

Gently, she laid a hand on Gault's arm. "John, I think Matt may have left you a message here in the *Lady-A*."

"Where, for Christ's sake?"

"Only a history buff would know about fifty-four forty or fight."

"So?"

"Look at the manufacturer's plaque, John." She pointed to the instrument panel. "There it is, the *Lady-A*'s number. And it's not flush with the panel."

With a trembling hand, Gault removed the screws and exposed a square of tightly folded papers.

"Son of a bitch!" he whooped.

"That's no way to talk to a lady," Paula said from right behind them.

Nick jumped, and for a split second, before reason took hold, she thought the plane had spoken.

"Paula, I didn't expect you," Gault said.

"I called her while you were scrounging doughnuts," Nick explained.

"She said she had a hunch about Matt's message," Paula added.

"She was right," he said, handing the papers to Nick. "I didn't bring my reading glasses."

Nick stared at him, wondering if glasses were the real reason he was delegating the job. She unfolded the papers. There were three onion-thin sheets.

"The first is a copy of a story from the *New York Times*," she said. "The headline reads, 'Americans used as human guinea pigs in radiation tests.'"

Both Paula and Gault moved closer to peer over her shoulder.

"'In sworn testimony before a congressional oversight committee,'" Nick read, "'Dr. Karl Maitland, a research scientist from the Los Alamos Laboratory, stated, "We no longer conduct human tests. That stopped in the mid-1970s. Since then only animals have been used for experimental purposes, and all in accordance with accepted humane practices. He dismissed as irresponsible, news reports that had compared his work to Nazi experimentations at Buchenwald.'"

"God damn it!" Gault said. "That's the bastard Matt was after. I know it."

Gooseflesh climbed Nick's spine. She remembered the cookies file had left a record that Matt had called up a biography of a Dr. Karl Maitland, who was now Director of the National Research Institute for Behavioral Statistics. She felt a horrible coldness overtake her. Congressman Hanlan had told them that Mesa d'Oro was the site for the Institute. And the holding area that had been so carefully sanitized at the base of that mesa, as the federal agent had put it, hadn't been designed to pen in animals, humanely treated or otherwise, but men. She'd seen it for herself.

The second page was a copy of another clipping, this one obtained through the Freedom of Information Act, from *U.S. News and World Report*. It connected Maitland with a government study entitled THE MORTALITY OF NUCLEAR WEAPONS TEST PARTICIPANTS. It detailed the incidence of leukemia among veterans who'd taken part in tests conducted in Nevada and at the Pacific Proving Grounds at Enewetak and Bikini.

The final page was a personal letter to Gault.

"You'd better read this one for yourself, John," Nick said, handing it to him.

Holding it at arm's length, Gault scanned it quickly. For a moment, he said nothing, but only stared though the bomber's windshield.

Finally, he cleared his throat and said, "I think you'd both better hear this."

" *'Dear Granddad, if you're reading this, I'm in trouble, or worse.'* "

Gault's voice cracked. He wet his lips before continuing.

" *'I'm on my way to a place called Mesa d'Oro in southeastern Arizona. It's called the National Institute for Behavioral Statistics and is run by a Dr. Karl Maitland. I suspect him of conducting illegal medical experiments on human beings. No, I take that back. I know that's what he's doing. I just can't prove it yet. That's why I'm on my way there, to meet an informant. I'm told that the experiments on the mesa involve illegal aliens. They are conducting terminal experiments on people against their will. I'm certain of it. This has got to be stopped if it's the last thing I do.'* "

Gault looked away. "Matt signs off saying, 'Give my love to the *Lady-A.*' "

"He always said that, in every letter he wrote to me," Paula said.

Carefully, Gault folded the letter and tucked it away in his wallet.

Nick felt sick. The sight of Matt's body flashed back to her. Again she saw the raw, angry-looking flesh, what she'd attributed to extreme sun exposure at the time. Now, she knew better. Now she knew that Maitland was still experimenting on human guinea pigs.

She shook her head to dispel the monstrous images. "What is it?" Gault asked.

She hesitated telling them. She'd seen John Gault's

anger at work in Ophir and feared what he might do. Yet her own anger demanded satisfaction. Because now, more than ever, she felt certain that the landslide that had nearly killed her and her father was no accident.

"John," she said as calmly as she could, "Do you remember me describing Matt's body?"

He nodded.

"I thought he was sunburned at the time," she explained to Paula. "Now, I think radiation killed him. I think he ended up as one of Maitland's experiments."

Paula turned away and stifled a sob, but Gault didn't say a word for a long time. He just sat there, staring through the *Lady-A*'s windshield. Finally, he took a deep breath, got up from his seat, and said, "I'm going to the office to call Bob Hanlan. I'll be right back."

It was a waste of time, Nick thought. The last time they'd spoken to the congressman he'd advised them to back off. Like all gutless politicians, she said to herself.

Nick and Paula sat in silence, Paula quietly crying, Nick unwilling to intrude on the younger woman's pain. In a few minutes Gault returned.

"Well?" Nick asked. His answer was aimed at Paula. "I'm going to need some bombs."

"Don't look at me, Dad."

"Your National Guard outfit is the only place I can get them."

"Hold it," Nick told Gault. "You can't be serious."

"You know me better than that. My entire crew has already volunteered for the mission."

"I take it the congressman wouldn't help."

"I only got as far as one of his aides. 'The congressman has never heard of you,' I was told. Now what about those bombs, Paula?"

"They're under constant guard. Even I can't get at them without written orders."

"Then we'll load the *Lady-A* with dynamite if that's all we can get."

"Listen to me," Paula said. "Matt wouldn't want you playing kamikaze."

"That's not my intention."

"I'm coming with you, then, to see that you don't."

Gault grasped Paula's hand. "Matt would never forgive me if I let something happen to you. As long as you live, something of him does too."

"And if I can get you the bombs?"

"Working miracles won't get you on board."

"I give up," Paula said, turning to Nick. "Stubbornness runs in the family, you know. Matt was the same way. As for you, John, miracles don't come into it. It's a matter of supply sergeants. Don't you remember your Air Corps days? Supply sergeants and their scrounging kept you flying, and supplied you with damn near everything else, too. In my experience, I've found that when it comes to juggling Air Force property, even losing a little of it, there's nothing like a master supply sergeant. And our outfit's got a beaut, name of Al Sawicki. A wheeler-dealer without peer. You've got to be prepared to trade though. That's his life's blood."

"He can have anything I've got left except the *Lady-A*."

"Okay, I'll sound him out on the subject. But even if you get your bombs, that mesa sounds like a difficult target."

"We've got a Norden bombsight."

"They weren't that accurate, except for saturation bombing."

"Maybe not from twenty-five thousand feet, but at low altitude Vic and his Norden won't miss."

Paula sighed. "Is there anything else you haven't told me?"

"Did I mention the cobra gunships that guard the mesa?"

"Jesus," Paula murmured. "You'll never make it."

Nick spoke up. "You're not really going to help him, are you?"

"Nick. Do you really think either of us can stop him?"

"We could turn him in," Nick said, but the look on Gault's face said he knew she was bluffing. Besides, she wasn't sure she wanted to stop him. Part of her wanted to volunteer to go with him.

Paula said, "I'll call you when I've set something up with Sawicki. Sergeants being what they are around officers, I won't go with you. The fact is, you'll be better off sending Nick. Sawicki likes women, and in case you haven't noticed Nick's got great legs."

"I've noticed."

"So will Sawicki."

48

They'd argued half the night and Nick wasn't sure whether she'd won or lost. John Gault had been outraged that Paula would suggest that Nick involve herself in arms dealing. She had quickly become annoyed with his overprotective attitude and found herself arguing against him. Everything she was doing was against her better judgment, but Paula had been adamant. Their best bet lay with enticement.

Nick ran her tongue along the inside of her incisors, hoping they'd withstand the acidity of Sawicki's coffee. For his part, the supply sergeant was eyeing her like a tiger after a six-day fast.

She'd played up to her part, hating herself. She'd ruined a perfectly good pair of jeans by cutting off the legs and converting them to short-shorts. She'd also undone the top button of her blouse and was flaunting herself. She felt like a complete idiot, but she had the supply sergeant's tongue practically hanging out. She also felt stupid for allowing herself to be talked into this. Procuring arms would make her an accomplice, for God's sake. Still, there was always the hope that Gault and his crew would come to their senses before anyone else got killed.

Sawicki's desk stood inside a chain-link security cage at the back of one of the National Guard hangars. There, he'd created an office of sorts by arranging eight-foot shelving around three sides of his desk. Parts, mostly electronic gear, along with hundreds of boxes marked with military nomenclature, crammed the shelves.

Sawicki set aside his coffee cup, put his feet up on the desk, and squinted at Nick between the toes of his spit-shined shoes. He was a short, wiry man, whose summer uniform had creases sharp enough to draw blood.

"Captain Latham tells me you're here speaking for John Gault."

Nodding, she leaned back in a pose she hoped he found seductive.

"The captain vouches for you," the sergeant continued, "or we wouldn't be here talking. She said you and Gault are interested in making some kind of trade." He raised an eyebrow. "Are you the merchandise?"

Nick had a panicky feeling that he might come over the top of the desk and wondered if she could use the desk lamp as a weapon. She gave him her best steely-eyed stare and replied, "You can't afford me."

Sawicki snorted. "The captain gave me your shopping list, but I can tell you, she's got me wrong. But that's officers for you." He looked Nick up and down. "No offense, but a good-looking woman is one thing, business is another. Hell, the moment I got your list I remembered Christmas when I was a kid. I always used to ask for everything. What I got was another matter."

Inwardly Nick cursed herself and felt a fool. Obviously, he'd been stringing her along, and Paula had certainly misread the man.

Nick forced a smile. "Are you saying you can't deliver?"

The supply sergeant smiled back. "I asked Santa for an airplane once."

"What kind?"

"I understand Gault Aviation runs Cessnas. Four of them, I think."

"You've done your homework," Nick said. Thank God Paula was correct about one thing—the extent of his greed, if not his libido.

"My folks didn't have much money when I was growing up," he went on, "so I always knew better than to ask for the top of the line."

The bottom, Nick knew from Gault's briefing, was the Cessna 150. It was a small two-seat trainer with a replacement value of about twenty thousand dollars.

"You're in luck. Mr. Gault has given me carte blanche. That means Christmas is early this year. A Cessna 150 is yours if we make a deal."

The sergeant grinned. "I like a woman who can make decisions."

"And our Christmas presents?" she asked.

"Talk about the holidays coming early. We were on a desert-warfare gig this spring, bombing the hell out of the salt flats west of here. Afterwards, I got stuck with some leftovers, not that they show on the books. Hell, that's expected. How else would us sergeants keep our units running, if we didn't have trading material?"

Sawicki opened his desk drawer and held out a manual, dog-eared to the appropriate page. Nick took it gingerly. One passage had been highlighted in advance. *The cluster bomb, type BL755, yields a high kill probability against a range of hard and soft targets encountered on the battlefield and immediate tactical areas.*

"I've got half a dozen." Sawicki retrieved a sheet of paper from his desk. "I've worked it out for you. Each bomb contains one hundred and forty-seven bomblets. Each bomblet produces two thousand fragments of shrapnel, bringing the grand total per bomb to ninety-four thousand. Multiply that by a kill factor of six, and you're in business."

Nick gritted her teeth. "That sounds like antipersonnel weaponry. Do you have anything that's designed to destroy buildings?"

"You want to shake 'n' bake, do you? Well, you haven't heard anything yet. Here's something called Hunting Area Denial Systems. HADES for short. Each one delivers one hundred and fifty bomblets. Whatever they touch burns—concrete, anything. So mix and match, that's what I say. A few HADES bombs along with your BL755s, and your target will be nothing but a barbecue."

Nick's stomach knotted at the thought of dropping such things. "There were a couple of other items on our list."

"No can do on the .50-calibers," Sawicki said. "One M-60 machine gun is all I've got. I can throw in an M-16 rifle, too."

"Ammunition?"

"Seven hundred and fifty rounds for the M-60. A little more than a minute's firing time. A dozen clips for the M-16."

"Tracers?"

"Sure."

"It will have to do. If you want to come to Gault Aviation with me, John will sign the 150 over to you right now."

"Hell," Sawicki said. "I like your style. For an extra five thousand dollars cash, I'll throw in a Stinger rocket. They're easy to use. All you have to do is point this sucker and pull the trigger."

Nick thought that over for a moment. "What about back-blast?"

"You're flying the old B-24, aren't you?" The sergeant scratched a closely shaven sideburn. "On second thought, scratch the Stinger. Chances are, firing it inside an airplane would blow you apart."

She took a deep breath. There was just enough money left in the kitty. "We'll take it anyway."

"It's your funeral, lady. But take it from me," he said, leering, "a nifty little number like you shouldn't let it all go to waste."

Nick felt the sudden need for a long, hot shower.

49

Frank Odell had been ordered off the mesa for an emergency meeting. After being helicoptered to a waiting Range Rover, he followed the directions provided. He drove north on a dirt road that led him deeper into the desert badlands. The only vegetation was the occasional prickly pear, cholla, and barrel cactus. There was no sign of animal life. Even a shot-up road sign would have been a welcome sight.

Finally, after what seemed like miles, he saw sun glinting on metal directly ahead. A quarter of a mile later he was looking at one of those aluminum-bodied, self-propelled mobile homes, forty feet long if it was an inch. Why the hell would it be out here in the middle of nowhere?

Because, Odell answered himself, that's the way the Chairman wanted it. He stopped the Range Rover twenty yards short of the trailer. He looked around for other signs of life. Nothing.

He was about to get out of the Range Rover when

men appeared, apparently out of nowhere, one on each side of his car. They both wore short-sleeve shirts and shoulder holsters.

One of them knocked on Odell's window. "You're expected inside," the man said, jerking a thumb at the mobile home.

Christ, Odell thought. What a way to earn a living. Maybe it was time to change occupations. Actually, he'd have to change lives first, using one of the new identities he kept stashed in safe-deposit boxes in Phoenix and Tucson, among other places. He thought of them as back doors to oblivion.

The men escorted him to the door. "Go on in," he was told. "It's all yours. We'll wait out here."

The inside of the mobile home was filled with television monitors, computers, and equipment totally unfamiliar to Odell. An innocuous-looking Bob Smith smiled from one of the screens.

"Take a seat, Frank."

With a sigh of relief at the efficient air-conditioning, he collapsed into a waiting chair and looked into the remote camera mounted on top of the TV monitor.

"You're sweating, Frank," Smith said.

"It's a hundred and ten outside."

"That's the desert for you. Turn up the air-conditioning if you'd like. Everything's there at your fingertips, computer controlled."

It was only then that Odell realized the mobile home's engine was turning over, providing power for all the equipment.

"I'm fine," Odell said.

"Let's get to it, then. I called you here to be doubly safe. The system is entirely scrambled and there sure as hell isn't any chance of eavesdroppers out here in the middle of nowhere."

Smith made a rumbling sound, a kind of mutant chuckle. "Now, give me your assessment of the Director and his security measures on the mesa."

Warnings sounded inside Odell's head. What the hell did the Chairman mean? What kind of assessment? In what context exactly?

Careful, Odell told himself. This had to be some kind of loyalty test. Thank god, he had back doors.

He cleared his throat. "He's very efficient."

"That goes without saying. Otherwise he wouldn't have been tolerated this long."

"We've only had one actual breach of security," Odell offered.

"The Cessna pilot, you mean?"

Odell nodded at the TV screen.

"I call that a disaster. Besides, you're forgetting the archaeologist who got close enough to talk to the old man."

"Who's to say that she wasn't imagining things?" Odell ventured.

"No witnesses, eh, Frank. That's your solution to our problems?"

"It's always an option."

"Like that botched attempt at Ophir?"

"I knew nothing about that," Odell protested.

"Let me show you something," Smith said. "Keep an eye on monitor number three, there to your right."

Monitor 3 steadied on a videotaped scene of the Director's office. The camera—positioned high up and at an angle to get both the Director and the man he was talking to, Odell—was obviously well concealed, because Odell had never noticed it.

"Progress always comes down to a matter of sacrifices," the Director was saying. "Think of how history will honor us if we come up with a cure. Think of what would have happened at Chernobyl if we'd had a cure for radiation poisoning. A Chernobyl could happen in this country, too, Frank. Then people would pay anything, do anything for a cure. If a few have to die here to save millions, wouldn't you say that's a cheap enough price to pay?"

"Absolutely, sir."

"That reporter was no different. He had to be interrogated. We had to know what he knew. After that, it would have been a waste not to use him in our work. Wouldn't you agree, Frank?"

"Of course."

The videotape stopped.

Smith cleared his throat. "Do you know what I call that, Frank? Evidence. It makes you a bona fide accomplice. Naturally, it shouldn't come to that if you work with me."

Odell nodded, wondering if it was too late to disappear through one of his back doors. Maybe not. There were only two men outside. If they didn't have orders to kill him already, he might be able to catch them by surprise. But he wouldn't make his move yet, not until he heard Smith out and knew all the options open to him.

"Let's get to the point," Smith said. "Do you have any indication that the Director is making progress on his project?"

"At the last staff meeting he said he was on the verge of a breakthrough."

"I've seen the tape, Frank. The Director's been saying the same thing for a year. So what I'm asking is, have you seen any evidence of a breakthrough?"

"No."

"I didn't think so. And my other people agree with you. So, Frank, let's get to the heart of the matter. Is there anyone on the mesa who would side with the Director against me?"

Odell hesitated. The implication was that Smith had other spies on the mesa.

"Stop worrying, Frank. I know you're too smart to back a loser. Just tell me who is loyal to the Director and not to me."

"The Blackbirds."

Smith nodded. "Voss and Wiley, you mean. You can leave them to me. Anyone else?"

"The Director's tight with his two chopper pilots. Some of the crazier security guards are with him too, I'd say."

"Is that it, Frank? The rest are ours?"

"You know scientists, sir. With them, the project is everything."

On screen, Smith steepled his fingers under his chin. "It's too bad the way things have worked out. The Scott woman has turned out to be much more resourceful than any of us could have imagined. That man, Gault, surprised me too. He's all but bankrupted himself getting that antique bomber of his into the air. And you know what that gives him, Frank, a weapon. The thing is, can we afford to let him use it?"

Odell was still thinking that over when Smith continued. "There are those of us who think that Director Maitland has become a liability. In that case, why not give Mr. Gault his head? I respect his grief. Losing a grandson is a terrible thing. So why not let him solve our problem?"

"That seems like a long shot," Odell said.

"Maybe so, but I want you ready with an evacuation plan for those loyal to me and the project. It's a contingency only at this stage, you understand."

Odell nodded, figuring maybe he wouldn't open those back doors just yet.

"Any questions?"

"How long do I have to get ready?"

"It all depends on those Blackbirds you mentioned." Smith raised his hand into camera range and tapped the face of his wristwatch. "About now, they're making their move. If they're successful, this conversation will have been moot. Otherwise"—Smith shook his head—"you'd better be ready to move in two hours."

50

Wiley ordered coffee and pie, paying the waitress as soon as she served him. That left him free to leave the truck stop whenever his target made a move.

He took his time with the pie, toying with the crust and pretending to sip coffee while studying himself in the mirror behind the counter. The image he'd created was perfect. Just another unshaven trucker. His boots, jeans, and T-shirt exposing press-on tattoos were well used and grimy.

His target, a size 40 regular by the looks of him, dropped money on the counter, joked with the waitress, then spun off his stool and started for the door. Wiley followed, hanging back a few feet until the target reached his truck.

"Excuse me," Wiley said, holding up a road map that hid the .22 automatic in the palm of his hand. "Could you give me some directions? This is my first run through Salt Lake, and this God damn map of mine is useless."

"Sure thing." The target beckoned him over. "I've got a good street guide in my cab." He turned away to open the door and lean inside.

Right behind him, Wiley vaulted onto the metal running board. From a distance, Wiley knew it would look like all he'd done was touch the driver's head. The shot was no more than a popping sound. No fuss at all.

Voss, who'd been waiting in the car, arrived to help cram the body into the foot-well on the passenger's side.

That done, they hopped out and looked around. No one was looking their way; no one had noticed a thing.

Voss went back to the car, while Wiley climbed into

the cab and drove out of the truck stop. A mile down the highway, he turned onto a side road they'd scouted in advance. There, he changed into the driver's uniform, dumped the body, and headed for the airport.

Once there, Wiley followed the driver's route and routine, delivering fuel to the small aviation companies in proper order. He didn't look for Voss. He didn't have to; he knew his partner would be close by, covering his back.

At Gault Aviation, procedure called for the driver to check in at the office before making his delivery. It was the moment of truth for Wiley's disguise, but no one paid any attention to him as he approached the counter. All seven photo subjects, as specified in the ISA packet, were assembled. A target-rich environment, if he'd ever seen one.

Wiley ID'd them as the Scott woman, Gault and his copilot, Roberts, all of whom he and Voss had been following for days. Also present were two of Gault's old crew buddies, Campbell and Yarbrough, plus his mechanic, Christensen, and Paula Latham, the Air Force pilot. Christensen was at the counter, while everyone else was clustered around a desk at the back of the office. They'd tried to look casual when Wiley entered, but he knew what they were up to. He didn't have to see the maps to know they were deciding on a flight plan. So much wasted effort, he thought. They'd never get off the ground. Probably they'd never know what hit them.

"Where's the regular driver?" Christensen asked.

"Ted's sick, I'm told." Wiley laid his clipboard on the counter. "The order says you have an underground tank, plus a truck."

"The tanker truck's damn near empty and the underground's down about half. So you might as well fill them both up. I'll show you the way."

As soon as Wiley was left alone, he attached the feeder hose to the tank and pretended to start the flow. When he was certain he wasn't being watched, he quickly entered the hangar and went to work.

51

Nick still couldn't believe what she was seeing, four men planning a peacetime bombing mission. Until they'd emptied the tanker truck into the *Lady-A*, she hadn't believed they'd actually go through with it. Even watching them load those damned bombs she'd wheedled out of Sawicki hadn't seemed real. It had been more like one of those old newsreels, remote and slightly off-speed. To make matters worse, they'd all armed themselves with .45 automatics, war surplus the same age as the *Lady-A*.

Nick moved away from the desk, hugging herself to hide her shakes from the others. More than anything she wanted Gault to give up his mission and stay with her. But she'd never ask it of him. At least they'd have tonight together, before tomorrow's takeoff.

Paula joined her to whisper, "You care about him, don't you? It shows on your face. Matt looked a lot like John."

"I know."

"He cares about you too, you know," Paula said.

"Maybe, but not as much as the *Lady-A*."

Paula smiled. "You're probably right. But I've seen the way he looks at both of you. Since the *Lady-A* isn't talking, that leaves it up to you. You're the only one who can talk him out of this mission. If you don't, chances are they'll all end up dead."

"He says the odds are fifty-fifty."

"I don't believe it and neither do you."

Christ, why couldn't Paula have waited? Tomorrow would have been soon enough to put into words what

Nick had been brooding about all day. That the mission was hopeless.

"Do you know what gives pilots nightmares?" Paula said. "Fire. And do you know how much gasoline a B-24 carries? Nearly three thousand gallons." She shook her head violently. "Every time I think about their chances, I see the Lady-A going down in flames."

"What are you two talking about?" Gault called to them.

"You, of course," Paula answered.

He crossed the room to hug them both. "Today, I feel twenty-one."

He swept Nick off her feet.

In midair, looking through the window, Nick spotted a fuel-truck driver leaving the Lady-A's hangar. Something about the way he moved alerted her. He looked like he was trying to sneak off unseen.

"John," she said, "behind you, the man coming out of the hangar. Should he be there?"

Gault set Nick down to look for himself.

Christensen joined them to say, "He's a new man. He's delivering fuel."

"He has no business in the hangar, then." Gault started for the door.

"John, relax," Paula called after him. "The man's probably never seen a B-24 before. He's a sightseer like everyone else around this airport."

"He looks suspicious to me," Nick said, sorry once the words were out because of their effect on Gault.

"God damn it!" he shouted. "Nobody goes near the Lady-A when she's getting ready for a mission."

It was Christensen who charged through the door first, with Gault right behind him. Nick jointed the exodus to keep from being trampled by the others.

"Wait up!" Christensen shouted at the driver, who was about to climb into the cab of his fuel truck.

The man swung around, facing them, and went into

a crouch. His hand came up as if to point at them. In that split second Nick saw the gun.

"Get down!" she shouted.

She didn't hear the shot, only Christensen's gasp as he collapsed onto the taxiway.

Gault dropped to one knee, tugging at his jacket to get at his .45. Roberts was doing the same.

Another silent shot ricocheted off the tarmac at Nick's feet. Christ, he was shooting at her.

As if in slow motion, Nick saw the robber's surprised look change to a smile as he redirected his aim at Gault. Please, she thought, not John. She threw herself at Gault as a shot snapped close over their heads.

Gault landed on his elbow. The impact jarred loose the .45. He scooped it up again, braced his elbows on the tarmac, and took careful aim.

Nick held her breath, but had no illusions. They were up against a professional.

Nick heard Gault gasp. God, he was hit, but he continued to aim the .45. By now, the gunman was firing continuously, a regular cadence. At any moment she expected to feel the impact. And with her lying prone like this, he'd be going for head shots, her head and John's.

A slug ripped out a chunk of asphalt inches from Gault's face. He didn't flinch, but calmly pulled the trigger. The .45's slide locked open. He was out of ammunition.

Even as the thought flashed through her mind that they were all as good as dead, Nick realized that Gault's shot had hit home, hurling the man into the side of the fuel truck. His eyes went wide, staring with disbelief as he toppled, face forward, onto the tarmac.

Nick twisted around to see if anyone else was hit. But everyone was down, flat on the tarmac. When she turned back to Gault, he was up on his hands and knees and crawling toward Christensen.

Nick followed. There was a hole in the mechanic's chest, but he was breathing.

"Is anybody else hit?" she shouted.

"Me," Paula said. "But Brad's worse."

Nick scrabbled to the copilot's side. He was dead. She picked up his .45, then went back to Paula.

"I'll be okay," Paula said. "No arteries hit, thank God." She was applying pressure to a thigh wound. "See to Theron first."

Before Nick could move, an automatic weapon opened up from the parking lot.

She fired back without seeing a target, hoping to God she didn't hit some hapless bystander. To her left, slugs gouged holes in the asphalt. She dropped flat but kept looking for a target.

Where are you, you son of a bitch? There, behind the Chevy. The bastard had an Uzi, and he was firing it at Gault and Christensen.

Nick raised up on one knee. Shoot me, you son of a bitch. Her sudden movement caught the second gunman by surprise, causing him to be a split second too late redirecting his fire. She shot him twice, once in the head.

Nick lowered the gun and turned to Gault, who was staring at her with a look of total disbelief. "I told you my father taught me," she said, trying to hold the shock at bay, not wanting to tell him that she'd never fired a gun under conditions like this. *So this is combat,* she thought, *this is what men go through in war,* and was happy to have never experienced it before.

In that instant, Nick realized she was the only one who'd escaped without a scratch. Campbell had rubbed his hands raw skidding on the tarmac. Yarbrough's pinkie finger was obviously broken. He straightened it with a grimace.

A siren sounded in the distance, probably one of the airport's emergency units.

"The police are going to be here any minute," Yarbrough shouted. "If we're going to fly, we'd better do it now."

Gault gestured at Nick. "Give me the gun."

Nick double-checked the safety before handing it over. Blood was streaming down his left arm. She moved forward to examine the wound, but he stepped aside.

"It's from a ricochet," he said as he rubbed the gun against his thigh to erase her fingerprints.

"For the record," he said. "I shot those two men. No one else had a weapon. Is that understood?"

"Stop playing hero," Paula said. "You can't fly without help in the cockpit, and Nick's the only one left."

"No."

"I'm going," Nick said. "I'm going to fly away with you, John."

"Whatever we do," Campbell said, "it has to be fast. That siren's getting closer."

Gault jerked a thumb at the dead man next to the tanker truck. "God knows what he did to the *Lady-A* while he was in there."

A second siren began to wail.

Nick knelt beside Paula. "Is it okay to leave you?"

"Time's up," Paula said. "I'd try to talk you out of it but I know you too well." She smiled at Nick. "Both of you. Now leave."

Gault looked to Yarbrough and Campbell. Both nodded their agreement.

"I'll stall them as long as I can," Paula said.

Nick hugged Paula goodbye. "*Omnia vincit amor*," Nick said. At Paula's startled look, Nick explained. "Love conquers all. I read it in the letter of a woman I'm researching."

Paula blinked back a tear. "Not death," she replied.

Gault grabbed Nick's hand and headed for the *Lady-A*, Campbell and Yarbrough right behind them. As soon as they were inside the building, Nick said, "I don't think that bastard had time to go aboard. If he did anything to the *Lady-A*, it's got to be out here."

They split up. Nick racked her memory for everything she knew about B-24s. Funny, she thought, it was easier to deal with them when they were in pieces.

Gault was searching the bomb bay when she noticed the scratches. The screws holding the underwing access panel in place had been disturbed.

"John," she called. "Take a look at this."

"You're right," he said as soon as he inspected the area. "Theron would never tolerate such sloppy work."

Gault went to work with a screwdriver. When the panel dropped open, Nick half-expected a booby trap to go off.

"Son of a bitch. Look what we've got."

The explosive wasn't large, about the size of a candy bar, but it would have snapped the fuel lines and ignited the gasoline.

They checked the other access panels, but nothing was immediately obvious.

"Do we keep looking?" Campbell asked.

Still more sirens sounded in the distance.

Gault looked directly at Nick and she knew that he was speaking only to her. "We've run out of time."

52

Odell's beeper went off. The signal, which caught him in the men's room, sent him running for his office, zipping up along the way. Inside, snap-locking the door behind him, he lunged for the secure line. Chairman Smith was waiting.

"Gault and his bomber are on the move," Smith's voice came over the line. "Like I said, a resourceful man, dangerous. He and the archaeologist both."

The Chairman's tone had a ring of finality to it. Unless Odell was mistaken, the panic button was about to be pushed.

"The bomber's movement would seem to confirm failure by those Blackbirds of yours."

"The Director's, you mean," Odell shot back.

"Of course. That's what I meant to say. They're probably dead in any case. Now, considering the cruising speed of a B-24 bomber, I figure you have two and a half hours to implement your evacuation. Maybe a bit less. You'll be picked up separately, Frank, after everyone else is gone. Except, of course, Director Maitland and his cronies."

"But—"

"I'll have a talk with them now, Frank. They'll think your evacuation plan is for their benefit. Now move!"

"Where will I be picked up?" Odell asked, wondering if he'd left it too late, wondering if all his back doors had slammed shut.

"On the pad, Frank, by my own personal helicopter."

Christ, Odell thought. Was he being set up? "I've taken precautions," Odell said. "I've left behind my own life insurance policies."

"Of course you have. I expected nothing less. Now stop worrying and start the evacuation."

53

Nick said a prayer as the *Lady-A* turned onto the taxiway and headed for the main runway. Engine start-up had been nerve-racking. With the turning of each propeller, she'd expected another booby trap to explode. But so far, everything had gone smoothly, even her help with the copilot's checklist.

Now, sitting there belted into the copilot's right-hand seat, she felt a fool. Not her career, not her father, and certainly not the Benson sisters could keep her from doing what she knew to be wrong. *I am a fool for love,* she decided, and wondered if this was what Pearl Benson meant when she'd told her daughter, "If love's a sin, so be it." Had she too abandoned all rational thought and run off to an uncertain future? Pearl's sister, Lillian, had never recorded a single word in her own diaries about what had happened to her twin. Instead, Lillian had called love a kind of madness.

And what will happen to Dr. Nicolette Scott? she thought. *Is she mad?*

Gault tapped her on the shoulder, held up crossed fingers, and asked the tower for takeoff clearance. If the police were there already, the B-24 would be grounded.

"Proceed to runway 34R," the tower said.

"That's the long runway," Gault told her on the intercom. "Ninety-five hundred feet long. We shouldn't need it, but with our bomb load it's good to have some leeway."

As he spoke, Nick scanned the instruments. She didn't know what to look for, really. After all, she belonged to the generation that expected warning lights on the dashboard, not real gauges.

Buffeting caused her to look up to see a jumbo jet ahead of them on 34R. Wide-eyed passengers were waving from their porthole windows. Nick waved back. *Hi there, folks, we're just on our way to drop a few bombs.*

Gault triggered his mike. "Crew check."

"Bombardier okay," Campbell said from the nose.

"Gunner on station," Yarbrough said from the waist.

"It's your last chance to back out," Gault told them.

"Are you kidding," Yarbrough shot back. "I've never had the pleasure of firing an M-60 before."

"Whatever you do, keep it out of sight until we're airborne."

"Roger."

"Vic?" Gault said.

"Me and the Nordeen are getting along just fine."

Gault reached across to clasp Nick's hand. "It's not too late," he said. "I can fly this by myself."

"You're still bleeding. Besides, first aid was part of my survival training."

"Nick, I—"

The jumbo started its takeoff.

"Stand by for takeoff," Gault said into the intercom, then swung the B-24 onto the runway. Quickly, he went through the same procedures he'd followed on their test flight, adjusting the control tabs and setting the rudder to compensate for engine torque.

Then he asked the tower for final clearance.

Nick was surprised to hear, "B-24, you are cleared for immediate takeoff." She'd half expected the police to intervene. Probably they hadn't sorted out the carnage at the hangar yet.

Gault turned to her. "Are you ready?"

"I wouldn't have missed it for anything."

His hand settled on the throttles. During takeoff, he'd told her to add her hand to his, a textbook precaution to keep the throttles from slipping.

"Lady Luck's still with me," he said, smiling at her. "I've got beautiful women at my fingertips."

Gradually, he engaged the throttles, her left hand on top of his right hand. The bomber rolled so slowly at first, Nick thought something was wrong. But the throttles were all the way forward, and the engines were roaring beyond anything she'd experienced on their first flight. Even so, halfway down the runway she had the feeling they were hardly moving. Frantically, she searched for the air speed indicator. Ninety, it said, inching toward one hundred. Impossible. What's takeoff speed, she wondered, but didn't dare ask for fear of breaking Gault's concentration.

Suddenly they were lifting off.

"Wheels coming up," Gault said on the intercom. "The serpent is airborne."

He banked west toward the Great Salt Lake, gaining altitude.

"From now on," Campbell said from the nose, "the Lady-A is gone. We're strictly poisonous."

"With fangs and stingers both," Yarbrough added from the waist.

Gault nodded at Nick. "You didn't know you'd landed yourself in a nest of vipers, did you?" On the intercom he said, "As soon as we reach cruising altitude, I'll bring the serpent onto the target heading. We'll check the M-60 when we hit the Arizona badlands."

"What about your arm?" Nick said. "It ought to be bandaged."

He pointed to the checklist. "Keep me honest, first."

At a thousand feet he said, "Fuel boosters off."

"Check," she confirmed.

At eight thousand feet he reduced power to 1600 RPM and Nick watched the serpent settle onto a cruising speed of two hundred miles an hour.

North of them, thunderheads were gathering along the Wasatch front. The forecast, however, called for clear skies over most of Arizona, including the target area.

On intercom Gault said, "How's the Norden, Vic?"

"As far as I can tell, the serpent's ready to strike," Campbell replied. "But I'd like to make one practice drop just to make sure."

"All right, we'll do that after we cross the border. Right now, I'm cutting in the autopilot. Vic, you'll have the serpent for a few minutes while Nick gives me a little first aid."

One by one he began throwing toggle switches. When the last one was engaged, he unclasped his hands from the control yoke.

"Autopilot engaged," he said into the intercom.

"Testing," Campbell replied.

Ever so slightly, the serpent veered to port. A moment later the plane changed direction to starboard.

"The serpent is behaving," Campbell said.

With a sigh, Gault leaned back and struggled out of his jacket, revealing a blood-soaked shirt sleeve.

"I'll get the first aid kit," he said. "If she makes a move while I'm gone, grab the yoke and hold her steady."

"I thought Vic was flying the plane."

"Serpents this age have been known to bite their own crews."

Before Nick could ask what qualified as a bite, Gault was out of his seat and into the fuselage. After that, she couldn't take her eyes off the yoke. What was Gault thinking about? Sweat ran down her forehead and into her eyes.

The yoke in front of her moved slightly. Was Campbell making the adjustment, or was the serpent getting ready to strike?

She scanned the gauges, looking for some telltale sign of rebellion. Nothing was blinking. Nothing was moving.

Wait a minute? Her head jerked up. Somebody had to look where they were going.

Thank God. The sky ahead was clear.

Again, the yoke quivered. She reached out, hands poised to grab hold.

"Stop!" someone said into her ear.

"Shit!" She swung around to see Russ Yarbrough standing behind her. "You scared the hell out of me."

"Relax. The scary part comes later. John asked me to keep you company for a minute while he roots out the first aid kit."

"I hope it's not as old as this plane."

Yarbrough shrugged. "The older antiques get, the more valuable they are." He leaned forward to study the instrument panel.

"Is everything okay?" she asked.

"Don't ask me. I shoot planes down, I don't fly them."

"You're all crazy."

"It takes one to know one," Gault said, sneaking up behind her. He handed Nick the first aid kit.

Thank God, she thought. It was brand-new and still sealed.

"Can we move back into the fuselage?" she said, "so I can have more room to work."

"Good idea," Yarbrough said, slipping into the pilot's seat.

Once Nick had poured disinfectant into Gault's wound and bandaged it, they did a quick check of the waist gun. Yarbrough had used bungee cords to suspend the M-60 in the firing window on the port side of the fuselage. The cords, one attached at each corner, gave the machine gun a wide field of fire.

The M-16 rifle had been bungeed to the starboard side. The Stinger missile was stowed nearby, secured to a fuselage strut.

"Russ is using his head," Gault shouted over the engines, whose vibrations were shaking the bomber like a wind chime. "By mounting his machine gun on my side of the ship, I can maneuver him into a better firing position."

"And if they come at us from the other side?"

"Russ will have to switch positions and go with less firepower."

"Don't forget I know how to shoot," Nick said.

"I haven't, but I'm counting on a little help from Lady Luck. If the Hueys come, chances are they won't expect us to have an M-60."

Sure, Nick thought. The serpent's attack would come as a complete surprise. Like hell! They'd left three dead men behind at the airport. Maybe four by now, if Christensen hadn't made it. And she had no doubt about those two gunmen. They had to have been working for Karl Maitland. Which meant, Maitland and his entire security force would be ready and waiting for the serpent's arrival at Mesa d'Oro. Gault had to know that, too.

So say something, she told herself. But she couldn't. To put the obvious into words might have weakened his resolve. If he turned back now, the lost opportunity would haunt him the rest of his life and haunt her, too.

She hugged him just as a downdraft shook the serpent.

"We'd better get forward," Gault said, "before Russ starts tinkering."

Back in the cockpit, Nick followed their progress on the map. Every so often, she'd touch her finger to a spot corresponding with some landmark below and check her reading with Gault, who'd either nod or shake his head.

She pinpointed them exactly as they flew over St. George, Utah, and crossed into Arizona. Thirty miles later, the map was virtually blank, just like the desert below. There were no roads, no rivers, no towns, nothing.

Gault triggered his mike. "Russ, it's time to check your gun."

A moment later, Gault lowered the wing to port,

allowing Nick to see the tracers streak away from the plane.

"Okay," Gault said when the firing stopped, "your turn's coming up, Vic."

"What are we going to drop?" Campbell asked.

"Russ and I have attached that booby trap we found to a small can of gasoline. That ought to give us a big enough explosion to see if you're on target."

"What altitude?"

"What would you suggest?"

"The lower we are, the more accurate I'll be."

And more vulnerable, Nick thought, but kept it to herself.

"How high's the mesa?" Campbell asked.

"The map says nineteen hundred and sixty feet," Nick said.

"Then twenty-five hundred ought to give us enough leeway."

"Twenty-five hundred it is," Gault said, easing the yoke forward and beginning their descent. "Everybody look for a target. Russ, let me know when you're in position to drop our bobby trap and I'll open the bomb doors."

"I'm there," Yarbrough said.

"Doors coming open."

"Roger. Doors are open. Just give me the word, and out she goes."

At twenty-five hundred feet the landscape looked as barren as the moon. The only possible targets were outcroppings of red rock, but most were small and too close together to single out. Just when Nick thought they'd have to alter course to find a suitable target, she saw a freestanding pinnacle of rock about a mile directly ahead.

Gault must have spotted it at the same time because he got on the intercom. "Do you see it, Vic? Straight ahead."

"How could I miss it?"

"I'll circle around for a bomb run."

"I hate to bomb a landmark like that."

"Okay. See how close you can come, then. I'm warming up the autopilot."

As soon as they were on the run, Gault turned the serpent over to his bombardier. They were about three miles from the target, Nick judged, and slightly to the left. But Campbell quickly corrected until their alignment looked good, at least from Nick's point of view. Or was that an illusion because she was on the starboard side?

Beside her, Gault appeared totally unconcerned.

She was about to nudge him when Campbell said, "Bombs away."

"Away," Yarbrough echoed.

"Bomb doors closed," Campbell said. "I'm giving her back to you, John."

"Got her," Gault answered, one hand on the yoke, the other switching off the autopilot, causing the serpent to lurch slightly.

To keep the target in view, he immediately banked steeply to port. A few seconds later, flame blossomed near the base of the pinnacle.

"Christ!" Campbell whooped on the intercom. "You can't get any closer than that with a make-believe bomb with lousy aerodynamics."

Nick glanced at Gault, who was nodding. Tears were in his eyes. He leaned over to speak into her ear. "Until this moment, I didn't really think we could do it. Part of me kept saying it was nothing but an old man's fantasy. Now, I know the serpent's as deadly as ever. And that scares me for your sake. Because now I can't turn back."

54

The Huey gunships came out of the sun. Nick's full attention had been focused on Mesa d'Oro, and she didn't realize anything was wrong until she felt the serpent shudder. A piece of cowling exploded from the outboard engine on her side of the plane. Smoke immediately began trailing out behind them. Gault leaned across her for a closer look.

"Cannon fire," Campbell shouted from the nose. "Hueys coming around for another pass. Watch it, Russ."

Nick held her breath. If they attacked on the port side, they'd come under fire from the M-60.

She looked to Gault to see if he was going to break off the bomb run. But his hands remained where they were, in his lap. Only his head was moving, swiveling constantly to catch a glimpse of the attacking helicopters.

He'd told her in advance what to expect. Once on the final bomb run, with the serpent properly trimmed and the PDI centered, there could be no maneuvering; no evasive action that might spoil Campbell's aim. From that moment on, they had to fly in a straight line and take their chances. During the war, that had included both fighters and flak.

The serpent shuddered again.

"Fuckers took a chunk out of one of our stabilizers," Yarbrough reported.

The serpent tilted momentarily, then righted itself.

"They're smart," Yarbrough said. They're staying out of range. Watch it, they're swinging underneath us."

Even as Nick watched, the outboard engine on her side of the plane took another hit.

Immediately, Gault cut in the fire extinguisher and feathered the prop. Then his hands moved to the yoke. "Vic, I'm coming off autopilot. We don't have a chance otherwise."

"Shit," Campbell said.

Over the roar of the three remaining engines, Nick heard Yarbrough open fire, a long burst. "Damn! The bastards are quick."

Nick released her seat belt. "I'm going back to help."

"Nick—"

"If we don't get them off us, it's all for nothing."

He started to reach for her, but missed as she plunged through the hatch. Ahead of her shafts of light began appearing as cannon shells punched through the fuselage. Sideslipping, the serpent took evasive action, coming off course and away from the target. Nick's stomach lurched.

When she reached Yarbrough, she was stunned at the number of holes around his firing window. His being untouched seemed a miracle.

She plugged into the intercom to hear him say, "Nick's manning the starboard gun. Now do your stuff, John, and give us a shot at the bastards."

Even on three engines, Gault handled the serpent precisely. Three times, he brought the Hueys into their field of fire. But now that the serpent was no longer headed toward Mesa d'Oro, the choppers seemed content to stand off and play a waiting game.

Nick clenched her teeth in frustration. At the best of times, the M-16 had an effective range of four hundred yards, and that was in the hands of an expert. On full automatic, at two hundred rounds per minute, its thirty-round magazine allowed about five seconds' firing time. Not much of a match for two Huey Cobras.

"Do you know anything about Stingers?" Yarbrough shouted without aid of the intercom.

She shook her head. "Too much back-blast."

"What choice do we have?"

"I'm not sure how it works," she said.

"I do. I read the instructions."

She helped him get it ready. When it was on Yarbrough's shoulder, she called Gault on the intercom. "We're going to try the Stinger."

"You told me Sawicki said we couldn't fire inside the plane."

"Russ thinks he can line it up so the back-blast goes out the firing window behind him. Now lure them in close."

"Jesus," Gault said. "Be careful."

Nick detached the M-16 and moved it and herself out of the back-blast area. Even as she did, the serpent turned toward Mesa d'Oro again. When the Hueys moved to intercept, they came in on Nick's side, forcing Yarbrough to reverse direction. Once he was braced again, he glanced over his shoulder to make certain he was lined up with the opposite firing window.

"Turn to port," Yarbrough said to Gault.

The serpent veered.

"A little more. Perfect."

At a nod from Yarbrough, Nick threw herself on the deck.

The back-blast blew out enough fuselage to double the size of the starboard firing window. It also blew away the M-60 machine gun that had been stowed nearby.

Through the surviving window, she watched the missile streaking toward the leading Huey. The chopper veered. So did the Stinger.

The initial explosion wasn't much more than a puff of smoke. For an instant, she thought they'd missed, or that the Stinger was a dud. Then flame erupted, and the helicopter turned turtle and fell like a rock, blazing into a fireball long before impact with the ground below.

"Okay, John," Yarbrough said. "That ought to give the other bastard something to think about. Now let's hit the target."

Like Yarbrough, Nick had expected the second Huey to turn tail rather than face the possibility of another Stinger. But it came right at them the moment the serpent turned toward Mesa d'Oro again.

"He must know we only had one," Nick said.

"We lost the M-60," Yarbrough reported to Gault. "All we've got left is a .45 automatic and the M-16."

Yarbrough looked at Nick, who nodded despite the fear gnawing at her.

Yarbrough triggered his mike. "Go ahead, John. Start the bomb run. We'll do our best back here."

"Autopilot engaged," Gault responded. "The serpent's yours, Vic."

The Huey's next pass was tentative, as if probing their firepower. He fired from long distance, his cannon shells coming in a lobbing arc. Only one struck home, blowing out a chunk of fuselage just behind the bomb bay.

Yarbrough opened fire with the M-16 rifle. He'd loaded the clips personally, with tracers every fifth round.

But his target wouldn't stay put. It kept darting in one direction, then another, until finally the chopper swept past them, beyond Yarbrough's field of fire.

Once out of sight, it must have turned sharply, because cannon fire immediately began raking the other side of the fuselage. Yarbrough was hit and flung to the floor.

A searing pain erupted along Nick's cheek, staggering her. When she reached up, her hand came away bloody.

Distantly, she heard Campbell say, "Fifteen seconds to target."

Gault was counting down to himself when the number two engine took a hit. The temperature immediately began rising. His hand hovered over the feathering button.

Internally his count reached five, then four, three, two, one. He held his breath.

"Bombs away," Campbell said.

At the sudden weight loss, the serpent rose as if riding an unexpected thermal. The sudden gain in altitude saved Gault's life as cannon shells slammed into the fuselage directly below him. The B-24 shook violently but still responded when he banked away. The turn gave him a clear view of Mesa d'Oro.

For a heart-stopping moment, he thought they'd missed. Then, in the next instant, explosions ripped the top of the mesa. A heartbeat later, the HADES bombs detonated. The entire plateau went up like an erupting volcano.

"You see that?" Campbell shouted. "I haven't lost my touch. Shit! I've got a warning light. The bomb doors won't close."

"It's just as well," Gault said.

"What?"

"I'll tell you later."

Gault switched off the autopilot just as the Huey attacked again. Number two took another hit and caught fire. Instinctively, he hit the feathering button, closed the fuel shut-off valve and booster pump, switched off the generator and ignition, and locked open the cowl flaps. In theory, without fuel the fire would blow out.

"I'm coming up," Campbell said.

Seconds later, he slid into the copilot's seat. By then the flames had subsided into smoke.

"She's still with us," Gault said.

Campbell nodded. "Lady Luck."

The Huey made another pass.

"Why doesn't the son of a bitch go home?" Campbell said.

"He doesn't have a home. We bombed it."

Cannon fire raked the fuselage directly behind them, blowing away part of the upper turret.

Gault squirmed, remembering the armor plating he and Brad had scrounged during the war. Sitting on it was the only way to protect your backside when the fighters came in for belly attacks.

"We're dead, John."

"Not as long as I can keep us in the air," Gault replied.

Campbell slipped out of his seat. "You keep flying. I'm going back to the waist and get myself a gun. Maybe we can take them with us."

Nick's legs were shaking hard enough to rattle the empty cartridge cases at her feet. Yarbrough lay half-buried in them, blood seeping from a wound in his chest. A second piece of shrapnel had sliced open his thigh, which Nick had tied off with a tourniquet. His survival, she figured, depended on how quickly they could get him to a doctor.

Miraculously, Yarbrough was still plugged into the intercom which, considering the hits they'd taken, was proof of yet another miracle.

"Nick's manning the M-16," he told Gault in a shaky voice.

"Vic's coming back," Gault answered.

The Huey gunship was holding position, five or six hundred yards off their starboard side. No doubt he was wondering, like Nick was, how long the serpent could stay airborne on only two engines.

When Campbell arrived, he knelt beside Yarbrough and held his hand.

"Goddamn," Yarbrough said, "we're still the best." He looked up at Nick and smiled. "Now if she'd do her job and take out that damned Huey with the M-16, we could all go home."

"Is there another gun?" Campbell asked.

"Only my pistol," Yarbrough said.

Campbell took it and stood up, bracing himself against a piece of fuselage that was still intact.

"Are you any good with that?" Nick asked.

"I fired one fifty years ago." He nodded at her M-16.

"But never one of those. With all that plastic, it doesn't look real."

"You saw how Nick handles a gun back at the hangar," Yarbrough said. "She's good. So all we have to do is get her a clear shot."

Just as he spoke, the gunship accelerated forward and out of Nick's field of vision.

"He's coming at me head-on," Gault said from the cockpit.

The bomber sideslipped first one way, then the other, but that didn't stop the cannon shells from striking home. Nick felt the plane stagger, then lurch to one side before slipping into a dive.

She caught her breath. They were going down. No plane could stay up with damage like this. Yet somehow the B-24 started leveling out.

Correction, she thought to herself. John Gault leveled her. His skill as a pilot was keeping them alive.

Campbell, who'd been thrown against the fuselage during the dive, scrambled to his feet. His intercom connection had ripped away, so he used Yarbrough's. "John, I've got an idea. I'm going to sucker the bastard."

"What the hell does that mean?"

"Just keep us in the air."

After disconnecting his headset, Campbell pulled his white T-shirt over his head and waved it out the firing window to get the Huey's attention.

"What's going on back there?" Gault asked.

"Vic's trying to get himself killed," Nick answered, shouting so Campbell could hear too.

"Don't worry about me," Campbell shouted back. "I'm a dead man already."

"What do you mean?" Nick demanded.

"John knows," he replied. "I got my death warrant from the doctors a few weeks ago."

He tossed away the T-shirt and unzipped his pants. "I'll piss on the bastard if I have to, just so he comes closer."

He glanced over his shoulder at Nick. "Get ready. Don't let them see you or the rifle. Fire through one of the cannon holes. If I do this right, you ought to get at least one clear shot at the bastard."

As soon as Nick moved into position, Campbell began urinating out the firing window and into the wind stream. "Come on, asshole. Get a little closer. See the whites of my eyes and die!" he yelled.

The hole Nick had picked was pie-size. Through it only a small patch of sky was visible.

"I can't see him!" she shouted.

"He's out there. Back toward the tail, out of your line of sight." Campbell leaned out dangerously far, gesturing obscenely. "He's moving up, but I've run out of ammunition."

"I see him," Nick shouted. He was still two hundred yards away, maybe three hundred. Too far, considering the way the B-24 was shuddering and shaking.

"Come on," Campbell yelled into the wind. "We're helpless. Come and get us."

Abruptly, Campbell dropped his pants. "I'll moon the bastard. Maybe that'll get his attention."

Risking a quick glance away from the target, Nick saw that he was doing just that. Quickly, she focused again on the Huey as it came in for a closer look.

"Wait until you can't miss, Nick."

The chopper stopped weaving and held a steady course, maybe fifty yards off their port side. At that range, Nick could see the pilot and his passenger laughing at Campbell. Nick clenched her teeth. The passenger, with his neatly trimmed black beard, looked very much like the Internet photograph of Dr. Karl Maitland.

She took a quick breath, let half of it out, and took careful aim just ahead of the copter.

"Now!" Campbell shouted.

Bracing herself against the recoil, she squeezed the trigger. The first tracer reached out, slightly in front of the Huey. Even as she corrected her bullet stream, flame erupted from the gunship's chin cannon. The impact of cannon shells at such close range was like a head-on collision. The serpent shuddered violently.

Out of the corner of her eye, she saw Campbell flung backwards. She knew, without having to look, that he'd been hurled out of the plane.

Screaming, she kept firing until her tracers were dead center on the Plexiglas. The Huey was adjusting too, its shells coming her way. Then suddenly blood exploded against the chopper's windshield where the passenger had been sitting. The Huey's nose dipped. Then it rolled over and fell from Nick's field of vision, trailing greasy black smoke.

55

Gault fought for control. She was the *Lady-A* again, not the serpent, and she was going down. That last burst of cannon fire had been her death blow. It was only a matter of time.

He checked the altimeter. Eleven hundred feet, and dropping steadily.

The yoke felt mushy in his hands. If he couldn't get her nose up, they'd wouldn't have time to jump. He pulled back on the yoke. Nothing. Christ, maybe the control linkage was shot.

"Annie," he said, "I need time."

He was panting now, half-blinded by the sweat flooding into his eyes. *Please*, he begged, *I'll be with you soon.*

He blinked. Was it wishful thinking, or was their rate

of descent slowing? Yes, by God, she was leveling off. Nine hundred feet and holding.

"Thank you, Annie."

He trimmed the plane as best he could, then switched on his intercom mike. "Crew check."

There was no response.

"Nick?"

Still nothing.

He said a silent prayer, and began switching on the autopilot. Engaging each toggle was a thrill. If the system had been hit, he'd lose control. At this altitude, there'd be no recovery.

But the autopilot engaged, holding the B-24 in level flight.

"You're the best, Annie."

He left his seat to look for Nick.

56

The *Lady-A* felt as if she were shaking to pieces. Air whistled through every hole inside the shell-torn fuselage. Loose pieces of jagged metal ricocheted with each jolt of the aircraft. Nick did her best to dodge them, but Gault stood his ground as he helped her with her parachute. He already wore his.

He nodded toward a backpack with parachute attached that lay braced against the bomb racks. Its rip cord had been secured to one of the struts so that the chute would open automatically.

"There's two gallons of water in there, and a map

and a compass," he shouted over the din. "I'll drop it just before we jump."

Thank God one of them had been planning ahead, Nick thought.

"What about Yarbrough?"

Gault knelt beside the gunner and felt for a pulse. After a moment he shook his head and closed Yarbrough's staring eyes.

The *Lady-A* lurched to one side, throwing Gault onto his face. The moment he got up, he grabbed her and pulled her toward the open bomb bay. "We don't have much time."

Below them, the desert floor looked very close.

"We're under eight hundred feet, so pull your cord the moment you're clear," he said into her ear. "You understand?"

She nodded.

"Wilcox is due north, maybe thirty miles. Can we make it that far?"

"With the water, easy."

He kissed her. "Remember, Nick, don't wait to pull the cord." With that, he sidestepped, grabbed her from behind, and held her over the opening as if she weighed nothing.

"Goodbye," he said. "If you survive, so do I." He dropped her out of the plane.

She fell, screaming her protest into the wind. Her hand, operating independently of her outrage, found the ring and pulled the rip cord.

The ground stopped rushing at her as the chute blossomed. Looking up, she saw another canopy suspended in the sky above her. The backpack. But Gault had stayed with the plane.

Already, the *Lady-A* was growing smaller. Soon the smoke trailing from her engines would be all that remained. When that dissipated . . .

The ground came up to meet her. The impact

knocked Nick flat. Scrabbling to her knees, she collapsed the chute.

"Damn you, John Gault."

The *Lady-A* looked very low now as it limped toward the horizon. *Please, John, make it to Wilcox. Wait for me there.*

Nick headed for the backpack, which had landed close by. The plastic water bottles, padded in bubble wrap, had survived intact.

But even with water, the rules for desert survival were absolute. Find shelter and wait for the cool of night. Don't expend energy. Don't sweat.

She started walking anyway, north toward Wilcox. By now, the *Lady-A* was out of sight. Even her smoke was gone.

Nick slowed. What happened if Gault did make it as far as Wilcox? What then? The police would be waiting for him—if not there, in Salt Lake. They'd be waiting for her, too, if they knew she'd joined the crew. After all, justifiable or not, they'd committed murder on Mesa d'Oro. No one could survive such a holocaust.

She stopped dead in her tracks. Gault was nobody's fool. *If you survive, so do I,* he'd said. His last words to her.

She scanned the landscape for shelter. A rocky outcropping was her best hope. Sundown wasn't far away. After that, she could move.

"All right, John. You win. If love is a sin, so be it."

As she settled against the rock, she heard a distant boom, like a jet piercing the sound barrier.

EPILOGUE

The *Lady-A* struggled on, her propellers clawing at the sky. This was what she was born for. In her final throes she was most alive. Meter by meter she lumbered on, the air tearing at the jagged holes in her skin. Her steel ribs vibrated to the thunder of her flight.

Depended upon; dependent on, the circle was complete. She'd waited these many years and had never forgotten. Together they were one, apart they were nothing.

He asked for everything she had, and she willingly gave it. She gave him the stern resolve of the men that had made her and the fearlessness of the band of pilots that had gone before. She scraped every inch of air above the deadly ground that she could cheat from gravity's greedy hold until she could give no more.

When it came, she accepted the final blow with resignation, not regret. She was beyond her time and knew it. She could no longer feel him, but somehow she knew he was still there. They were together again and always would be.

ABOUT THE AUTHOR

VAL DAVIS studied anthropology and archaeology at the University of California at
Berkeley and now lives in Northern California.

If you enjoyed FLIGHT OF THE SERPENT,
watch for the next Nicolette Scott mystery,
WAKE OF THE HORNET,
coming from Bantam Books in fall 1999.

VAL DAVIS

Track of the Scorpion

A NICOLETTE SCOTT MYSTERY

NICOLETTE SCOTT is an archaeologist with an unusual passion—uncovering lost airplanes. When a prospector brings word of such a find, Nick is eager to investigate. What she discovers is an American B-17 bomber, shot down over friendly territory, it's long-dead crew still inside. The sensational news story, and Nick's investigation, trigger a massive cover-up. Within days, the bomber disappears, the newspaper that reported the story prints a retraction, and Nick finds herself in serious jeopardy. People who saw the plane are starting to die. It will take all of Nick's instincts to keep her from being next....

.

On Sale Now

____57728-x $5.50/$7.50

- -

GRACE F. EDWARDS

If I Should Die

A MALI ANDERSON MYSTERY

"Excellent . . . Edwards expertly creates characters who leap to instant, long-remembered life."
— *CHICAGO TRIBUNE BOOK REVIEW*

"This girlfriend really cooks!"
— *MYSTERY LOVERS BOOKSHOP NEWS*

"A gorgeous, sassy heroine and a plot that doesn't quit . . . V. I. Warshawski look out!" — *WOMAN'S OWN*

HARLEM HAS NEVER BEEN HOTTER!

On Sale Now   ___57631-3 $5.99/$7.99